onward, I, **Ars**, shall succeed my father Raven as the **head** of House Louvent!"

As a Reincarnated Aristocrat,
I'll Use My Appraisal Skill to Rise in the World

1

By Miraijin A
Illustrations by jimmy

Translated by Tristan K. Hill

As a Reincarnated Aristocrat, I'll Use
My Appraisal Skill to Rise in the World 1

A VERTICAL Book

Translation: Tristan K. Hill
Editor: Maneesh Maganti
Production: Shirley Fang
Proofreading: Micah Q. Allen

Copyright © 2020 Miraijin A

All rights reserved.

Publication rights for this English edition arranged through Kodansha, Ltd., Tokyo.
English language version produced by Kodansha USA Publishing, LLC, 2023.

Originally published in Japan as *Tensei Kizoku Kantei Sukiru de Nariagaru ~Jakushou Ryouchi o Uketsuidanode, Yuushuuna Jinzai o Fuyashite Itara, Saikyou Ryouchi ni Natteta~* by Kodansha, Tokyo, 2020.

ISBN 978-1-64729-194-5

Printed in the United States of America

First Edition

Kodansha USA Publishing, LLC
451 Park Avenue South, 7th Floor
New York, NY 10016
www.kodansha.us

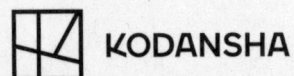

Design: **AFTERGLOW** Illustrations: **jimmy**

Contents

Prologue ··· `009`

Chapter 1 ·· `017`

Interlude: Rietz's Postscript ···················· `057`

Chapter 2 ·· `061`

Interlude: Charlotte's Postscript ············· `090`

Chapter 3 ·· `093`

Interlude: Rosell's Postscript ··················· `136`

Chapter 4 ·· `139`

Chapter 5 ·· `193`

Chapter 6 ·· `233`

Prologue

This summer, my father died. Though he was born a peasant, his innate courage and valorous deeds allowed him to deftly climb the ranks of society. He was even granted a noble title, albeit a minor one, before his life was cut short at the age of thirty-nine.

My father had long suffered from a chronic illness. Before he took ill, he was a strong and sturdy man, but as the days passed by and his sickness took its toll, his vitality faded. He was eventually an emaciated husk, barely recognizable as the man I once knew.

When he passed, his final breaths came so quietly and softly that I almost thought he'd fallen asleep. My father had suffered so terribly for so long, but at the very end, as he slipped away from us, he looked peaceful—tranquil, even. The moments before death, it would seem, have a way of relieving us of all our anguish.

The day of his funeral service arrived, and my father was laid to rest atop a bonfire. Cremation was far from a universal practice in the Summerforth Empire, and some regions went so far as to prohibit it, but it was simply the way things were done in our territory. Watching the flames crackle and dance before me, watching the plume of smoke waft up overhead, drove in the reality of the situation: my father was dead and gone.

Truth be told, thanks to certain complications in my personal history, I had never fully accepted the fact that he was my father. That didn't change the fact that he was the person I trusted and respected above all others in this world, though. Tears welled up in my eyes, but I held them back.

I can't allow myself to cry.

I knew what I had to do next, and if I was going to pull it off, I couldn't break down. Not here.

After the funeral, I gathered my father's closest subordinates. I stood before them, clad in the most impressive outfit I owned, doing everything in my power to present myself as a grown man—or at least as close to one as I could manage. Then, head held high, I made my declaration.

"From this day onward, I, Ars, shall succeed my father Raven as the head of House Louvent!"

It was the twelfth year since my life in Japan had ended. Twelve years after I died and was reborn in this world.

○

My own death had come so abruptly that it was downright anticlimactic.

I was a thirty-five-year-old man, living out an utterly mediocre existence in a country called Japan. I was born into an average family, went through elementary, middle, and high school without incident, graduated from an average college, and found a job at an average company that paid me a salary of around four and a half million yen a year—a perfectly unexceptional wage.

The only part about my life that *wasn't* ordinary to a fault was the fact that I never got married. Considering Japan's rapidly declining birth rate, though, for all I knew, that might have also been

I WILL USE MY APPRAISAL SKILL TO RISE IN THE WORLD

within the realm of average.

The fact that I never had a girlfriend either probably counted as abnormal, however. I'd describe my looks as, well, average, so I suppose my personality must've ruined any chance at romance for me. I'd often been told that I was too passive for my own good... and that I was too absent-minded just as often.

The people who told me that weren't wrong, either. I never found anything that really sparked my enthusiasm, aside from my lifelong love of books, and I just didn't have it in me to be proactive about things that didn't catch my attention. That might have had something to do with why I never found a girlfriend, actually. After all, I never met a girl who I genuinely fell for.

Anyway, let me set the scene for you: it's Monday morning and I'm just about to walk out the door, dejected at the thought of going back to work after a blissful weekend of freedom. I step outside, my favorite briefcase in one hand and my key in the other, and just as I'm about to lock the door behind me, *wham*! I gasp in shock and pain as a jolt of unbearable agony shoots through my chest! My hands tremble, and my key and briefcase fall to the ground. I clutch at my chest, but it doesn't help—it hurts so much I can't breathe or even remain standing. Moments later, I join my bag on the concrete.

What is this?! What's going on?! I try to process the situation, but the pain is so intense that I can't focus. I can't even think. The world goes dim, my consciousness fades, and I sink into a pit of darkness, tormented by pain worse than anything I've felt before, not even understanding what just happened to me.

○

When I woke up, the first thing I saw was a woman's face. I couldn't even begin to make sense of why *that* would be, so I tried to take a step back and put the pieces that had brought me there together.

I remembered leaving for work, to start, just like I always did. Then I remembered trying to lock my door, being overcome by pain, collapsing, and passing out. The next thing I knew, I was waking up with a woman's face in front of me. Her features were attractive, but clearly indicated she wasn't Japanese. She was probably Caucasian, as best as I could tell.

Okay, so if the chest pain knocked me out, I guess this is probably a hospital?

If that were true, though, you'd think the woman would have been wearing a nurse's uniform or something. I definitely didn't know her, either—I'd remember if one of my friends was a Caucasian woman.

Perhaps the weirdest part of it all was the way she was looking at me. It was the sort of gentle, loving expression an affectionate pet owner might give their beloved dog. It certainly wasn't the look you'd give some random guy who'd passed out and gotten himself carted off to a hospital.

It didn't take long for the woman to say something, but that didn't answer any questions. I couldn't understand a single word that came out of her mouth. It was a foreign language, obviously, but it wasn't one I'd ever heard. I was pretty confident I could have picked out one of the world's more commonly-used languages, even if I couldn't speak any of them myself, so whoever she was, I assumed she must have been from some smaller nation.

I tried to say something to her…and failed. I could move my mouth just fine, but for some reason, I couldn't form words. I could make a sort of "ahhh" noise, and I could manage "oooh" just fine, but that was my limit. I tried moving the rest of my body without

I WILL USE MY APPRAISAL SKILL TO RISE IN THE WORLD

much more luck. I *was* moving, technically, just not how I wanted.

Hmm?

As I squirmed about, my own hand entered my field of vision. It was small. Shockingly small, even. Almost like a baby's hand, in fact.

My mind was a mess of question marks. At long last, I convinced myself that *surely* I'd just been seeing things, but when I took another look at my hand, that theory crumbled away. It was just as tiny as before.

What the hell? Is this some kind of joke? Or, could it be...I died? Have I been reincarnated?

I knew enough about Buddhism to be familiar with the concept of the souls of the dead being reborn in a different form. The historical Buddha taught that to live is to suffer—that human souls are bound to the cycle of reincarnation, doomed to be born, die, and be born again, over and over, trapped in a cycle of pain all the while. Only through training and discipline could enlightenment be reached, and only through enlightenment could a soul escape the cycle.

I wasn't enlightened, that was for sure, so apparently, I'd been shipped off for another trip through the cycle. That didn't explain why I had all of my memories, of course, but at the very least, I was convinced of one thing: something extremely abnormal had happened to my body. That understanding, however, didn't change the fact that I couldn't speak, move, or do anything. All I could do was wait.

And, as I waited, the powerful urge to sleep washed over me. I *was* in a baby's body, after all. Unable to withstand the intense fatigue, I quickly drifted off into the land of slumber.

Chapter 1

Several months had passed since my birth, and I'd gradually picked up an understanding of the local language. In doing so, I'd begun to answer some of the many, *many* questions that plagued me.

To start, I learned that my new, post-reincarnation name was Ars Louvent. Though oddly enough, I couldn't actually remember my *former* name at all. I remembered my old life itself easily enough, but my name was just *gone*, somehow. That didn't really bother me, though. Having two names for myself would probably have just been confusing, so I quickly convinced myself that the bout of forgetfulness was for the best.

The next piece of info I picked up: there was a high likelihood that I wasn't on Earth anymore. My main point of evidence in favor of that conclusion came from the fact that this probably-new world's technological level was *extremely* low compared to Earth's. Not only did they not have TVs, radios, or smartphones, but they hadn't even worked out electricity! Oil lamps were the most advanced form of lighting available.

It went beyond just lighting, too. On the whole, I couldn't find any of the conveniences of modern society I was so used to in my new home. I'd be able to rationalize that away if we were poor, but the house I lived in was huge and opulent, tech level aside. I had a hard time believing that a family living in a house like *that* could be impoverished. I suppose I might've just been born into an exceedingly eccentric family, though, so it was hard to draw any definitive conclusions.

I did have one other reason for believing I wasn't in my old world anymore: my family was keeping an animal the likes of which I'd never seen as a pet. It was *almost* like a dog, but I'd definitely never seen a dog with a pair of wings sprouting from its back during my time on Earth. They weren't just for show, either—it could fly several feet in the air by flapping them. Though, wings aside, it bore a striking resemblance to a breed of dog called the Japanese Chin, and its name was Ahsis.

Now, I didn't know *everything* about Earth, but I was still pretty confident that we didn't have winged, flying dogs back there. The conclusion that I was probably in another world seemed more or less inescapable. I didn't know what sort of world I *was* in yet, but the winged dog made me suspect it landed somewhere on the fantasy side of the spectrum.

In short: I'd gotten wrapped up in a situation I was *extremely* unprepared for.

○

And so, three years passed by in the blink of an eye.

As you'd probably guess, by the age of three I was totally capable of talking and walking around on my own. I finally had a solid grasp of the local language, and I'd begun to reach an understanding of the state of the world around me, as well.

To start: as expected, the world I'd been born into was indeed definitely not the Earth I used to know. My new home was appar-

I WILL USE MY APPRAISAL SKILL TO RISE IN THE WORLD

ently in a nation called the Summerforth Empire, located on the continent of Summerforth. I'd definitely never heard of a country with a name like that on Earth, much less a continent, and I knew my history well enough to be pretty sure they'd never existed at all.

Then, of course, there was the discovery that magic was real in this world. It was a power that could bring about mysterious, inexplicable phenomena—starting fires, manifesting water from nowhere, that sort of thing. Seeing real-life magic used right before my very eyes was what finally convinced me beyond a shadow of a doubt that I was in another world.

Another revelation: apparently, the Louvent family I'd been born into was a noble household. House Louvent ruled over a territory called Lamberg, a small region consisting of around two hundred households and a total population of about a thousand. I was the family's first son, which meant that I would one day inherit the area.

Frankly, I was *very* worried about that whole business. I lived my last life as an office drone, after all! How could somebody like *me* end up ruling over anyone? Maybe I could just delegate the practical affairs of rulership to a trusted subordinate or two and spend the rest of my life idling my time away?

Oh, and there was one last thing I discovered during the first three years of my new life: the fact that I was born with a power that people around me definitely did not possess.

○

"G'morning to you, Young Master!"

"Good morning!"

One day, I decided to pay a visit to the training grounds right next to my family's estate. House Louvent technically had about a hundred and twenty troops ready to mobilize, but the vast majority of them were really just farmers. The only thing that made them soldiers was the fact that they'd occasionally steal a moment out of their busy schedules to make their way over to train for battle, running through drills on swordsmanship and archery.

"You really spend your fair share of time here, don't you, Young Master?" noted one of the soldiers.

"And he's only three!" added another. "He'll be a fearsome warrior when he grows up, I tell you!"

The soldiers were always happy to see me. Apparently, the idea of a three-year-old taking an interest in martial arts was enough to give them a good first impression of me. Truth be told, though, I was never interested in martial arts at all. I was interested in *people*.

I looked out over the training grounds and focused my gaze on a man who was thrusting a spear. Then, I activated my power: the power of Appraisal.

Appraisal was the name of the special ability I'd been born with. All I had to do to use it was stare at someone for long enough, and then I would instantly learn all sorts of information about whoever I was appraising. When I say "someone," by the way, I mean it. I could only appraise people.

To be clear, it wasn't like someone came up and told me, "Oh, that power you're using is called Appraisal!" or anything like that. I named it myself, actually. "Appraisal" just seemed like an appropriate name for a skill that let me peer into a person's detailed abilities and traits.

As I stared at the man, a sort of black screen materialized before my eyes with all the information I could obtain about him displayed on it. I knew from experience that I was the only one who

I WILL USE MY APPRAISAL SKILL TO RISE IN THE WORLD

could see the screens. That particular man's looked like this:

> Millais Cristal
> Age: 21
> Male
> **Status:**
> LEA: 21/35
> VAL: 60/62
> INT: 22/32
> POL: 15/31
> Ambition: 3
> **Aptitudes:**
> Infantry: D
> Cavalry: D
> Archer: B
> Mage: D
> Fortification: D
> Weaponry: D
> Naval: D
> Aerial: D
> Strategy: D

The format of the status screens just so happened to bear a striking resemblance to that of the menus in a historical strategy game I was quite fond of, so I knew exactly how to interpret them.

LEA stood for Leadership: the ability to effectively command an army.

VAL was Valor: a person's combat prowess.

INT meant Intelligence: ergo, how quick-witted they could be.

POL was Politics: their ability to conduct negotiations and handle administrative work.

Finally, Ambition represented how likely they were to betray their superiors if the opportunity arose.

The numbers on the left indicated their current score, while the numbers on the right indicated their maximum potential. Breaking the numbers' meanings down, the scale went something like this:

100+: Inhuman
90: Excellent
80: Great
70: Good
60: Average
50: Mediocre
40: Bad
≤30: Hopeless

Or something to that effect. At the very least, that was how the scale went in the game I used to play. I'd gone out of my way to appraise as wide a variety of people as I could manage, and everything had seemed to more or less line up with the game's systems so far.

Next up, the Aptitudes. They were scored on a letter-based system, with D representing the lowest possible score and S the highest:

Infantry: the ability to fight at close range.
Cavalry: the ability to fight on horseback.
Archer: the ability to fight at range with a bow and arrow.
Mage: the ability to wield magic for combat purposes.
Fortification: the ability to construct and maintain castles.
Weaponry: the ability to both create and handle weapons.

I WILL USE MY APPRAISAL SKILL TO RISE IN THE WORLD

Naval: the ability to battle aboard a ship.

Aerial: the ability to battle in the air...probably? I wasn't entirely sure what that Aptitude referred to, as it wasn't from the game.

Strategy: the ability to think tactically and turn the tides to your advantage.

Incidentally, the one person I *couldn't* appraise was myself. Looking at my hand or my abdomen didn't allow me to bring my status screen up, and looking at my face in a mirror didn't do the trick, either. It was a real disappointment, honestly—I would've loved to know what my own talents were.

Anyway, back to Mister Millais, who I'd just appraised. His Valor satisfied the bare minimum standards for decency, at least, but everything else was more or less a wash. On the other hand, stats like his were probably just about normal for a rank-and-file foot soldier. Pretty much all of his fellow soldiers fell into the same basket: middling Valor, terrible everything else. Some of them didn't even have a decent Valor score.

There was one thing that caught my attention about Millais, though: his aptitude as an Archer was remarkably high. In other words, he'd probably be pretty skilled with a bow, if he got his hands on one. And yet, there he was, out on the field training with a spear. He'd been practicing his spearmanship the last time I saw him, and I couldn't remember ever seeing him so much as hold a bow. Was he just not interested in archery? I decided to ask.

"Millais?"

"Huh? D-Did you need something, Young Master?" Millais stammered in a panicked reply. "And wait, you know my name?"

"Why don't you ever use a bow?" I asked, pushing past his confusion.

"A bow? 'Cause bows are a coward's weapon, of course! Real men don't stand off in the back lines, shooting away when their enemy can't even reach 'em—they fight up close and personal!"

Wow, what an incredibly banal answer.

If *that* was all that was keeping him from making use of his talent, I figured stepping in to intervene was probably best. He had a B-rank aptitude for bows, so surely he'd be reasonably effective fighting with one.

"You should give bows a try!" I urged him.

"Ugh, seriously?" Millais moaned.

"You have the talent for them! Just try it!"

"Look, kid, just because you're the lord's son—" began Millais, almost certainly intending to turn me down again. But just then, the other soldiers who were training nearby started giving him a *look*. Specifically, it was the "You know you can't *actually* turn down a personal request from Lord Louvent's son, right?" glare.

Millais hesitated for a moment, then sighed and replied, "All right, fine, I'll do it."

The soldiers didn't know about my appraisal ability, of course. They probably just wanted to get on their lord's good side by way of his son.

"Never drawn a damn bow in my life," grumbled Millais as he picked up a nearby bow, then turned to face the archery targets and nocked an arrow.

"Oi, Millais!" shouted one of the other soldiers, who specialized in archery himself. "You're way too far for a beginner! You're not even gonna reach the targets at that range, much less hit 'em! Move closer!"

"No, stay right here," I commanded.

This was all my idea in the first place, so Millais stayed rooted

to the spot. He drew the bowstring back as far as he could, then let it loose.

The arrow sailed cleanly through the air…and landed dead-center in the target. He'd hit the bull's eye. Everyone except me was stunned.

"The hell…?" whispered one of the more experienced soldiers. "How's a beginner shoot like *that*…?"

"B-Beginner's luck, that's all! Oi, Millais! Let's see you do that again, eh?!" shouted another of them.

Millais drew his bow once more, and again, his arrow thudded perfectly into the target's center. One perfect shot might've been a fluke, but two in a row was too much to write off so easily. The nearby soldiers were flabbergasted all over again. Even Millais's jaw had dropped so far that it was practically touching the ground.

"Millais? Do us all a favor and use a bow from now on."

"You've got the knack for it, man!"

"I hate to break it to you, but you were always lousy with a spear."

The other soldiers clustered around Millais, and it wasn't long before he caved in the face of their praise.

"W-Well, I guess being an archer wouldn't be *that* bad! What's a little cowardice on the battlefield if it keeps you breathing, eh? Ha ha ha!"

And just like that, the matter was settled. It was almost shocking how quickly he went from "archers aren't real men" to "maybe bows are fine after all." Honestly, he seemed a little too shallow for his own good.

"But anyway, how'd you know, Young Master?" asked one of the soldiers. "What tipped you off that Millais was a born marksman?"

The rest of the soldiers turned to face me as well, looking more

I WILL USE MY APPRAISAL SKILL TO RISE IN THE WORLD

than a little curious.

I wonder—if I explain that I have a special power that allows me to see their stats, will they believe me?

There was no telling how that revelation might go over, so in the end, I settled on a simple, one-word answer.

"Instinct!"

○

I was sitting down with my family for a meal the day after my encounter with Millais. My father in this new world, Raven Louvent, sat directly in front of me.

Raven was an exceptionally tall man with a rugged face and a sharp, dangerous glint in his eyes. To be completely honest, I was rather scared of him. This was, after all, a man who had been born at the bottom rung of society, a mere peasant, and yet he'd managed to climb all the way up to a noble title by virtue of his valorous deeds alone. He was a terror on the battlefield, capable of engaging ten average soldiers on his own and emerging from the brawl unscathed.

His stats, incidentally, looked like this:

AS A REINCARNATED ARISTOCRAT

> Raven Louvent
> Age: 30
> Male
> **Status:**
> LEA: 86/86
> VAL: 94/95
> INT: 44/56
> POL: 23/31
> Ambition: 67
> **Aptitudes:**
> Infantry: A
> Cavalry: S
> Archer: B
> Mage: D
> Fortification: D
> Weaponry: D
> Naval: D
> Aerial: D
> Strategy: D

In short, he had the exceptional leadership and valor required to rally an army of any size and lead them to victory: a natural-born general, through and through. On the other hand, his grasp of political matters was rather tenuous. That was probably why he'd contented himself with his status as the lord of a small, unimportant territory.

After we finished eating, my father looked over at me and said, "Ars. I've been told that you discovered Millais has a talent for archery yesterday."

"Yes, that's right," I replied.

I WILL USE MY APPRAISAL SKILL TO RISE IN THE WORLD

"And you did so by 'instinct,' was it? It seems those instincts of yours are nothing to scoff at. Polish that skill, Ars. The ability to identify people's talents is invaluable for a lord."

Is that really the sort of advice you should be giving to a three-year-old? I guess I'm not exactly acting my age, though, so I should probably cut him some slack.

I was still Raven's only child, and it occurred to me that I might've given him the misapprehension that *all* kids developed as quickly as I had.

"I'll take that advice to heart," I replied.

○

Several months came and went, over the course of which I turned four. As I grew, I learned more and more about the circumstances I'd been thrust into, and, well, let me put it bluntly: my future looked grim.

It might have been more accurate to say that the future of the entire Summerforth Empire looked grim, actually. From what I could tell, the odds of some sort of strife breaking out in the nation in the immediate future were incredibly high.

The empire dominated the entire continent of Summerforth. In other words, it had no external enemies to speak of at all. There *were* other nations out there, of course, but mounting an invasion of Summerforth would have involved sending their armies on an extended voyage beforehand, making the empire a less-than-attractive target.

The strife I was worried about, then, was internal: a civil war. The upper echelons of the Summerforth Empire's power structure were so flagrantly corrupt that it was almost laughable. As a result, several peasant uprisings had already broken out all over the nation. My father had been sent to suppress one just recently, in fact.

With each revolt that was put down, though, another sprung up, and the emperor's hold over the nation was growing weaker and weaker with each passing day. Local lords, in consequence, were growing more autonomous and less inclined to bow to the empire's word.

Small skirmishes between feuding local lords had already begun to crop up on occasion, and the ruling authorities just didn't have the power or influence left to do anything about them. In short, the country was a mess, and battles were breaking out all over the place at the drop of a hat. Troubled times indeed.

At the rate things were going, I could easily picture the empire collapsing entirely. Free from the threat of intervention, the lords of each region might escalate their minor skirmishes into all-out wars. Speaking as the first son of a noble family, I was *incredibly* distressed to realize what sort of era I'd been born into. The odds of me getting sent out into battle over and over were horrifyingly high, and if I'd inherited my father's title by that point, I'd be commanding our army as well.

Part of me desperately wished that I'd been born into a peaceful era, fated to live out a mundane life pushing papers, but I was in no position to fantasize about what could have been. The last time I was born, I wound up in modern Japan, a nation that was about as peaceful as possible. I didn't know the first thing about battle! I wasn't even convinced I'd be able to function on a basic level on a battlefield!

Just how long will I be able to survive in such a turbulent era?

My mind was full of worries, but one thought took precedence above all else.

I don't want to die.

I WILL USE MY APPRAISAL SKILL TO RISE IN THE WORLD

My last life had ended abruptly at the early age of thirty-five. I had a laundry list of goals I'd left unaccomplished and experiences I'd failed to have. I did *not* want to let my second shot at life end as early as my first did! I wanted to fade away into the grasp of senility, surrounded by a small army of grandchildren!

What could I do to stay alive, though? I thought as hard as I could, desperate to find *something* I could do, when suddenly, my father's words echoed through my mind.

"The ability to identify people's talents is invaluable for a lord."
That's it! People!

I just had to gather up all the most talented and exceptional individuals I could find, make them into my retainers, and let them bolster Lamberg's power and influence! That would lower my chances of meeting a sudden and violent end for sure! After all, in the sort of turbulent times the empire was rushing toward, the most important resources you could have were power and influence.

That settled it. I'd put my Appraisal ability to work, gathering up all of the most talented subordinates I could get my hands on! I got right to it, too: the moment I set that goal, I left our estate and wandered out into town, looking for my first recruit.

The territory the Louvent family ruled over, Lamberg, was home to a town of the same name. About eighty percent of the region's population lived in the town of Lamberg, and my family's estate happened to be located nearby. Even on foot, it only took about five minutes to reach the town.

I set off on my own. Lamberg was a relatively peaceful region, so wandering around without anyone there to supervise me wasn't especially dangerous. My parents told me not to go out on my own, of course, but taking a guard into town would've made me stick out like a sore thumb. My whole goal was to keep quiet and observe the townsfolk, so the last thing I wanted was to draw attention. I even made sure to pull my hood up, just to minimize the chance anyone would recognize me as the local lord's son.

It took me about eight minutes to make it to town. I *was* just four years old, so you couldn't blame me for walking a bit slower than an adult.

The town of Lamberg was about as ordinary as provincial villages got. Its populace was primarily made up of farmers, ranchers, hunters, and the like, and its atmosphere was calm and peaceful across the board. There was plenty of food to go around, too, which might have had something to do with why the villagers seemed quite healthy on the whole.

With a population of somewhere near eight hundred people, it was on the large side for a village. I knew that appraising *everyone* who lived there would be an infeasible task, so I decided to start by checking out anyone who seemed to be on the younger side of things. Conveniently enough, a young man was busy toiling away nearby, so I appraised him on the spot.

Hmm… Not exactly great numbers, huh?

At a second glance, I realized that I'd actually seen that young man at our estate's training grounds. That made me realize something: since the village's young men were all liable to be conscripted if things took a turn for the worse, most of them probably came over for training every once in a while. In other words, the odds were good that I'd already appraised the majority of the village's young men.

I guess I should move on to the women, then.

By this world's standards, women were judged as being unfit for the battlefield, and it was close to impossible for them to climb the social ladder. Things were more or less the same here as they were in medieval Japan, in that sense. I'd yet to find a woman with a high

I WILL USE MY APPRAISAL SKILL TO RISE IN THE WORLD

Valor score, but women seemed just as likely to have high Leadership, Intelligence, or Politics scores as the men, so I wasn't about to rule out recruiting a woman to be one of my retainers.

I set off once more to appraise all the women I could find, but unfortunately, pretty much everyone was on the low end of average. I even appraised a few kids, but none of them had any eye-catching, exceptional stats, either. It appeared my quest was going to be harder than I'd initially thought.

The ability to appraise people was great in practice, but being able to pick out exceptional talent wasn't actually useful at all if I couldn't *find* anyone with talent. I'd appraised so many people that I was starting to feel a case of eyestrain coming on, too—using my Appraisal skill was apparently sort of hard on my vision. I was just about to throw in the towel for the day when suddenly, an angry shout rang out.

"Get the hell outta my store! I don't have nothin' to sell to the likes of you!"

I glanced in the direction of the commotion just in time to see a boy get thrown out of a nearby shop, landing on his hands and knees in the street. His dark complexion and distinctive facial features set him immediately apart from the Lamberg locals. I and the people I'd grown up around were fairly close to Caucasian, appearance-wise, whereas the boy looked more like a heavily-tanned Japanese person.

"That kid's a Malkan, isn't he?"

"Ugh, disgusting! What's one of *those* doing in our town?"

"Probably just drifted along until he wound up here."

The nearby villagers broke out into hushed conversation, which finally reminded me that I'd heard of the boy's ethnicity before. The Malkans were a race of people who lived in an overseas nation, far away from the continent of Summerforth. The boy before me was the spitting image of how I'd heard them described.

Malkans were extraordinarily rare in the Summerforth Empire, but it wasn't like there were none around. Most of them were the descendants of slaves who'd been brought to the empire against their will generations ago, and the people of Summerforth bore a deep-seated prejudice against Malkans on the whole. Seeing such open and undisguised discrimination turned my stomach, honestly, but I knew that if I tried to step in and help him, I'd be putting my own reputation at risk. I *did* decide to appraise him, though, just for good measure.

Rietz Muses
Age: 14
Male
Status:
LEA: 87/99
VAL: 70/90
INT: 72/99
POL: 78/100
Ambition: 21
Aptitudes:
Infantry: A
Cavalry: S
Archer: A
Mage: C
Fortification: S
Weaponry: A
Naval: D
Aerial: C
Strategy: S

I WILL USE MY APPRAISAL SKILL TO RISE IN THE WORLD

For a moment, I couldn't believe my eyes.

It's... It's...

"It's Nobunaga himself!"

This mystery boy's stats were so overwhelmingly high, so flawless, *and* he was the spitting image of a warlord so legendary there wasn't a single person in Japan who didn't know his name: Oda Nobunaga! Obviously, I just meant his stats were the spitting image of Nobunaga's in that one historical strategy game I used to play, but still. He was young, and had yet to reach his full potential, but what bone-chilling potential he had!

To think the random boy I saw getting tossed into the street like a stray cat would turn out to be Nobunaga's doppelgänger! Life really does throw you curveballs! Looks like his name's Rietz Muses. Well, I can't let him keep languishing away on the streets! I'm making him my retainer one way or another!

Considering his race, recruiting him was a surefire way to draw no small amount of scrutiny toward myself, but weighed against the merits of having him on my side, I honestly couldn't have cared less about all that stuff. I sprung into action right away, trotting right over to him!

"You're having a hard time, aren't you?" I called out to him.

Rietz shot a sharp glare in my direction, but his expression softened as soon as he realized that I was a child.

"You shouldn't talk to people like me," he replied, picking himself up off the ground. "The adults will get mad with you. This isn't your problem, so hurry up and get out of here."

Apparently, he was actually concerned that I'd get myself in trouble. Now that I'd had a closer look at his face, I was struck by just how handsome he was. If this were Japan, I figured he'd probably have gotten scouted as an idol or something. His black hair was cut short, and he was quite tall—probably somewhere above 5'6" or so. Considering the fact that he was only fourteen, surely he'd push past six feet by the time he was fully grown.

Of course, his looks weren't exactly a priority, as far as I was concerned. With stats like those, I'd want to make him my retainer no matter *what* he looked like!

"I knew the risks before I approached you. I'd like you to become my retainer," I replied, cutting straight to the chase.

"Uh, umm, you mean you want to play make-believe?" asked Rietz with a somewhat strained smile. "L-Look, I'd love to play with you, honestly, but this really isn't a good time for me."

It seemed he'd taken my request as the nonsensical ramblings of a child who didn't know better. Which, to be fair, was a reasonable conclusion. I hadn't even told him I was the local lord's son yet, after all!

"No, that's not what I meant," I quickly clarified. "My name is Ars Louvent, and I am the son of the lord who presides over this village. I believe that you are an individual of incomparable talent, so I would like you to become my retainer."

Rietz's forced smile vanished in an instant.

"The lord's son? *You*?" he asked, shooting me a skeptical look.

Again, I couldn't blame him. I hadn't wanted to let my identity be exposed, so I'd disguised myself in a set of threadbare rags. The locals might've recognized me if they took a good look at my face, but Rietz was almost certainly not from Lamberg, so there was no way he would have known who I was.

"*Anyway*," I said, cutting off his objections, "if you need help, I'm offering it. Come with me!"

"I'm not so sure about this," replied Rietz. Most likely, he was

I WILL USE MY APPRAISAL SKILL TO RISE IN THE WORLD

hesitating over putting his faith in a literal child. Before he could turn down my offer, though, he was interrupted by a loud growl from his stomach.

"Are you hungry?" I asked.

"W-Well, yeah. So?" Rietz replied.

"We have plenty of food at my family's estate. Come with me, and you can eat your fill."

"W-Well..." Rietz mumbled hesitantly. The prospect of a meal was hard for him to pass up. Finally, he made his decision and replied, his face slightly flushed, "Umm, well...all right. Lead the way."

○

As we walked back to my family's estate, Rietz took the opportunity to introduce himself.

"Come to think of it, I never told you my name, did I? I'm Rietz Muses. You said you're called Ars Louvent, right?"

"Yes, that's right!" I replied. This seemed like as good of an opportunity as any to ask him about himself, so I decided to dig a bit deeper. "How did you end up in Lamberg, Rietz?"

"It's a long story. I was traveling with a band of mercenaries until just recently, but most of our group was wiped out in a war we were hired to fight in. Everyone capable of leading us was killed, so the survivors ended up going our separate ways. I don't have anywhere to go home to, so I ended up more or less wandering at random until I happened to find my way here."

I could only imagine how hard going through all that had been on him. Considering his capabilities, though, surely he would've been able to make a living easily enough in a different band of mercenaries, or maybe as a bodyguard? I went ahead and asked, but Rietz was less than optimistic about his prospects.

"No way," he replied. "Nobody would hire a no-name Malkan kid like me. My kind aren't trusted around these parts. I was only allowed in my last band because my parents were part of it."

It made sense when he put it that way. Nobody would hire a bodyguard they felt they couldn't trust, and most mercenary leaders probably wouldn't be excited about the idea, either. Of course, most people also wouldn't reach out to a random boy on the street and ask him to be their retainer, so weird things happened sometimes! Though, to be fair, if I hadn't been able to appraise him and didn't know that he had Nobunaga-level capabilities, I probably wouldn't have been that reckless.

A short period of walking and talking later, we arrived at my family's estate. Rietz's jaw dropped as my home came into view.

"Y-You live *here*?" he asked, gaping all the while.

"I do! I told you I was the lord of Lamberg's son, didn't I?"

"That's actually true...? Uh, I mean, please excuse my behavior! I wouldn't have spoken so flippantly if I'd realized!"

"Think nothing of it!" I proudly replied.

"Huh? Wait, hold up..." said Rietz. "If you really *are* the son of a lord, then does that mean all that talk about making me your retainer wasn't a joke, either...?"

"Of course! I was entirely serious."

"Wh-What?!" Rietz shouted in astonishment. It was such a shocking revelation that he obviously had no clue how to react.

I decided to take him inside, find him something to eat, and then go petition my father to make him into one of our family's retainers. Before I could follow through on my plan, however, a man burst out of the house and rushed over to me.

I WILL USE MY APPRAISAL SKILL TO RISE IN THE WORLD

"Master Ars!" the man shouted. "Were you gallivanting around outside *again*?! For the love of mercy, *please* put an end to this behavior! You realize it will be *my* head on a plate if anything happens to you, don't you?!"

The man's name was Krantz, and he was the Louvent family's steward. A man of almost fifty years of age, Krantz had served my family for decades and had been entrusted with the task of serving as my caretaker.

"I'll be happy to listen to your lecture in a moment, Krantz," I replied. "But first, would you mind preparing a meal?"

"A meal? Have you not eaten yet?"

"Oh, not for me," I clarified, gesturing toward Rietz. "I meant for him, actually."

"Hmm?" said Krantz, glancing behind me. "*H-Him*?! Why, he's a Malkan! What are you thinking?! How could you bring a filthy wretch like him into your lord father's estate?!"

Krantz's face flushed red as he reprimanded me. I wasn't at all happy about Rietz being treated with such open contempt, but I knew that protesting it then and there wouldn't get me anywhere. Hatred for the Malkan people was deeply rooted in Summerforth's culture—or, at the very least, everyone I'd met thought Malkans to be an inherently inferior race. It was considered common sense, so it wouldn't be easy to change people's minds. It would take a lot more than a debate with a child, that was for sure.

"I appreciate your concerns," I replied, "but for the moment, please bring him a meal on the double. He's teetering on the brink of starvation!"

I didn't know if Rietz was *actually* anywhere close to starving to death, of course, but I thought that appealing to the urgency of the situation would be my best shot at getting through to Krantz.

AS A REINCARNATED ARISTOCRAT

"Very well," Krantz replied, after a moment of hesitation. "Malkan or not, it would pain my conscience to see a child starve to death. He'll be driven out the moment he's finished eating, though!"

Krantz stormed back into the house to prepare a meal, and I was left to wonder about just how astonishingly prejudiced the man had turned out to be. Would I even be allowed to make Rietz my retainer if *that* was how an otherwise reasonable person reacted to him?

No, whether or not I'm allowed to isn't the question. I will make him my retainer, no matter what! Rietz has the sort of talent I can't possibly afford to pass up! I only just met him, and I can already tell how indispensable he'll be for my future! I will not let him slip away from me over something like this!

Eventually, Krantz returned with bread and water for Rietz, who thanked him and dug in without hesitation. The bread was obviously old, stale, and flavorless, but watching Rietz devour it, you'd have thought it was the most delicious thing in the world.

"Now then, send him away!" demanded Krantz, turning to me.

"I'm afraid that's not an option," I replied, standing my ground. "You see, I brought him here to make him my retainer."

"Wh-What?! Have you gone mad?! How could you—what?!" Krantz babbled in incoherent shock.

"I intend to discuss the matter with my father!" I declared. Ignoring Krantz, I grabbed Rietz by the hand and pulled him toward my father's room.

"Father!" I cried as I burst into his room. "Please make this boy into one of our retainers!"

My father, as best as I could tell, had been writing a letter. My sudden entrance didn't break his concentration in the slightest,

I WILL USE MY APPRAISAL SKILL TO RISE IN THE WORLD

though. He didn't even look up until he'd finished writing, at which point he finally turned his attention to me.

"By 'this boy,' I presume you're referring to the Malkan child?" asked my father.

I nodded, prompting him to shake his head and reply, "I will do no such thing. Making a Malkan into one of our retainers would be an act of unprecedented foolishness. Send him away."

He concluded with a sigh and a scowl that told me he was unamused by me disrupting his work with this nonsense.

I guess it's not going to be that easy after all. I can't afford to back down, though!

"Father, this boy—Rietz Muses—is exceptionally talented! Failing to take him into our service would be an immense loss for our family!"

"Listen to me, Ars," replied my father. "Malkans are overwhelmingly inferior to us Summerforthians in every aspect. There is *no such thing* as a talented Malkan."

That was the widespread belief regarding Malkans throughout the whole Summerforth Empire: that Malkans were clearly and fundamentally inferior as a race. Now, I'd only met one Malkan so far, that being Rietz himself, but he alone was enough to make me doubt the narrative that society at large was feeding me. If a Malkan could be as exceptional as Rietz was, then how could there possibly be that much of an inherent difference between them and Summerforthians?

"I cannot speak for Malkans on the whole," I replied. "However, I *can* say that Rietz has undoubtedly been blessed with incomparable talent and wisdom. I appreciate that you have your doubts, so why not put him to the test? That way you can see for yourself how exceptional he is."

My father paused for a moment to consider my proposal. Eventually, he spoke up once more and said, "What makes you so certain that this boy is talented?"

"I can just tell."

"I recall you picked out Millais's talent with the bow in much the same way, yes?"

"That's right! I feel the same sort of hunch about Rietz as I did back then. My instincts are telling me that he has talent beyond anything I've ever seen before."

My father looked me straight in the eye. His gaze was sharp and intimidating, but I didn't let it sway me, and stood my ground. A moment later, he turned to Rietz, who also met his gaze unflinchingly. Perhaps the trials his life had put him through had prepared him for this sort of probing scrutiny.

"Very well," declared my father. "If you're so certain, then I shall put him to the test, as you suggested. If I'm convinced that he is indeed talented, I will employ him as a soldier."

All right! I actually got his permission!

Being hired as a rank-and-file foot soldier wouldn't exactly put Rietz at the top of the social ladder, but whatever my father claimed about Malkan inferiority, I knew for a fact that he was a man who valued ability above all else at heart. There wasn't a doubt in my mind that Rietz would prove himself in battle and rise to a higher standing in the long run. Plus, even if the opportunity didn't present itself, I could just give him a boost as soon as I inherited my father's title.

"The test will be a simple one," my father continued. "The boy and I will spar. If he defeats me, he passes."

All that confidence I'd just built up came crashing down. My father had a score of 94 in Valor, while Rietz was sitting at 70

I WILL USE MY APPRAISAL SKILL TO RISE IN THE WORLD

points in total. He had a maximum score of 90, so with proper training, he might have had a chance. However, as things stood, his odds of success were slim.

"Umm, Father?" I nervously spoke up. "You should know that Rietz is still young—he's only fourteen. I'm afraid that winning a duel against a man of your age and skill may be next to impossible for him."

"You said he's talented, didn't you?" replied my father.

"Well, yes, but...you're *also* gifted with an incredible, innate talent for combat, Father. I believe that Rietz will be well-matched against you once he's had time to grow and mature, but without that opportunity, he would hardly stand a chance."

"Then I won't fight seriously," my father conceded. "I'll give the boy an advantage."

What sort of advantage he'd give and to what extent he'd be giving it weren't exactly clear to me, but I still felt reassured. As long as Rietz had a leg up somehow, he had a shot. I had a feeling my father had already given all the ground he was willing to offer, anyway, so taking him up on these terms seemed like my best bet. Thus, I nodded in agreement.

"We'll have our bout in the training grounds. Follow me," said my father, standing up and walking out of the room. Rietz and I hurried along after him.

As we walked, Rietz leaned over and whispered, "Umm, Ars... err, that is, Master Ars, why would you go so far to make someone like me your retainer? Are you doing this out of sympathy?"

"I explained my reasons to my father just a moment ago," I replied. "Weren't you listening?"

"You mean all that talk about me having talent? But...there's no way I actually—"

"You're good at fighting, aren't you?"

"Y-Yes. I've been told I have a deft hand in battle more than once, but that's all! I don't have any other talents to speak of."

"That's where you're wrong. Not only are you a skilled warrior, but you can command troops, you have an astonishing intellect, and the instincts of a seasoned politician dwell within you! You have it all!"

"I'm telling you, I *definitely* don't!"

"You just haven't had the opportunity to put those skills to use, that's all! Fortunately, you'll have plenty of chances to show off while you're serving House Louvent."

"W-Will I...?" asked Rietz, his skepticism written all over his face. I could tell he wasn't satisfied with my explanation.

Come to think of it, I never actually asked him if he wanted to be my retainer, did I? I was so excited to have him around, I brought him all the way here without even thinking to check! This certainly won't do!

"Are you opposed to working for House Louvent?" I asked, looking over at Rietz once more. "If so, I can tell my father to call the whole test off."

"Oh, no, I'm honored by the offer," said Rietz. "If anything, it seems too good to be true! But, well...that raises questions, you know? Malkans like me aren't welcome anywhere on this continent, so we have to be cautious about these things."

"I'm not trying to trick you, I promise! And I'm afraid it's not set in stone whether we'll even be able to follow through with this. I should warn you that my father's test is likely to be a harsh one. I have faith that you'll pass, though!"

Hearing all of that from me seemed to help Rietz gather his resolve. I, meanwhile, was just relieved that he wasn't going to turn

I WILL USE MY APPRAISAL SKILL TO RISE IN THE WORLD

down the job. Shortly thereafter, the three of us arrived at the training grounds.

Several soldiers were running through drills when we arrived. The moment they noticed us, their expressions stiffened up in unison. My father coming down to the training grounds wasn't unheard of, so they weren't surprised by his appearance—no, they were *worried*. My father was an exceptionally harsh instructor, and things always got a bit tense when he decided to stop by.

"I'm not here to train you today," said my father. Instantly, all that ambient tension faded away. "I'm here to test this boy, that's all."

The soldiers had been so focused on my father that they hadn't even noticed Rietz, but at that point, their gazes finally turned to him.

"You're *testing* a Malkan kid?" one of the soldiers asked incredulously.

"I am," replied my father. "According to Ars, he's exceptionally talented. Assuming that's true, I don't see any reason not to take him in as a foot soldier."

A hushed clamor rose among the soldiers.

"A Malkan, *talented*?"

"*Hah*, as if!"

"The young master gets some wild ideas in his head sometimes, eh?"

None of them believed in Rietz's talent.

Eh, that's fine. He'll just have to prove it to them!

"We have wooden swords over there. Take one," said my father.

"All right," replied Rietz.

The two of them took up their training blades and faced each other.

AS A REINCARNATED ARISTOCRAT

"I told you I would give you an advantage, and here it is: our match will continue for three minutes. If you manage to land even a single blow on me, we'll consider it your victory. You can receive as many hits as you like until time runs out, or until you surrender. Gratz! Bring me an hourglass!"

"Right away!" said Gratz, one of my father's men. He sprinted over to the nearby storehouse and quickly returned with a three-minute hourglass.

An unskilled swordsman would have been hard-pressed to land a single strike on my father. As a matter of fact, none of the soldiers gathered around us had ever managed the feat in single combat. Considering Rietz's Valor and his A-rank aptitude in Infantry, though, I had a feeling he'd be able to pull it off.

"Come to think of it..." said my father. "You have yet to declare your name to me. If I'm going to fight a man, I want to hear his name from his own mouth first."

"My name is Rietz Muses," Rietz replied.

"And I am Raven Louvent, head of House Louvent. Now then—show me what you're capable of!"

A moment later, Gratz turned the hourglass and the match began. My father took the initiative, bringing his sword down with crushing force in a swing that betrayed a level of agility you wouldn't have expected from a man of his musculature. A blow like that to the head could easily knock a man unconscious, or even kill him in the worst case.

Faced with that level of technique, an amateur would likely panic and fall over backward, but Rietz had clearly seen his fair share of battle. He kept his cool, stepping away and avoiding my father's swing entirely before immediately springing forward again and going on the offensive.

AS A REINCARNATED ARISTOCRAT

My father, however, was not so easily caught off guard. In spite of the force of the attack he'd unleashed a split-second before, he regained his balance and evaded Rietz's attack with ease. Rietz's eyes widened in shock—it was probably sinking in that my father was a top-tier swordsman, not just a simple musclehead.

Once again, my father went on the attack. Rietz was shaken, but he didn't let his surprise get the better of him, and intercepted my father's blade with his own. A spectacularly fast exchange of blows began.

The nearby soldiers had been making a mockery of the match at first, but as they watched the duel unfold, they quickly fell silent. Not one of them had ever managed to hold their own against my father in single combat. My father went well out of his way to not kill or even seriously injure his opponents when he sparred, and they knew it, but even when he was holding back, they almost always ended up disarmed and defeated in a matter of seconds.

Not only could the soldiers not land a hit on my father, but they were also hardly even capable of having a proper match with him! These were actual soldiers who'd undergone no small amount of training, but against my father, they might as well have been children. But now there he was, fighting at what was certainly closer to his full strength than they'd ever seen against an actual, literal child who never retreated so much as a step. Nobody who knew how strong my father was could possibly have heckled a match like that.

As well as he was fighting, though, Rietz was gradually beginning to lose ground. At the beginning of the match, he'd attacked about as much as he defended, but as time went by he gradually shifted more and more to the defensive. About half of the hourglass's sand had fallen, but neither fighter had landed a clean blow. That was no surprise in Rietz's case, but the fact that my father hadn't gotten in a

I WILL USE MY APPRAISAL SKILL TO RISE IN THE WORLD

single strike was something else entirely.

As I watched, it struck me that in a real fight, your opponent landing a hit could very well mean instant death depending on where they hit you. Both Rietz and my father were likely experienced with live combat, and given they'd lived to see another day, it stood to reason that neither of them had taken very many hits, if any at all.

That led me to wonder if the so-called "advantage" my father had given Rietz would really make much of any difference. I was starting to worry.

Is Rietz going to lose? I can't rule out the possibility!

After going as far as I had to strike the deal, backpedaling and renegotiating if Rietz lost probably wasn't going to fly. My father would surely acknowledge Rietz's talent after a fight like this, but he was the sort of person who never went back on the letter of his word, its spirit be damned. Any chance of him taking Rietz in would be sunk.

I kept my eyes glued to the match, praying that Rietz would *somehow* manage to land a strike, even if only by pure chance. The sand in the hourglass was depleting rapidly, and it wouldn't be long before the match concluded. Not even my father could fight at full strength forever, though, and it seemed fatigue was setting in—his movements were beginning to slow ever so slightly.

It was almost like Rietz had been waiting for that opportunity. He mustered up his strength and swung his blade with all his might. It was an attack born of resolve, of the fact that he knew it might be his last chance. He aimed for my father's leg, and my father must not have seen a targeted blow coming. He couldn't defend in time, so Rietz's sword struck his shin true.

The soldiers stood stock-still, paralyzed in dumbfounded astonishment. They couldn't understand what they'd just witnessed. My father was still on his feet, and showed no sign that the blow to the shin had hurt him. It was an old truism that the shin was so hard to toughen up that even the legendary warrior-monk Benkei couldn't help but cry when he was hit there, but apparently, my father wasn't so easy to bring to tears.

In any case, Rietz had undeniably succeeded at landing a blow. Not only had he won per the rules of the match, but he'd also won the duel by *any* reasonable standard of judgment. I imagined that if they fought a few more rounds, my father would probably have come out ahead in total victories, but this time, Rietz had won the day.

"The bout is yours," admitted my father, though not without a moment of frustrated silence beforehand. "As promised, I'll take you into my employ as a soldier."

I breathed a sigh of relief. Rietz had done it—his position as a soldier of House Louvent was secured. The soldiers around us, meanwhile, were stunned.

"G-Gods above, that kid's incredible!"

"Did you see that? He *won*!"

"A *Malkan*, of all the people...?"

Not one of them could object to taking Rietz in after the display they'd just witnessed. None of them would've had the guts to stand against my father's decision in the first place, of course, but having someone as strong as Rietz on their side could be nothing but beneficial for them; I didn't imagine they would've complained regardless. Adding even a single capable soldier to your side reduced the odds of your horrific death on the battlefield, after all.

My father returned his wooden sword to the rack, then approached me and stated, "It's just as you said. Rietz has an undeniable talent for battle. He'll be a swordsman to be feared someday,

I WILL USE MY APPRAISAL SKILL TO RISE IN THE WORLD

I'm sure."

One fight was all it took for my father to appreciate the depths of Rietz's abilities. In truth, of course, fighting was only one of Rietz's many talents—he was actually even *more* stunningly capable when it came to his skills as a commander, tactician, and politician.

"You perceived Millais's talent with a bow before, Ars, and this time you saw something in Rietz that no one else could. I'm starting to suspect that you have something, yourself—a power that makes *you* truly special," my father continued. Had he realized that I was capable of Appraisal? "I've told you this before, but the ability to identify people's strong points is a truly indispensable skill for a lord to possess. Identifying them is merely the first step, though, and if you stop there, you won't last long in this line of work. You have to know how to *use* those talents, not just how to pick them out."

Once again, my father was throwing the sort of concepts at me that most reasonable people would never even consider discussing with a four-year-old. That said, his words really did give me some food for thought.

Knowing how to use your people's talents... He's absolutely right.

However many talented individuals I gathered up, if I couldn't help them make full use of those talents, they'd be nothing but pearls before swine—the swine, in this instance, being none other than me. And wasting their talents wasn't even the worst-case scenario. If someone as exceptional as Rietz decided I wasn't worth their service, I could very well find myself shipped off to the slaughterhouse before I knew it. This was a lesson that I would have to take to heart.

"That said," my father added. "If your power to perceive the strengths of those beneath you is genuine, and if you *do* learn to make full use of those strengths, there's no telling how high you could rise in society. We live in an era of strife and chaos, but even in these turbulent times, you could climb to the pinnacle of the aristocracy...or even claim the emperor's throne."

The emperor.

In other words, my father believed that I could quell the discord that was sweeping through Summerforth, and become a leader fit to define an epoch.

I couldn't believe it. I couldn't picture myself becoming someone that important, and I wasn't interested in doing so, either. Could you imagine just how much of a pain in the ass being an emperor would be? I'd be perfectly content gaining just as much influence as it took to keep me alive, and no more, thank you very much!

"Ha ha ha ha ha! I'm *joking*, Ars," my father suddenly bellowed. "A noble from a backwater like this, becoming the emperor? *Hah!* I wouldn't expect *that* much from you. So long as you stay alive and carry on the Louvent family's name, I'll have no complaints."

My father, cracking a joke?!

It was a relief to know he wasn't serious, in any case. For a moment, my father kept cackling and patting me on the head, then finally left to return to his room.

After he departed, the soldiers descended upon Rietz, swarming around him and asking him to spar with them as well. It seemed they were eager to get a taste of his capabilities firsthand. Unfortunately for them, the intensity of his match with my father had left him so exhausted that his hands were shaking too hard to even hold his sword properly. His next bout would have to wait until another day.

○

Thus, Rietz officially became one of my family's retainers! That was

I WILL USE MY APPRAISAL SKILL TO RISE IN THE WORLD

an achievement, to be sure, but there was one problem left to solve: his housing situation. The rest of my family's soldiers were all Lamberg folk with homes in the village, so they all lived in town. Our only two options were to find an unoccupied house and have Rietz stay in town, or find a place for him to live on our estate.

I asked my father what we should do, and he told me that Rietz could live in a currently unoccupied room in the servants' quarters. I was all for that plan—he'd almost certainly face all sorts of persecution if he had to live in the village, and sparing him that treatment was for the best. In exchange for his lodgings, he would work around the house in addition to fighting as one of our soldiers.

"I'm still not so sure about this," said Rietz after everything was settled. "Do you really want someone like *me* working for you?"

"This again?" I replied. "I swear, I must have told you that I want you here thirty times by now!"

I was giving Rietz a tour around our estate. One of our servants was initially tasked with the job, but it seemed like the perfect opportunity to chat with Rietz and get to know him better, so I volunteered to take over those duties.

"You have, but I just can't believe it! Never in my wildest dreams could I have imagined serving a noble family!"

"We may be nobles, but our territory is tiny, and our influence even smaller," I countered. "Plus, you've technically only been hired on as a soldier! It's not exactly a dream position."

"Y-You don't understand. I'd just about given up on finding someone willing to give me the time of day, much less hire me! *Any* position is a dream come true for a person like me."

A wistful look appeared on Rietz's face. He was probably thinking back on all the misery he'd suffered through. A moment later, he knelt down on one knee and bowed his head to me.

"If it weren't for you, Master Ars, I'm certain I would've died in a ditch somewhere out in the wilderness. I cannot possibly thank you enough for giving me this chance."

"You don't have to thank me," I replied. "I made you my retainer because I expect great things from you! I'm confident that you'll be an incredible asset."

"I will be! I swear that I'll work myself to the bone to repay you for the kindness you've shown me today!"

Rietz pledged his service to me, and I chose to take his oath at face value. I knew that he was a man I could trust to never betray me—a man who would pull me back from the brink of defeat time and time again. In that moment, it felt as if our future together had been set in stone.

Interlude: Rietz's Postscript

About a week has passed since I, Rietz Muses, entered the service of House Louvent through what I can only describe as a series of miracles.

Malkans like me are scorned and despised no matter where we go. I don't even want to think back on everything I've gone through as a result of society's contempt for people like me. That didn't entirely change after I began my life in the Louvent estate, to be fair, but the fact that I'm consistently well-fed and clothed makes my new lifestyle feel downright heavenly.

I'm only able to live in such comparative comfort thanks to Ars and his decision to make me one of his retainers. I swore to pay him back with a lifetime of service, and each morning, I quietly reaffirm that oath to myself.

"Rietz?" says Ars one morning. "I'll be going into town today to scout for talent, and I'd like you to accompany me as my guard!"

Ars, the boy I consider my benefactor, is a mere four years old. He looks the part, as well, with childish features and big, round eyes that are, frankly, downright adorable. The elevated manner in which he speaks betrays an unusual level of thought and sophistication for a boy of his age, though, and he conducts himself with an astonishingly stately bearing.

It's like a grown adult is lurking within his childlike shell, so I can hardly believe he's really a child at all. I have to wonder just how in the world he'd been raised to turn out this way, and whether the process can be replicated.

"Understood," I reply. "I would be happy to accompany you."

The thought of turning down his request doesn't even cross my mind.

The two of us set out for the village, which is just a short walk away. The locals look upon me in a less-than-kind manner, as always, but with Ars by my side, nobody dares to openly harass me. I'm used to being glared at, so I don't pay them any mind in particular as we stroll through town. Eventually, Ars chooses a place by the side of the road to stop, and carefully watches the people as they pass by.

"Umm, Master Ars? I understand that we're here to look for talented individuals...but do you intend to do so by simply, well, *looking*?" I ask. I had assumed we would be seeking out people with an interest in serving the nobility, then giving them some sort of test. Literally just watching people come and go strikes me as a strange way to go about this.

"I can tell what a person's talents are just by looking at them," Ars replies.

"You can...huh?

Just by looking at them? Is that even possible? I suppose he *did* discern my talent with a sword at a glance, so maybe it is?

Not only had Ars never seen me wield a blade at the time he declared I had a talent for them, he hadn't even seen me *hold* one.

If he's telling the truth, though, and possesses a truly astonishing

I WILL USE MY APPRAISAL SKILL TO RISE IN THE WORLD

ability, then I can only imagine how incredible his achievements will be in the long term. We live in a world where the vast majority of people's futures are decided for them the moment they're born, so there could be vast numbers of talented individuals stuck in jobs that don't suit them, just waiting to be discovered.

"Oh, that man has a seventy in Intelligence!" Ars exclaims as a young man walks past us. "I thought I'd already checked all the men—I must have missed him somehow."

"What in the world does that mean?" I ask, perplexed.

"To put it simply, it means that there's a high likelihood that he's smart. I'm going to talk to him!"

This time there isn't a doubt in my mind: judging how smart somebody is at a glance is, quite frankly, impossible. Ars, however, really does run over to speak with the man, and as I listen to their discussion, I realize that he really *is* quite sharp. Certainly more intelligent than your average passerby, as far as I can judge.

Ars invites him to become one of House Louvent's retainers, but the man shoots the offer down without a second thought. Apparently, he isn't interested in serving anyone other than himself.

"Well, that's just how it goes sometimes," says Ars with a shrug. "On to the next candidate!"

He doesn't seem especially perturbed by the man's refusal, and immediately moves on with his search.

Ars calls out to several people over the course of the day, and each time, they prove that his judgment is on the mark. Eventually, I realize I may well have entered the service of a truly incredible person.

Chapter 2

Several months had passed since Rietz became one of House Louvent's retainers. Over that short period, he'd already proven himself in battle, and the people around him were finally beginning to realize that his intellect was just as exceptional as his skill with a blade.

My father had fought by Rietz's side several times, at that point, and was among those who had realized how clever he really was. He ended up tasking Rietz to read a book as a test, and Rietz responded by breezing through it at record speed and summarizing its contents in perfect detail. Even my father was astonished by *that* spectacle!

It was quickly decided that Rietz would be given as high a level of an education as possible, and his standing in the household grew to the point that even though he was still a mere soldier in theory, nobody would have thought to call him one in practice. A formal education had done wonders for his Intelligence, as well, which was sitting at a current score of 89. It wouldn't be long before he broke into the 90s, at the rate things were going. Finally, my father gave Rietz a new position in the household, which meant he would no longer be going out into battle.

"Now then, Master Ars, it's time for us to begin your studies for the day!" said Rietz.

Right, he had been appointed to oversee *my* education!

At that moment in time, Rietz was the most knowledgeable member of the Louvent household. Considering he'd only started focusing on his education a matter of months beforehand, the leaps and bounds he'd taken were truly mind-bending. Meanwhile, as the house's eldest son, my education was considered a priority, so Rietz was entrusted with the job in the hopes that he would train me to be skilled with both the pen and the sword.

I, by the way, had spent the past several months so absorbed in my search for talent that I'd unfortunately let my quest to learn everything there was to know about my new world fall to the wayside. Having Rietz around to teach me the ways of the world couldn't have suited my purposes better.

Rietz stood before me, a book in hand. "Today, we'll be discussing the current state of the Summerforth Empire," he explained, opening the book up and setting it down on the table in front of me.

A map of the empire, and by extension the entire continent of Summerforth, was drawn on his chosen page. It wasn't much of a map, though—in fact, it seemed downright slipshod. Apparently, this world had yet to master the art of cartography.

"Let's see," began Rietz. "I believe we've already discussed how the continent used to be home to seven kingdoms, and how their unification signified the birth of the empire?"

"That's right!" I replied.

I already knew the seven countries that formerly occupied the continent. The Kingdom of Rofeille had been in the continent's northeast regions, to start. The northwest was home to the Kingdom of Canshiep, while the Kingdom of Ansel was in the eastern-central region, and the Kingdom of Scheutz took up the central-west. Between Ansel and Scheutz, at the very heart of the continent, sat the Kingdom of Paradille. Finally, the Kingdoms of Seitz and Missian were down south, with Seitz in the southwest and Missian in the southeast.

The nearest continent to Summerforth was across a channel, and the Kingdom of Ansel, which was located closest to that channel, had gained an edge over the other kingdoms by way of foreign trade. Ansel gradually amassed more and more power, and ultimately mounted an all-out invasion of its surrounding nations. The ensuing war of conquest proved successful, and the king of Ansel, Anathis Bydoras, proclaimed himself an emperor. Thus, the Summerforth Empire was born.

The old kingdoms' names weren't just a historical curiosity, incidentally. They were still used to refer to regions in the modern era. The Kingdom of Rofeille, for instance, corresponded to a modern-day duchy of the same name. The Kingdom of Canshiep became the Duchy of Canshiep, and so on and so forth.

Each duchy was ruled by a governor formally known as a duke. The dukes tended to be either descendants of the imperial line, or the descendants of monarchs who chose to surrender and swear fealty to the Kingdom of Ansel in the early stages of the war.

The territory we lived in, Lamberg, was located in the Duchy of Missian. Missian was characterized by its seasonal climate and expansive flatland, which made the territory ripe for agriculture. Its population was quite large as well, so it struck me as a pleasant region all around.

"This year marks the two hundred and thirtieth anniversary of the Summerforth Empire's founding," explained Rietz. "Of course, the empire currently stands on its last legs. The dukes hardly lend an ear to the emperor's orders, and the duchies grow more and more independent with each passing day. Nevertheless, the power wielded by the imperial line is still far from insubstantial. The Bydoras family holds direct control over a considerable swath of territory, and it's not entirely unthinkable that the empire could regain its former glory under the command of an especially capable leader."

"Is the current head of the Bydoras family capable?" I asked.

"The current head of the family, Bydoras XII, is an eight-year-old child. His retainers hold the true power, it would seem. I don't know the details myself, but it would seem there's no single individual who holds all the cards. A variety of factions are vying for influence, and frankly, I don't get the impression it's going especially well for any of them."

They're focusing on political infighting while the empire falls to ruin around them? Sounds like I shouldn't expect much from the imperial family.

"To be clear," Rietz continued, "the Bydoras family is hardly exceptional in that sense. In fact, it's quite likely that we'll be seeing a conflict of succession here in Missian before long."

"What do you mean by that?" I asked.

"The current Duke of Missian, Lord Amador Salemakhia, is quite old. There's been no word of him falling ill, but the odds are very good he'll pass away before the decade is done. Furthermore, Lord Amador has two sons. Under ordinary circumstances, the eldest would inherit his title, but the younger of the two is exceptionally talented when compared with his elder brother. Word has it that Lord Amador himself is unsure which son he intends to name as his successor.

"Needless to say," Rietz went on, "if he passes away before reaching a decision, war is all but guaranteed. And even if he does name

I WILL USE MY APPRAISAL SKILL TO RISE IN THE WORLD

an heir, the odds of conflict breaking out are considerable. Both brothers have expressed a desire to inherit the title, after all."

A war of succession...

That was the sort of conflict that could spiral horribly out of control. Small-scale skirmishes weren't particularly uncommon, from what I understood, but a real, large-scale war had yet to occur in my lifetime.

If such a war were to break out, and if my family were to throw their weight behind the losing side, then it was possible we'd lose our territory. On the other hand, if we were to ally with the victors and prove our worth in battle, *expanding* our territory was very much also on the table. Of course, my father would almost certainly still be alive if any of this ever happened, so deciding which side to support would fall on his shoulders. I had to wonder if he was already planning for that eventuality.

"Who do you think my father would choose to support?" I asked.

"I understand that Lord Raven is inclined to back the elder brother, but regardless, he wouldn't be in a position to make that decision," Rietz answered.

Oh, that's right!

It had entirely slipped my mind that my father was not, in fact, a direct vassal of the Duke of Missian. Each duchy of the Summerforth Empire was divided up into counties. Around ten or so counties per duchy was typical, and each county was managed by a local count. Lamberg was a part of the County of Canarre, and my father's direct superior was the Count of Canarre. I guess if I were to write it out like a modern address, it'd go something along the lines of: Lamberg, County of Canarre, Duchy of Missian, Summerforth Empire.

Anyway, the point was that the count would be responsible for choosing which of the brothers Canarre would support, so my father had no say in the matter. I suppose he at least had the count's ear, though, so his opinion might play a factor in the final decision.

"Who do you think should inherit the title, Rietz?" I asked.

"Y-You want *my* opinion? Hmm... I've never met either of them, so I'm afraid it's hard for me to judge."

I'd thought Rietz would have an answer ready for me, considering how high his Intelligence and Politics scores were, but I supposed that was asking too much when he had so little information to work with. I had a feeling that when the time finally came, my Appraisal skill was going to come in handy.

If I could get a chance to evaluate their skills, and the skills of their closest allies while I was at it, I figured I'd be able to easily determine which brother had the higher odds of coming out on top. Then I'd just have to convince my father to see things my way and have him convince the count in turn. We'd be on the road to certain victory in no time!

"For local lords with small domains like House Louvent, I believe this state of affairs presents an opportunity. In a war of this nature, proving yourself in battle could be all it takes to be promoted all the way to count. It may well be in our interests to be as prepared as possible for that development," concluded Rietz.

We spent a while longer immersed in our studies, and finally, the day's lesson concluded. I, of course, wasted no time in suggesting our next activity.

"All right! I think it's time for us to head out on our usual personnel hunt! We'll need as many skilled subordinates as we can gather if we want to be prepared for a war of succession, after all!"

"Very well, then. I'll accompany you," replied Rietz. He'd been

I WILL USE MY APPRAISAL SKILL TO RISE IN THE WORLD

coming along on my headhunting missions more often than not recently, largely to serve as my personal guard.

I'd appraised the vast majority of the local villagers already, so I'd started expanding my search to the nearby towns, as well. A few Lamberg locals were skilled enough to be of some use, and I'd recruited a number of them, but unfortunately, I'd yet to find a single person with the sort of raw talent Rietz had. Venturing out to the nearby towns posed a certain degree of risk, of course, but I knew I had nothing to fear with Rietz there to protect me.

"Shall we?" I suggested.

"All right," agreed Rietz.

As the two of us stepped out from the estate, a voice rang out.

"Ars! Going into town again today, are you?" called my father from the training grounds. He'd just finished running through his swordsmanship drills, it seemed, and he wiped the sweat from his brow as he walked over to us.

"That's right!" I replied. "I'm off to look for more talented new recruits!"

"I see," said my father with a nod. "As it happens, I have a favor to ask. I want you to find someone proficient with magic, next."

"With magic?" I parroted.

"Right. Magic will be a critical factor in the battles to come, and a force that can't use it may as well not even take to the field. I don't have the knack for it, myself, and I don't have nearly enough men serving under me who do. If you find anyone with a talent for magic, I want you to bring them to me."

Magic...

I was far from knowledgeable in that field. I'd only used it once, on my father's orders. I'd had to pour a mysterious red liquid into some sort of strange device and chant a short spell, which produced a tiny ball of fire that leaped through the air.

Unfortunately, it seemed that the test was something of a failure. My father told me that I clearly wasn't suited for magic, and he never let me use it again. That was pretty disappointing, honestly—I'd been downright moved to cast my very first spell, and I really wanted to give it another go someday.

I guess I just didn't have a talent for magic, in the end. That said, if it was possible to determine someone's talent in the field with a single, simple test, I had to wonder why my father even had to bother sending *me* out to hunt for a magic user at all. Or maybe I had it wrong—maybe it wasn't easy to find talent, and my results made that fact painfully clear.

"All right," I agreed. "I'll search for someone who excels in magic!"

"Best of luck," my father replied with a nod.

And so, I set off for town with Rietz, eager to make my father proud.

○

We made the journey to town on horseback. I couldn't actually ride yet, so Rietz had to more or less hold me in his arms as he literally took the reins. Thankfully, his S-ranked Cavalry aptitude wasn't just for show, and he was an impressive enough horseman to make even my father sing his praises.

On horseback, the trip from Lamberg to the next town took roughly two hours. We were planning on staying there for two days.

"I don't know much about magic, Rietz. Is there anything you can teach me?" I asked partway through the trip. We had all that time, so a crash course on the subject seemed like the perfect way to use it.

"Magic? Let's see…" replied Rietz. "Are you already familiar with the basics?"

"Yes! I've used it once, myself. I poured some sort of red stuff into a weird device, chanted a spell, and it just worked."

"Yes, that sounds about right. The 'weird device' was a catalyzer and the red liquid is called aqua magia. Magic is cast by loading a catalyzer with aqua magia and reciting an incantation. The aqua magia is expended in the process."

Catalyzers and aqua magia, huh? I have a feeling I should remember those words.

"In the past, the incantations required to cast spells were incredibly long, so their output was considered insufficient to be used in battle. As a result, magic was more or less considered a party trick," Rietz continued. "The invention of catalyzers, however, rewrote the rulebook. They allow for shorter incantations and amplify the effects of spells, making magic a practical and lethal weapon. The proliferation of magical warfare in Summerforth began about a decade ago, and it has spread to a dramatic degree since then."

Oh, so magic's a new thing? It hasn't been used for ages? That's sort of a surprise.

"So aqua magia's like magical fuel?" I asked. "Is it easy to get?"

"Aqua magia is made by liquefying a type of stone called magistone. Magistones aren't especially rare, but the demand for it has skyrocketed in recent years, so the price has risen accordingly. Supplying a magical combat unit with aqua magia would cost a considerable sum of money."

"So it's expensive, huh…? And House Louvent doesn't exactly have the highest income…"

Lamberg was a small territory to begin with, and we didn't have any local specialties or notable natural resources to boast of. The territory brought in very little money, all things considered. We were scraping by; that was the best I could say for our finances.

"Even if we can't put an entire unit together, having just one skilled mage in our army could make all the difference," said Rietz. "I'm sure we'll be able to find at least one person to fill that role. Let's make that our priority for this excursion."

"Sounds like a plan," I quickly agreed.

A long, bumpy horse ride later, we'd arrived at our destination: Canarre, a city that served as both the namesake and central hub of the County of Canarre. It was a properly fortified city, too, surrounded by a spectacular curtain wall.

The wall didn't contain the entirety of the city, to be clear—plenty of large, well-constructed buildings stood outside the fortifications as well. I took that as a sign of how long this region had been at peace. The people here didn't see a need to keep their homes all that soundly defended, it seemed.

The walls themselves were built in the era before the unification of Summerforth, and were naturally more than a little time-worn as a result. At the very center of the town stood Castle Canarre: the home of House Pyres, the head of which served as Canarre's count.

I started by strolling around the part of town that was outside the walls. In the present day, the only people who were allowed within the walls were those of the upper class. As the son of a lord, I qualified, of course; I could have gone inside if I'd wanted to, but my goal was to find personnel, and going into the walls didn't seem necessary for that purpose. There were plenty of people in the city outside, after all.

And there really were *plenty* of people. The total population of the town was supposedly somewhere in the vicinity of fifty thou-

I WILL USE MY APPRAISAL SKILL TO RISE IN THE WORLD

sand, and the thought of appraising all of them was already making my eyes water. Thankfully, appraising literally everyone wasn't even on the table—I was planning on centering my search around the poor in particular.

The problem with coming out to a city like this was that even if I did find someone exceptional, the odds were high that they'd refuse to enter into my family's service. After all, who would want to move from the big city to a provincial hamlet like Lamberg? It wasn't like we had the funding to offer an enormous salary in exchange or anything, either.

As such, I knew that I wouldn't be able to hire anyone unless they were in serious need of money. The people who'd been living in Lamberg all their lives were basically the only exception to that rule. And if scouting out affluent individuals was a lost cause, I just had to turn my eye to those in need!

"All right, let's get searching!"

"Very well."

I scanned the crowd from horseback, keeping a keen eye out for anyone who looked relatively destitute. I didn't hit pay dirt right away, though. I found some people with reasonably remarkable talents, don't get me wrong, but I was looking for someone with talent as a mage in particular, and I wasn't planning on chatting up anyone who didn't fulfill that requirement. I didn't need them to be as incredible as Rietz or anything, but if their highest stats were in the mid-60s, I didn't feel the need to go out of my way to scout them.

All that squinting and eye strain got the better of me eventually, and I happened to also have worked up an appetite. We decided to take a break and dismounted to find something in the market to fill our stomachs. As we walked into the marketplace, though, I noticed something surprising out of the corner of my eye.

"Wait, is that...?"

I took a closer look, and indeed, I hadn't been seeing things. A cage stood in the market, and within that cage stood a cluster of people with placards hung around their necks.

"A slave trader," muttered Rietz as he followed my gaze.

Slaves.

Slavery was a common practice in the not-so-distant history of certain cultures back on Earth, but I'd never been confronted with the reality of the slave trade until that moment. My first impulse was revulsion at the thought of buying a human being, but a moment later, a second thought struck me: *Who's to say that slaves can't be just as talented as any other person?*

Going this route would certainly simplify the negotiation process for bringing them in as a retainer, as well. The problem, of course, was the question of price. I'd brought a chunk of funding with me to serve as an advance payment for anyone I recruited, but would that be enough?

No point speculating—I should take a look at them before doing anything else.

"Let's have a look at the slaves before we eat," I said to Rietz.

"The slaves?" asked Rietz. "Are you planning to buy one?"

"One of them might have talent, for all we know!"

"That's...true, I suppose," Rietz replied. He seemed more than a little hesitant, but he didn't try to dissuade me, so we approached the cage.

I took a moment to appraise everyone there, one by one. None of the numbers that were coming up were particularly impressive, though. Just as I was about to give up, my gaze fell upon a particular girl.

I WILL USE MY APPRAISAL SKILL TO RISE IN THE WORLD

> Charlotte Lace
> Age: 11
> Female
> **Status:**
> LEA: 65/92
> VAL: 93/116
> INT: 34/45
> POL: 31/40
> Ambition: 1
> **Aptitudes:**
> Infantry: D
> Cavalry: D
> Archer: D
> Mage: S
> Fortification: D
> Weaponry: D
> Naval: D
> Aerial: D
> Strategy: D

My eyes widened in shock.

A 92 in Leadership, a 116 in Valor, and an S-ranked aptitude as a mage...? Those numbers are insane!

Her other stats weren't anything to write home about, to be fair, but her strong points were undeniably out of this world. Hell, her Valor was on par with my father's, and she hadn't even reached her full potential yet!

A person's capability in combat was determined by a combination of their Valor score and their aptitudes. As such, no matter how high your Valor was, if you were fighting in a field you had a D-ranked aptitude in, you wouldn't be very effective at all. All of the girl's aptitudes other than Mage were D, so in all likelihood, she wouldn't be useful for anything other than magic on the field of battle, but that Mage aptitude! That alone would make her an overwhelming force in battle!

She had long, blue hair and a face so perfectly proportioned you'd think she was a living doll. She'd surely be beautiful when she grew up...not that I even cared. I was set! I'd buy her no matter what, bring her back to Lamberg, and have her be our army's resident mage!

"How much for that Charlotte girl?" I asked the slave trader.

"Huh? Oh, her? Five silver. Why, you want 'er?"

Five silver...

Five gold coins—with each being equivalent in value to ten silver—was enough to cover a typical adult's living expenses for a year. From that perspective, five silver was hardly an outrageous price. I checked on the other slaves' prices as well, and found that on average, the men were priced higher than the women. People probably thought men would be more valuable for manual labor purposes, I assumed. Charlotte was young and attractive, which was most likely why her price was set a little higher than the other female slaves.

At the moment, I had five gold coins on hand. In other words, more than enough money to make the purchase feasible.

"P-Pardon me, Master Ars?" said Rietz. "I hope you're not actually planning on buying that girl..."

"I am!" I replied immediately. "She has an *unbelievable* talent for magic!"

"I, uh, don't mean to doubt your eye for such things, but she *is*

I WILL USE MY APPRAISAL SKILL TO RISE IN THE WORLD

a girl. We can't exactly send her out onto the battlefield... Or rather, I don't believe Lord Raven would ever allow us to do so."

In this world, it was broadly accepted that women were not suited for combat. It wasn't an unfamiliar perspective to me—plenty of cultures back on Earth had similar values, after all. If I were to bring a girl back with me and say I planned to have her serve as a soldier, I'd probably raise even more eyebrows than I did when I brought in Rietz the Malkan to be one of our retainers.

People might start thinking I'm some sort of maniac, in the worst case! But then again, no matter what they think of me at first, seeing her literally work her magic should shut them up nice and quick.

"What's important, Rietz, is that she has an unmistakable aptitude for magic that we can't ignore! Passing up this chance just because she's female would be foolish!" I declared.

Rietz frowned, but remained silent. Apparently, he'd given up.

I passed the slave trader a gold coin. He gave me five silver in return, thanked me, then brought Charlotte out of the cage. Leading her over to me, he passed me the chain connected to the collar around her neck as well as the key to the collar itself.

I wasn't about all that collar business, though. I knew that if I was judging her correctly, she'd go on to accomplish truly incredible feats in battle. Having a woman like that wear a collar just felt *wrong* to me, so I immediately reached up to unlock it.

"Whoa there, kiddo, not so fast!" snapped the slave trader. "She might be obedient, but trust me—you'd be better off keeping her on a leash!"

"I'll be fine, thank you," I replied, removing Charlotte's collar without a second thought. She just stood there, not running away or even moving at all.

"Why did you take it off?" Charlotte eventually asked. That was my first time hearing her voice.

"Because I have no intention of keeping you as a slave," I replied. "I paid for you because I want you as one of my family's retainers. A collar isn't appropriate attire for someone of that station, right?"

Charlotte cocked her head. I got the impression she didn't really understand what I was talking about.

"Tell you what—I'm pretty hungry. Let's go get some food, and I can give you the details while we eat!"

I found some food at a nearby market stall, and we had a quick meal. Well, Rietz and I did, but it seemed Charlotte wasn't hungry, as she declined to eat with us. After we finished, I decided it was time to formally introduce ourselves.

"Now then, my name is Ars Louvent and this is..."

"Rietz Muses. Nice to meet you."

"My name is Charlotte Lace. Likewise," she replied. The way she spoke was sort of flat—almost monotone, even.

"As I said a moment ago, I bought you from that slave trader because I want to make you one of my family's retainers," I explained. I went on to tell Charlotte that I was the son of the lord of Lamberg. "So, if possible, I'd like you to come back with us and work for my household. What do you say?"

"The son of a lord? Okay," replied Charlotte immediately. "I don't have anywhere else to go, so I wouldn't mind being a retainer. I'm a girl, though. I don't know why you'd want me for a position like that. Did you think I was a boy or something? I know I don't have much of a chest, but I'm a girl through and through. Should I prove it?"

Before I even had time to ask her *how* she planned to prove it to me, Charlotte had already stood up and started pulling down her trousers.

I WILL USE MY APPRAISAL SKILL TO RISE IN THE WORLD

"No, no, stop!" I shouted frantically. "I already know you're a girl! You don't have to prove anything!"

"Oh...?" replied Charlotte, cocking her head. "I guess that makes sense. Nobody would mistake a girl as pretty as me for a boy."

Did she just call herself pretty? I mean, she's not wrong, but still, wow.

At that point, Rietz leaned in, his voice a whisper, and said, "M-Master Ars, don't you think this girl is...a little strange? Are you really sure about this?" he asked with concern.

"I don't care if she's a little strange, as long as she has talent!" I replied, though it didn't seem to do much to assuage Rietz's worries.

"So tell me, why do you want a girl like me as a retainer?" asked Charlotte.

"Because you have a talent for magic," I replied.

"For magic?" said Charlotte, cocking her head again. "I've never used magic at all, though. How could I possibly have the talent for it?"

I could immediately tell she was speaking the truth—she'd genuinely never used magic before.

That's weird, I thought. *With a Valor score that high, I assumed she had some real combat experience. Her maximum value's crazy high, sure, but that doesn't explain how someone so inexperienced could have a current Valor score that's that huge!*

I didn't have any doubts about my own Appraisal skill, but just in case, I decided to have her use some magic for us and see what happened. Fortunately, I'd had Rietz bring the necessary materials along.

"Rietz? I'd like to have her use some magic for us, as a test," I said.

"Very well. However, the middle of the city is hardly the place for such a thing. We should leave town first, Master Ars."

"Oh, right! Good point."

Rietz, Charlotte, and I made our way out to a plain just outside the city limits.

"All right," I said the moment we arrived and confirmed there wasn't anyone else nearby. "Let's do it! Think you can show us some magic?"

Rietz produced the tools Charlotte would need for her test: a catalyzer and a leather flask full of aqua magia. The catalyzer was a sphere that was about the same size as a baseball, with writing in an alphabet I didn't recognize inscribed across its surface. A chain was attached to it, and all you had to do to use it was loop it around your neck.

To start, Rietz had to fill the catalyzer with aqua magia. Part of the catalyzer was basically a lid, and removing it allowed access to the reservoir inside. Rietz took off the lid and poured a very small portion of the thick, viscous liquid into the device. Catalyzers were made to use up all of the aqua magia you put into them, regardless of how much. As a natural result, people couldn't cast multiple spells in a row with one.

"Now then, put this on," said Rietz, recapping the catalyzer and passing it over to Charlotte. She did as he said and hung it around her neck.

"What do I do now?" she asked.

"Once you're wearing it, all you have to do is recite an incantation," explained Rietz. "I only brought flame aqua magia with me today, so you'll want to use some form of fire magic."

"Huh?" I interjected, my ears perking up at a new piece of information. "Wait, does that mean there's more than one type of aqua magia?"

I've only ever seen the red stuff! Could there be a bunch of them?

I WILL USE MY APPRAISAL SKILL TO RISE IN THE WORLD

"Yes, there is. Some are blue, some green—there's all sorts, really," Rietz confirmed.

"What do the different colors mean?" I asked.

"Different types of magic have different aspects, and the color of the aqua magia indicates what magical aspects it's capable of evoking. Red aqua magia, for instance, allows you to use flame-aspected magic. For simplicity's sake, people tend to call it flame aqua magia as a result. Blue aqua magia allows you to use water-aspected magic, so it's water aqua magia, while green allows the use of wind magic, and is wind aqua magia."

"How many aspects are there?"

"Too many to list. The three I already mentioned aside, there's lightning, darkness, light, ice, sound, poison, shadow, profane, healing, force, etcetera, etcetera."

Rietz was pretty much blowing my mind. He'd listed off more magical aspects than I could've imagined, and there were even *more* of them he hadn't bothered mentioning. And wait, how were dark-aspected magic and shadow-aspected magic even any different?!

"Flame magistones are commonly mined in Missian," Rietz continued. "So most of the aqua magia in circulation in this region is flame-aspected. I believe the second most common form of aqua magia in the area would be sound-aspected, if memory serves."

Sound... What would you even use sound magic for? I guess you could send signals on the battlefield with it, or something? Or maybe you could make noises loud enough to burst people's eardrums?! No, wait, that would be just as bad for your troops as it would be for your enemy's. Scratch that plan.

"Can you teach me the incantation?" asked Charlotte. I was so caught up in Rietz's impromptu lesson that I sort of forgot about her for a minute there.

"Oh, excuse me. Right away," said Rietz, who turned back to her and began instructing her on the process. "The spell I'd like you to use today is called Fire Bullet. The incantation goes, 'O bolt of flame, burn my foe to ash.'"

I knew that incantation. It was the same spell that I had used. When I cast it, an orb of flame had whizzed out in a straight line ahead of me and detonated the moment it hit something. "Detonated" might have been overstating it a bit, though—it was more of a pop than an explosion, really. That was probably on account of me rather than the spell, however, and considering Charlotte's sheer, raw talent, I had a feeling we were about to witness a much bigger fireball.

"Oh, and when you cast magic, you have to hold a hand out before you," added Rietz. "The catalyzer won't activate otherwise."

"Left? Right?" Charlotte asked bluntly.

"Whichever your dominant hand is. It'll be easier to aim that way."

"Left, then."

Guess Charlotte's a lefty.

The field we were standing in was dotted here and there with trees, and Rietz told Charlotte to use one of them as a target. She picked the tree nearest to us, held her palm out toward it, and chanted the spell.

"O bolt of flame, burn my foe to ash."

For just an instant, the catalyzer let out a flash of light, and at the exact same moment, the Fire Bullet burst out from Charlotte's hand.

And I mean it *burst* out, at a tremendous speed. It rocketed across the field, hitting the tree dead center.

AS A REINCARNATED ARISTOCRAT

Before I could even process that, a thunderous roar swept across the field as an enormous explosion engulfed the tree. When the dust settled and the smoke cleared, there wasn't even a charred trace of the trunk left. All that remained was an enormous crater, centered upon the point where a tree had stood tall a couple of seconds ago.

Rietz and I stood there, stock-still, our mouths agape. When I cast that spell, its destructive potential was roughly equivalent to that of a firecracker. I knew that magic could be more or less effective depending on who was using it, but I was aghast that the difference could be *that* stark.

"That was...pretty good, right?" I mumbled in amazement.

"P-Pretty good doesn't even begin to describe it..." muttered Rietz in response. "I've seen plenty of mages on the battlefield, but I've never seen a Fire Bullet like *that* before... Was that *really* your first time casting a spell?"

Charlotte simply nodded in reply.

"Then there's no doubt about it. She's a magical prodigy," said Rietz.

I didn't really need the confirmation, honestly. Watching her cast a single spell was enough to sell me.

"Once again, Master Ars, your eye for talent has proven its worth," added Rietz, turning to me with a look of the utmost respect in his eyes. "I'm beyond impressed—you truly are incredible."

Charlotte's aptitude for magic was the real deal, and with firepower like *that* on the table, I couldn't possibly imagine my father turning her away, girl or not. I was convinced that I'd be able to make her one of our retainers without much fuss. We'd initially planned on staying in Canarre for two days, but I considered our mission thoroughly accomplished, and we decided to return to the

I WILL USE MY APPRAISAL SKILL TO RISE IN THE WORLD

estate immediately.

The three of us mounted our horse together. I was barely bigger than a toddler, and Charlotte was far from fully grown as well, so the horse didn't have too much trouble bearing all of our weight. It couldn't quite gallop at full speed, though, so the trip back was noticeably slower than the journey to Canarre had been.

"I can't believe I had this sort of talent hidden away in me," Charlotte suddenly muttered to herself. "They say the heavens never grant two blessings at once, but I guess I'm an exception."

"Huh? Wait, then what's your other blessing?" I asked, my curiosity piqued.

"My face."

"Oh."

Somebody sure has tons of self-esteem. Like, a weirdly high amount of it.

Again, though, she wasn't *wrong*, so I couldn't bring myself to call her out on it.

Charlotte was hard to get a handle on in general, really. I still had no idea what sort of person she was. I remembered what my father had told me: finding people with talent was the first step, but it wouldn't amount to anything if I didn't know how to *use* their talents, as well. That meant that having a solid grasp on my retainers' personalities was an absolute must.

I decided to start by asking about Charlotte's history, and one question on that subject immediately sprang to mind.

"How did you end up getting enslaved, Charlotte?"

"That's a long, tragic story," she replied. And of course it was, so she most likely didn't want to talk about it. I decided not to pry further, but she surprised me by continuing her story. "I never knew my parents, and I grew up in the slums."

AS A REINCARNATED ARISTOCRAT

Oof! Yeah, we're off to a pretty heavy start. I bet slum life was so hard that she eventually had no choice but to let herself get sold off, or something along those lines.

"Life in the slums was hard...for pretty much everyone else, but I was more or less the boss of all the town's slum brats."

Well, scratch that theory. She was a boss? *I guess it doesn't make much of a difference whether you're a boy or a girl when you're a little kid. And considering her crazy Leadership score, it's not a surprise that she'd end up in that sort of position.*

"The lord who ruled over the area was a real tightwad. He taxed his people to their last copper while he lived in luxury. I hated his guts, and it'd been so long since we'd managed to get food that my kids were on the brink of starving, so I decided to go steal from his mansion's kitchen. Long story short, I got caught. Most thieves get executed on the spot, but since I'm a real looker, he decided to sell me off instead."

I couldn't say she'd brought it upon herself, but I also couldn't say she hadn't walked right into it. Then again, if the lord in question really was that much of a tyrant, and if her only choices were to steal food or die, I couldn't blame her for turning to theft.

"So? Did you shed a tear?" asked Charlotte.

"Not quite, sorry... You don't sound all that torn up about it, either."

"Huh. True enough."

Once again, I met with a wall of impenetrable indifference. Talking to her wasn't doing much at all to help me figure her out as a person, and the circumstances of her enslavement didn't give me very many clues, either.

A few hours of getting tossed around by our horse's canter later, we arrived at my family's estate.

I WILL USE MY APPRAISAL SKILL TO RISE IN THE WORLD

○

We made it back around dusk. The moment we arrived, I hurried off to find my father and ask him to make Charlotte one of our retainers.

"Absolutely not," said my father, just as I expected. "What are you thinking, Ars? You'd make a girl a mage? Men fight to protect women, not to see them driven out onto the field of battle!"

"I thought you would say that," I replied. "However, I believe that her talent for magic will fill that crucial void in your army! That's why I brought her back with me."

My father gave me a skeptical glance. Just then, Rietz stepped in to back me up.

"Master Ars speaks the truth, Milord. The girl, Charlotte Lace, possesses a talent for magic the likes of which I've never seen."

Thankfully, our desperate appeal finally seemed to get through to him.

"Very well," my father sighed. "I'll give her one chance to demonstrate this supposed talent of hers. If she's the unprecedented genius you claim her to be, I'll take her under my command as a mage."

It was time for another test! We moved outside to find an appropriate location for Charlotte to show off her magic. Knowing what she was capable of, I figured that having her cast anything on the training grounds would be incredibly dangerous, so I decided to find a different, wide-open space for the event.

In the end, we settled on an abandoned field. It had been cultivated at one point, but was now overgrown with weeds and thick undergrowth. We put a wooden box out into the center of it to serve as her target. Meanwhile, the rumor that we were putting Charlotte to the test had spread among my father's men, who all gathered to watch.

"A girl? And she's supposed to be a *mage*?"

"I wouldn't be so hasty—she's another one that the young master hand-picked for the job!"

"Right, but come on! This time he *has* to be going a step too far."

"Can women even *use* magic?"

"Take a close look at her! With a face like that, maybe the young master's planning on taking her as his bride?"

"He's *four*, jackass!"

I decided to disregard their color commentary. Charlotte's magic would shut them up before long, anyway.

"Go on, then," said my father.

At his prompting, Charlotte began preparing to cast her spell. Setting up a catalyzer was a simple enough process that she'd learned how to do it just by seeing Rietz run through the steps once.

Charlotte extended her arm, holding her palm out toward the box, and chanted her incantation. A Fire Bullet burst forth from her hand, sailing across the field and scoring a direct hit on the box.

The ensuing explosion was, somehow, even more enormous than on her first try. It seemed that lone attempt had been enough practice for her to improve her magical ability substantially. It was hard—and terrifying—to imagine just how dangerous she'd become if she had the chance to get some real practice in.

The soldiers, by the way, were all gawking in bug-eyed horror. I could literally see the nervous sweat begin to drip down their faces. Even my father was openly shocked, for once. I'd never seen his jaw drop like that before.

I WILL USE MY APPRAISAL SKILL TO RISE IN THE WORLD

For a moment, silence reigned. Then, at last, my father pulled himself together enough to speak.

"Very well, then. We have ourselves a mage."

Interlude: Charlotte's Postscript

My name is Charlotte Lace, and about a week ago, I got recruited to be some lord's retainer. Couldn't even begin to explain how or why. I've lived hand to mouth my whole life—even before I was enslaved—so if this new job of mine means I get to live in a big, clean mansion and eat an actual meal every single day, I'll count myself lucky.

"Hey, Charlotte! Are you getting used to the lifestyle here?" asks the source of my newfound fortune, a little lordling called Ars. I nod and give him a grunt of agreement.

He's the one who paid my way out of slavery, all to "make me his retainer," so it's thanks to him that my life's taken a turn for the better. He looks like a cute little brat at first glance, but I figured out pretty quickly that he's actually more of a cute little weirdo. He talks like a fully-grown adult, for one thing.

Speaking of Ars being weird, there's one question I still haven't gotten a decent answer to. When we first met, he told me that he wanted me to work for his family because I have a talent for magic. Turns out he was right. I guess I really *do* have more of a knack for it than most people. I thought he was just talking me up, but after arriving at his estate, I got the chance to see a couple other folks cast a few spells.

I WILL USE MY APPRAISAL SKILL TO RISE IN THE WORLD

Honestly? They were sorta pathetic. At the very least, they didn't have anywhere close to the sort of power my spells seem to pack.

So, yeah, I guess Ars was right, and I really do have a talent for magic. But how the hell did he figure *that* out? I'd literally never cast a single spell before we met. Anyway, since he's around and apparently up for a chat, I may as well ask him.

"I can tell what people's talents are at a glance! It's an ability of mine," he explains. "That's why, the moment I laid eyes on you, I knew for a fact that you had a talent for magic."

"Huh, really?"

I've never been good at, like, showing my emotions or any of that stuff, so he probably can't tell, but I'm honestly really shocked on the inside. I mean, what? He can just look at people and tell their talents, just like that? Didn't know that was a thing.

"Just for magic?"

"You mean, your talents?"

"Yeah."

Ars hesitates for a moment, then shakes his head and replies, "No, that's not all. You probably also have a talent for leading soldiers into battle."

"Do I have any talents that *aren't* all about fighting?" I ask.

"I, uh…can't say for sure, but you don't have any that my power can discern."

"Oh… Too bad."

That's kind of a letdown. Then again, I'm enjoying myself plenty with magic already. If I can only have one big talent, at least I got a good one.

"I'm off to practice," I say, giving Ars a wave and heading toward the training grounds.

If magic's my thing, I may as well get real good at it.

Chapter 3

A very eventful year had passed since Charlotte began working as a mage for House Louvent. Canarre, the county that Lamberg belonged to, was situated on the westernmost edge of the Duchy of Missian. In other words, it shared a border with Seitz, the duchy to the west. As a natural consequence, territorial disputes were common and small skirmishes were surprisingly frequent...and whenever one of those skirmishes arose, my father was called upon to ride into battle.

Over the past year, he'd had to sortie in that manner no less than five times. Charlotte went along with him, and quickly proved herself both an invaluable asset on the battlefield as well as an indispensable presence in the Louvent household. She'd grown on a personal level, as well—her Valor score had reached a total of 101.

Before I knew it, she'd also ended up becoming something of a boss to the very few mages who served House Louvent, and her Leadership score had risen to 73. Something about her strange, hard-to-pin-down personality drew people to her, for reasons I couldn't quite fathom.

Her contributions were so dramatic, in fact, that I'd heard that other noble families had made efforts to hire her away from us.

She turned them all down, thankfully. I wasn't entirely sure why, but part of me sort of hoped that she did it out of a sense of gratitude toward me.

Rietz, meanwhile, was still serving as my personal tutor. As a natural result, he hadn't had the chance to go out and make a name for himself on the battlefield the way Charlotte had. He had the skills for it, no question about it, and part of me wondered if he wasn't secretly chomping at the bit to get out there and accomplish something, but when I asked him about it, he just said there could be no greater honor than educating the next head of the family. He might have been just trying to make me feel better, but I didn't get the sense he was outright lying.

Speaking of the family, the year brought with it one very happy event: the birth of my twin siblings, a boy and a girl! They'd been born two weeks ago. I'd already turned six, myself, so we were rather far apart in age—though, of course, if you took my mental age into account, I might as well have been their father.

My little brother's name was Kreiz, and my little sister's name was Wren. Kreiz was born just a little while before Wren, so I suppose she was his little sister as well, technically. Needless to say, I appraised both of them the first chance I got!

Kreiz's status screen looked like this:

I WILL USE MY APPRAISAL SKILL TO RISE IN THE WORLD

Status:
LEA: 1/82
VAL: 1/89
INT: 1/33
POL: 1/21
Ambition: 77
Aptitudes:
Infantry: S
Cavalry: B
Archer: A
Mage: C
Fortification: D
Weaponry: D
Naval: D
Aerial: D
Strategy: D

And Wren's looked like this:

AS A REINCARNATED ARISTOCRAT

> **Status:**
> LEA: 1/22
> VAL: 1/21
> INT: 1/91
> POL: 1/85
> Ambition: 33
> **Aptitudes:**
> Infantry: D
> Cavalry: D
> Archer: D
> Mage: D
> Fortification: C
> Weaponry: B
> Naval: C
> Aerial: B
> Strategy: A

They were still infants, of course, so all of their stats were currently stuck at 1, but they both had a couple of truly remarkable maximum values!

Kreiz clearly took after his father. His Leadership and Valor were both outstanding, but his Intelligence and Politics scores weren't exactly exceptional. He also had an S-ranked aptitude as an infantryman, so I had a feeling that he'd prove to be a master with the sword or the spear when he grew up.

Wren, in sharp contrast, had incredible Intelligence and Politics scores, but wasn't anything special when it came to Leadership or Valor. Her A-ranked aptitude in Strategy made me hopeful that she was a master tactician in the making, however.

I WILL USE MY APPRAISAL SKILL TO RISE IN THE WORLD

In short, the twins' strong and weak points seemed to complement each other extremely well. The one problem with that theory, of course, was that women born into noble families in this world were raised with a very particular purpose in mind: marrying into other noble households. Thus, I knew that keeping Wren around in the Louvent household might prove challenging.

Part of me seriously considered marching up to my father and telling him that Wren had the brains to be a master tactician, and that he should raise and educate her to fill that role. Another part of me, however, couldn't help but wonder if that was really in her best interests. A militaristic upbringing like that would almost certainly hurt her chances at marriage, after all. Would I be spoiling her best opportunity to find happiness?

As it turned out, deciding how a child should be raised wasn't a task I was especially prepared for! There was another factor weighing on my mind, as well: Kreiz's remarkably high Ambition score. He was sitting at a value of 77, and a high ambition carried with it a heightened chance of betrayal. If we gave him any reason to take issue with his living situation, he might defect to another household...or even start a rebellion!

As best as I could tell, anything above a 60 in Ambition was on the high end of the spectrum. A score in the 70s was just about unprecedented. I had to make getting a handle on Kreiz's personality a top priority, then keep him on a short leash at all times!

○

"That's enough for today, I believe," said Rietz, lowering his sword.

We were out in the training yard, and had just finished up a lesson in swordsmanship. Knowing how to defend myself in a pinch could save my life someday, so it seemed like an important skill to obtain...but unfortunately, I hadn't turned out to be a very fast learner. Rietz and my father were unperturbed by my lack of talent—I *was* only six, after all—but *I* could tell that age wouldn't cure this problem. It seemed I just hadn't inherited my father's knack for martial arts.

Then again, it wasn't like I was hoping to charge out into battle and reap my foes like a field of grain. I didn't really *need* that sort of ability, either. I could leave those matters to the people who were better suited for them, and focus on my own strong points. That perspective made me feel at least a little better as I wiped the sweat off my brow and collected myself.

"Incidentally, Master Ars, I wonder if you've heard the news..." began Rietz.

"News? What news?"

"A family of hunters has moved into town recently. They're known as the Kischa family, apparently, and they have three sons. The eldest and second eldest—a twelve-year-old and an eleven-year-old, respectively—are purportedly tall, muscular, and all but certain to become incredibly strong men in the future. Do you suppose we should go take a look to judge them for ourselves?"

"Let me think..." I muttered. This wasn't the first time I'd caught wind of a supposedly incredible person of interest, only for them to turn out to be nothing special at all when I appraised them. Still, though, if these wonder-sons were already in Lamberg, I didn't exactly have anything to lose by heading out to take a look. "Yes, we might as well go see them!"

"Understood. I'll prepare for our excursion immediately."

And so, Rietz and I set off for Lamberg proper. We strolled into town and made a beeline directly for the Kischa family's home. Un-

I WILL USE MY APPRAISAL SKILL TO RISE IN THE WORLD

like the first time I went into town, I made no effort to disguise the fact that I was the lord's son. Somewhere around the sixth time I went scouting in the village, I got found out and caused a bit of a scene, and I'd been back several times since then.

The villagers seemed to be used to my presence, and didn't think much of my visits at all anymore. The disguise would've seemed superfluous at this point. Unlike that first incident, Rietz and I weren't getting swarmed by excited townsfolk, and we were walking around in the open without making any effort to hide our identities.

"We've arrived," said Rietz. "This is the Kischa family's home."

We'd stopped in front of a somewhat run-down old house. Even by the village's low standards, it was far from a luxury dwelling. I stepped up to the door, ready to knock, only for it to be flung open in my face before I had the chance.

A child burst out from the house, bawling his eyes out. He was young and scrawny enough that I couldn't actually tell what gender he was with total certainty, but my best guess was that he was a boy. His golden hair was in dire need of a good combing, and he was even shorter, and presumably younger, than me.

The child took one look at me, then spun around and sped off down the street, still crying incessantly. I didn't even have time to appraise him before he made it out of sight.

I guess that's one of the Kischa kids? He didn't look eleven or twelve, though... Oh, right! Rietz said they had three *children!*

The rumors claimed that the two eldest children were tough as nails, but they also mentioned a younger child who I'd almost forgotten. He certainly didn't seem to live up to his brothers' reputations, but then again, he was still just a kid. Who could say how he'd grow?

"Rosell! Get back here, boy!" roared an enormous man who emerged from the house just a moment later. He glanced down, noticing my presence. "Who're...? Wait—aren't you the lord's son?!"

I guess my outfit must've given me away.

The man's expression shifted dramatically the moment he realized my identity.

"Indeed I am!" I replied. "My name is Ars, and it's a pleasure to make your acquaintance."

"What's the lord's son doing in front of *my* home...?" the man asked, clearly skeptical.

"I've caught wind that the sons of the family that lives here are truly remarkable individuals, so I decided that I would like to see their capabilities for myself."

"Oh! Well, that's—that's wonderful! My name's Greg Kischa. Please, come inside!"

Greg's attitude pivoted on a dime, and he welcomed me with open arms. A moment later, he noticed Rietz and made a face like he'd taken a big bite out of a lemon, but Malkan or not, Rietz was dressed the part of a lord's retainer, so Greg didn't try to turn him away. Incidentally, I checked Greg's stats and found, aside from a slightly above-average Valor score, that he was perfectly unremarkable in every regard.

"By the way," I asked as I strolled inside. "Was the boy who ran away in tears a moment ago one of your sons?"

"Yeah, the boy's name is Rosell," Greg replied. "He's my third son, but he's not worth your time. The brat's nothing compared to his brothers. He was born weak, he's a crybaby, and nothing I tell him seems to make him shape up. Y'know why he was crying a minute ago? 'Cause I told him off for pissing the bed! The boy's *five*! Hate to imagine what he'll be like when he's an adult."

I WILL USE MY APPRAISAL SKILL TO RISE IN THE WORLD

"If he's only five, then he still has plenty of time to grow," I said.

"You think? Well, he's no lord's son, that's for sure! Just one look at you, and I can tell you've got a good head on your shoulders. Rosell'll never match that! You look to be about his age, too."

That "good head" on my shoulders has a solid thirty years on Rosell's thanks to my reincarnation, though.

I couldn't remember perfectly, but I had a feeling I'd still wet the bed every once in a while when I was five, too.

Greg went on to introduce me to his other two sons. The eldest was named Gatos, while the second eldest was Marcus. The rumors certainly weren't exaggerated: both of them were remarkably tall and sturdily built for their age, and when I appraised them, their numbers were much better than I'd expected.

Both of their Leadership attributes had maximum scores in the 40s, and while they weren't quite natural-born commanders, Gatos's maximum Valor was 77, while Marcus's was 75. Their current Valor scores were nothing to scoff at, either—Gatos had a 67 and Marcus a 65. All that said, their Intelligence and Politics scores were pretty awful.

As far as aptitudes went, Gatos had an A-rank as an infantryman. The rest of his were all Cs or Ds, though. Marcus had an A in Archer, but Cs and Ds for everything else across the board as well. In short, Gatos would likely excel in melee combat, while Marcus would be better off as a long-distance fighter.

Honestly, I wasn't expecting them to be anything incredible. Hell, I wouldn't have been shocked if they'd been totally useless! But apparently, sometimes rumors really were right on the money.

"So, what do you think?" asked Rietz.

"Both of them have real potential!" I replied. "If either of them has any interest in being a soldier, then I say they should be sent off to the training grounds as soon as tomorrow!"

"Oh, perfect! You two were just telling me you wanted to go out in battle and make a name for yourselves, weren't you?!" exclaimed Greg, who was absolutely beaming. I knew he was a hunter, but apparently, he wasn't too particular about his sons carrying on the family trade. He seemed downright excited for his sons to become soldiers, even. Gatos and Marcus were just as enthusiastic, so they immediately agreed to begin training at my family's estate.

"Perfect! In that case, feel free to stop by tomorrow. No time to waste!"

"Yes, sir!" they exclaimed.

With that, my business with the family was complete. I stepped outside…only to find Rosell, the boy who'd run out in tears earlier, making his way back home. On a whim, I decided to give him an appraisal. His brothers were both exceptional, after all, so perhaps he had some talent lurking deep down as well.

I glanced at Rosell's stats and very nearly choked.

I WILL USE MY APPRAISAL SKILL TO RISE IN THE WORLD

> Rosell Kischa
> Age: 5
> Male
> **Status:**
> LEA: 35/88
> VAL: 11/32
> INT: 45/109
> POL: 32/95
> Ambition: 21
> **Aptitudes:**
> Infantry: D
> Cavalry: D
> Archer: C
> Mage: C
> Fortification: A
> Weaponry: A
> Naval: C
> Aerial: A
> Strategy: S

Not only did he have talent, he had the overwhelming ingenuity necessary to become a tactician the likes of which the world had never seen! The only word that could possibly describe his maximum Intelligence score was "absurd." I couldn't imagine there was anyone on the continent of Summerforth with a score higher than 109!

And that wasn't all—his Politics and Leadership scores were also incredible. Valor was his only low stat, and I got the impression that he just wasn't much of a fighter. He was also five, of course, so his current stats were all on the low side, but with the right upbringing, he could be a truly invaluable retainer in the long run.

I thought I'd found an excellent crop of candidates in his brothers, but Rosell was simply on another level. The Kischa family moving to Lamberg was a godsend, no question about it!

"Has that boy caught your attention, Master Ars?" asked Rietz, who'd noticed my astonished stare.

"He really has," I replied. "He has a mind like nothing I've seen before, and his potential is breathtaking! If we can give him the training he needs, he'll be an incredible tactician someday."

"A tactician, you say...? Well, I wouldn't dream of questioning your judgment."

"It *is* just a matter of potential at this point, though," I clarified. "Still, I'd like to give him the education that he deserves."

"In that case, why not have him attend your lessons?" suggested Rietz. "If he's as bright as you say, I'm sure that teaching him will be worth my time."

Having him study with me? That's a great idea, actually!

Rietz was an incredible teacher, and I was certain that under his tutelage, Rosell's Intelligence would improve by leaps and bounds. The problem, of course, was his father. Would Greg permit us to take over his child's education?

Throughout that whole exchange, Rosell had been standing nearby, staring at me and shivering. Tears were pooling in the corners of his eyes. It seemed that, in his mind, Rietz and I were more than a little intimidating. We hadn't done anything in particular, though, so I was at a loss as to what could be scaring him so much.

It's not like my father's here with us—though, if he were, I could definitely understand the impulse to break down and cry.

"Oh, Rosell!" Speaking of terrifying fathers, Greg arrived just in

I WILL USE MY APPRAISAL SKILL TO RISE IN THE WORLD

time to give Rosell the third degree. "Where've you been?! And did you remember to greet the young master?!"

Rosell shook his head.

"Are you daft, boy?! That's the son of Lord Raven you're looking at! How could you not even bother to *greet* him?!"

He's probably just shy, right? Okay, maybe really *shy, considering how scared of us he seems. Then again, with a Politics score like that, I'm sure his shyness will go away with a little training. You can't exactly be a master politician if you can't look a stranger in the eye!*

In any case, Greg's arrival was quite timely for my purposes. I decided to speak to him about Rosell's education right away.

"Greg, Rosell," I began, "There's something I'd like to discuss with you, if you have a moment."

"Huh? You aren't finished? And wait, with me and *Rosell*?" Greg exclaimed incredulously.

"Quite!" I replied. "You see, I can tell that Rosell has the talent to be a tactician. He's still a child, of course, so his talent is still underdeveloped, but I'd like to give him the education that he needs to make the most of it."

"*R-Rosell*?! This wimpy little bedwetter, a *tactician*?! Y-You're pulling my leg, right?"

"Everyone wets the bed at some point in their life. I don't think it's anything to be embarrassed about," I chided.

"Right, but you don't understand! The boy's useless! He can't even look a man in the eye, he's built like a twig, and he's barely grown at all since he started walking! His brothers were a thousand times better put together when they were his age!"

Greg's opinion of Rosell was even lower than I'd thought. I had a feeling that Greg judged his sons purely by their physical strength, and didn't spare much thought for their smarts. Even at his current status, Rosell was surely remarkably bright for a child of his age, and if he'd been born into a family that valued education, they might have found him to be a genuine prodigy. A shame, then, that a hunter's household didn't offer many chances for that sort of education.

His brothers and their exceptional Valor scores probably hadn't helped the situation, either. I'm sure he looked like a downright disappointment in comparison. And, to be fair, if you solely compared their Valor stats, he *was* the least capable by a mile. I had a feeling that convincing Greg of Rosell's true potential was going to be a difficult task, which meant that my only option was to ask him as sincerely as possible, and hope he'd cut me a break.

"It's true that Rosell has talent—of that, I'm extremely confident. If you allow him to study under me, I can guarantee that he will make a splendid tactician in the future. Will you let him attend lessons at my family's estate?"

Greg hesitated for a moment, then replied, "Well… If you're really willing to teach him, I guess I don't have any reason to say no. You're good with that, right, Rosell?"

Rosell looked up at his father, then nodded silently. It didn't feel like he was interested so much as he was unwilling to defy his father's wishes, though, and he didn't exactly look enthused. I was hoping to have him cast the deciding vote, but maybe asking a five-year-old to make their own decisions was a little much.

"I appreciate it," I replied. "In that case, I'd like to begin Rosell's education tomorrow as well. Please bring Gatos and Marcus to the training grounds tomorrow morning, then bring Rosell to my family's estate proper. Thank you for your time."

"Right, will do."

Starting his education so soon seemed like asking for a lot, but

I WILL USE MY APPRAISAL SKILL TO RISE IN THE WORLD

I couldn't resist. With Greg as on board as I could've expected, I returned home and spent the rest of the day practically trembling with excitement for the next morning.

○

And before long, the next morning arrived!

"Rosell is here, Master Ars," reported Rietz. I immediately hurried outside, where I found Greg and his son waiting for me.

"Oh, Master Ars! Sorry to make you come all the way out to welcome us. Come on, boy, say sorry with me!" said Greg, giving me an apologetic bow and shoving Rosell's head down in an imitation of the gesture. "Well, I've got work that needs doing. You listen here, Rosell: you are *not* to make a nuisance of yourself! There'll be hell to pay if you do, y'hear?!"

With that parting comment, Greg went on his way. I turned to Rosell.

"Thank you for coming today, Rosell!" I said, stepping toward him. "Now then, let's head inside and—"

"Eek!" Rosell whimpered, shrinking away from me.

Am I really that scary?

His condition was a little too extreme for me to call it plain shyness. It seemed he had an almost phobic aversion to meeting new people.

"Rosell, it's all right. I'm not planning to hurt you. There's no need to be afraid of me, I promise," I said, flashing the least intimidating smile I could manage.

Rosell, unfortunately, wasn't buying it.

"Y-You're lying!" he snapped. Which, incidentally, were the first proper words I'd heard him speak out loud.

"I'm not," I calmly replied. "I'm telling the truth."

"N-No you're not! You're a dirty liar! You s-said I have talent, but that's impossible! Y-You called me to your house to kidnap and enslave me! Or maybe you just did it because you thought bullying me would be fun! Y-You're up to no good, I just know it!"

It seemed that once Rosell's mouth opened, there was very little you could do to make him shut it again. I was stunned by both the speed at which the little motor-mouth could talk when he put his mind to it and the sheer degree of pure pessimism he was spouting at me. I was obviously not dealing with the most trusting of individuals.

Then again, a healthy dose of pathological skepticism could very well be an asset for a tactician, from a certain point of view. It'd certainly serve him better than being too optimistic or too credulous, at the very least. I just had to convince him that *I* was a person he could let his guard down around.

I walked up to Rosell and planted my hands atop his shoulders. I felt him jump in fright, but I held him in place, looked him directly in his teary, sky-blue eyes, and said, "That wasn't a lie. I am certain beyond a shadow of a doubt that you *do* have talent, and that is the reason why I called you here. I swear that I will do you no harm."

Rosell whimpered, but it seemed that going into full-on serious mode had finally gotten through to him at least a little. His shivering felt like it was growing at least a little less violent, anyway. It couldn't be *that* easy, though, and a few seconds later, Rosell broke eye contact. I could tell by that point that standing around and talking at him wasn't going to gain me any more ground.

"All right, follow me," I said, then turned around and began making my way to the room where Rietz taught me my lessons.

I WILL USE MY APPRAISAL SKILL TO RISE IN THE WORLD

Rietz, incidentally, had been accompanying me all the while, and leaned down to whisper in my ear as we walked.

"I'm a little concerned about that boy, Master Ars. Are you sure he's ready for this?" he asked. He had a point. Entering the estate had done nothing to clear up Rosell's obvious anxiety, and he was glancing about wildly, keeping a constant eye on his surroundings. His guard was up impossibly high.

And then, with superbly terrible timing, my family's pet fledgehound, Ahsis, showed up to make a mess of things.

"Arf, arf!"

"*Augh,* no! A b-b-beast!"

The instant Rosell spotted Ahsis, he was on the move, zipping over to take cover behind a nearby statue.

"No need to be scared! It's perfectly all right. Ahsis isn't a *beast* or anything of the sort," I explained, kneeling down and patting Ahsis's head in an effort to prove that our pet really was, well, just a pet. Ahsis's wings fluttered happily in response. "See? Cute, right?"

Wings aside, Ahsis looked like a Japanese Chin, which was far from the scariest of breeds out there.

"I-It's cute *now,* sure," admitted Rosell. "B-But, umm…i-it might transform, for all I know! M-Maybe when it smells prey, it shapeshifts into a mighty cerberus! Wait…I see now! You brought me here to feed me to your beast, I'm sure of it! I bet it has a taste for small, tender prey! It all makes sense now!"

Once again, Rosell was descending into a spiral of remarkably talkative negativity. I was starting to realize that he was just as much of an eccentric as Charlotte, albeit in a very different sort of way. In any case, Ahsis was terrifying him, so I called one of our family's servants over to take the fledgehound out for a walk.

"Okay, it's gone. Nothing to be scared of anymore, right?" I said, trying to reassure him. However, Rosell was still glancing compulsively around at his surroundings. It took way longer than I'd expected to guide him to our study, in the end.

Speaking of the study: as we walked inside, the books that filled the chamber reminded me of an important question I had to ask.

"By the way, can you read, Rosell?"

I'd gathered over the years that this world's literacy rate wasn't even close to that of Japan's. Considering the fact that he was only five, I figured that the odds of Rosell already being literate were extremely low.

"Only a little," he replied, more or less as expected.

Looks like teaching him to read will be our first order of business, then.

Rietz had been illiterate at first as well, technically, but he managed to pick up the skill after only five days of studying. Meanwhile, it took *me* about three weeks to learn the local writing system. I really came to appreciate just how talented Rietz was after he pulled that little feat off.

Rosell's maximum Intelligence score was outrageously high, so I figured that he *had* to be pretty quick on the uptake. He was still a kid, too, which meant that his mind was a sponge for new information. I wouldn't have been surprised if he picked up reading even faster than Rietz had.

"I'll study on my own today so that you can teach Rosell how to read," I told Rietz. Leaving the task up to him while I did my own thing felt like my best bet.

"Very well," Rietz replied.

Surprisingly, Rosell was actually quite obedient when it came to Rietz's lessons...possibly on account of the fact that he was scared stiff of his teacher. I was a little worried about whether he'd actually

I WILL USE MY APPRAISAL SKILL TO RISE IN THE WORLD

remember any of the things he learned in that condition, but I had faith that Rietz would figure something out, so I tried to focus on my own studies.

Emphasis on *tried*, unfortunately. Without Rietz the super-teacher on my side, I wasn't making much progress at all. Studying tactics was all well and good, but since I'd never even *seen* a real battle in person, a lot of the descriptions I was reading didn't really click.

Hmm. Yeah, I think it's time to shake things up. I'll leave the tactics to the tacticians.

I decided to focus on history and geography instead…but that resolve didn't last long. I ended up moving from one subject to the next without ever grasping anything new about any of them.

I probably should've seen that coming, frankly. In my previous life, I'd consistently ranked in the lower-middle portion of my class, grade-wise. Some people had the sheer, dogged diligence to focus on their studies to the exclusion of everything else, and I was most certainly not one of them.

Quite a fair span of time had passed before I decided to check in on Rosell and see how many letters he'd learned while I was being unproductive. I set down my own study materials and looked over, only to find Rosell hunched over a book in complete silence. Rietz wasn't saying a word either—just standing there, staring at his new protégé.

"What's going on over here?" I asked. "Don't tell me he's memorized all the letters already?"

My new world's standard alphabet had far fewer characters than Japanese. It was closer to English, in that respect, and since it didn't have Japanese's excess of written characters, it was a little easier to pick up, from my perspective. Not *that* easy, though! It'd been less than a single day!

"Y-Yes, he has, difficult though it is to believe," stammered Rietz. "He is...*abnormally* adept at grasping new concepts, it would seem. He learned the whole alphabet before I knew it, then said he was interested in the books, so I let him read one, and, well..."

"You mean he's *actually* reading a whole book already?"

"Yes. As a matter of fact, this isn't the first one. He's currently working his way through his third book of the day."

"You're *kidding* me," I gaped at Rosell. "That means he's gotten through at least three hundred pages!"

"Yes, his pace *is* quite impressive. I've checked, though, and he genuinely understands and absorbs everything he reads. His ability to concentrate is remarkable. Speaking of which—I tried to speak to him while he was reading, and it was like he couldn't even hear me! I had to wait until after he finished the volume to quiz him on its contents. Frankly, I've more or less been sitting here and waiting while he reads on his own. I suppose that's just how it goes when you're dealing with a genius..."

Rietz shook his head and shrugged. I could hardly believe that Rosell was smart enough to make even *him* feel awed.

"I'll admit," continued Rietz. "I was worried that this might be too drastic of a step for him, but you've proven me wrong yet again. Your ability to perceive talent really does seem infallible."

Rosell took to books like a fish to water. He finished several more tomes before the day was out, only to abruptly run out of energy around dusk and collapse into a deep sleep on the spot. I ended up having to ask one of my family's servants to carry him back to his house for me.

Ever since then, Rosell started visiting my family's estate daily to study alongside me. He remained wary of me and my family for

I WILL USE MY APPRAISAL SKILL TO RISE IN THE WORLD

the first two or three days, but eventually, he decided that we weren't an immediate threat to his life and limb and started warming up to us. By around twenty days in, it felt like he'd completely opened up to me.

As Rosell settled into the rhythm of his new routine, he eventually started calling Rietz Mr. Rietz—a sign of respect toward his teacher, apparently—and calling me just plain Ars. He also blazed through the books in our study at such an astonishing pace that I was worried it wouldn't be long before he ran through all of them! Books were fairly precious and hard to come by in this world, so we didn't exactly have a fully-stocked library on our hands, but it was still preposterous to think he could work his way through *that* many of them in less than a month. Why, he was already picking up pieces of knowledge and trivia that even most adults wouldn't know.

All that said, his Intelligence score hadn't gone up all that much. It was sitting at a value of 48, currently. It seemed that it took a little more than having a good memory or knowing a lot of random facts to raise your overall Intelligence. My best guess was that it had more to do with how you *used* the knowledge that you'd gained, and Rosell was still an inexperienced boy of five. He knew all sorts of things, sure, but he hadn't learned how to make use of any of them, and until he managed to do so, his Intelligence was unlikely to make any significant advances.

Considering his maximum Intelligence, though, I was very confident that he wasn't wasting his time hitting the books. A value like that meant that he had the potential to gain some life experience and start putting the fruits of his studies to use before too terribly long, and the moment he started doing so, I expected his Intelligence to skyrocket.

In short: learning as much as he possibly could while he was still young seemed like it would prove very important for Rosell's growth, and happily enough, he'd turned out to be a major bookworm. That had the added benefit of speeding along his studies even more than ever—after all, it was always easier to learn proactively than it was to learn because you were being forced to do so. Rosell's studies were going just about as well as I could've possibly expected them to...but that didn't mean that *everything* was proceeding as swimmingly.

○

"I kn-knew it!" Rosell sobbed. "I really *am* a waste of space... I never should've been born..."

He'd come over to my family's estate to study as per usual, but when he arrived, we found him even more down in the dumps than we'd learned to expect from him. Something must have happened to him at home. Not only was he not reading, but he'd also actually curled up in a fetal position. It was like he was non-verbally screaming, *Look at me, everyone! I'm depressed, okay?!*

This wasn't the first time he'd shown up in that state, to be fair. Whenever his father chewed him out, he tended to mope his way over to my side. Then, I ended up hearing him out and doing what I could to cheer him up.

"Did Greg get mad at you again?" I asked. "What was it this time?"

Rosell didn't reply, so I knew it was probably something pretty awkward.

"Did you wet the bed again?"

"Ugh!" grunted Rosell.

Bingo.

I WILL USE MY APPRAISAL SKILL TO RISE IN THE WORLD

"I told you before, remember? Bed-wetting's totally normal for kids. It's nothing to be ashamed of."

Rosell hesitated for a moment, then asked, "Do you do it too, Ars?"

Now it was *my* turn to lapse into an awkward silence. As far as I knew, bed-wetting was a developmental issue. Little kids just weren't built to hold it in overnight, so being mentally an adult didn't do squat to stop it. I absolutely did wet the bed until I was around three, and I came dangerously close to keeling over dead from the shame of it every single time.

Thankfully, though, my body had apparently developed on the faster side of the spectrum, and it had been quite some time since my last bed-wetting incident. That was actually a bit of a problem for once, though, since telling him that I *didn't* was sure to hurt his feelings. Just as I was trying to decide whether or not I should lie to him, the silence had dragged on for long enough that Rosell put the pieces together on his own.

"You *don't*, do you?! I *knew* it! It really *is* just me! I can't take this—if my weenie isn't going to work right, I'd rather just *chop it off and be done with it!*"

"You *what* now?! N-No, stop! Don't do anything crazy! Oh god, put the knife down!"

I had *no* clue why he was carrying it in the first place—for self-defense, I assumed—but Rosell pulled out an *actual goddamn knife* and began preparing to, well, let's just say dismember himself. I, of course, freaked the hell out and rushed over to stop him.

"Let go of me! Once I get rid of *this,* I'll never have to be humiliated again!"

"N-No, it doesn't work like that! Cutting it off won't *stop* you from wetting the bed! If anything, it'll do the opposite, and it'll also really, *really* hurt!"

Rosell froze in place and replied, "...I-It will?"

"*Yes*, it will! Do you even have to ask?!"

"H-How much? Worse than getting kicked in the shins?"

"So much worse. You can't even compare the two!" I shouted. Not that I'd ever actually cut mine off, mind you, so technically speaking, I couldn't actually say for sure whether or not that was true.

Thankfully, though, Rosell was a major scaredy-cat when it came to pain, so he eventually put the knife away. I heaved a sigh.

Who knew he was the sort of person who'd go to extremes that easily? And who knew that dealing with a kid would be this exhausting?

It was becoming increasingly clear that Rosell's extreme case of pessimism was going to be an issue going forward. Being excessively optimistic would be a problem for an aspiring tactician, of course, but he was going so far in the opposite direction that it felt like it'd be trouble in its own right. I had to do *something* to inject a little positivity into the kid's mindset, and I had a feeling that if I didn't do it soon, he might be stuck this way for life.

I'll talk strategy with Rietz later.

○

After Rosell went home for the day, Rietz and I got together to discuss his personality defect.

"I certainly agree that it's a problem," said Rietz. "Even setting aside its potential impact on his worth as a tactician, seeing somebody with such an appalling excess of talent act like he's inferior is, well...rather hard to stomach."

Oh, good. Looks like we're on the same page.

I WILL USE MY APPRAISAL SKILL TO RISE IN THE WORLD

"It seems clear to me that Rosell's negativity is entirely the fault of his father, Greg," Rietz continued. "The way he belittles Rosell over every little thing has taken a toll on Rosell's confidence."

"I was thinking along the same lines," I agreed with a nod. "But what can we do about it? Would getting Greg to compliment him solve the issue?"

"Even if we were to order Greg to praise him, it wouldn't be *genuine* praise, and I believe that Rosell is smart enough to tell the difference. Personally, I think the most effective means would be to have Rosell do something that prompts his father to praise him."

Getting Rosell to impress his father himself, huh…? What's the best way for Rosell to show off how smart he is? His dad's a hunter, so maybe catching a wild animal with some sort of clever trick is the way to go?

"Here's an idea," I said. "How about we have Rosell come up with some new sort of trap that Greg can use to hunt more efficiently? That would prove how smart he is, no problem. What do you think?"

"A trap…?" muttered Rietz. He sounded a little skeptical. "I'm afraid that might prove difficult. I'm confident that Greg is already well-versed in the art of trap-making, and no matter how smart Rosell is, asking him to invent an entirely new trap out of thin air might be setting our expectations impossibly high."

"Hmm… Fair enough."

Rietz *did* have a point. Inventing a new type of trap wasn't exactly the easiest of tasks, especially for a child.

"That said," continued Rietz. "I doubt proposing the challenge to Rosell would be a bad idea in and of itself. True knowledge can't be gained from books alone, after all. You have to apply what you learn to the real world. In that sense, having Rosell apply his newfound knowledge for hunting purposes could prove to be beneficial."

Plus, that sort of practice might be just what he needs to raise his Intelligence score.

If Rosell exceeded our expectations and invented some spectacular new trap, he could make his father acknowledge his talents, and if he didn't, he'd still be gaining practical skills out in the real world. As far as I could tell, there were no downsides. That settled the matter in my mind, so I asked Rietz to have Rosell start designing a trap first thing tomorrow.

○

The next morning, when Rosell arrived to study, Rietz proposed the plan we'd come up with the day before.

"A trap…?"

"Indeed. You were raised in a family of hunters, so I imagine you're familiar with the basic principles of trap-making?"

Rosell shook his head and replied, "No. What do you mean by 'trap,' anyway?"

That certainly wasn't the first question I'd expected him to ask.

"You don't know what traps are?" Rietz asked. "Your father must use indirect methods of hunting sometimes… You know, something other than simply shooting animals with a bow."

"He doesn't," Rosell replied bluntly.

"Hmm. I'm surprised, to be honest. Then again, I'm hardly an expert when it comes to hunting myself," admitted Rietz.

This wasn't necessarily a bad thing, in my mind. If Greg didn't know how to make traps, then Rosell probably didn't have to make anything particularly complex to impress him.

"So, what're traps, Mister Rietz?" Rosell asked again.

I WILL USE MY APPRAISAL SKILL TO RISE IN THE WORLD

"In the context of hunting, the word 'traps' refers to devices or methods that allow you to indirectly capture your prey. A particularly well-known example you may be aware of is a pit trap. You dig a deep hole in the ground, cover it with a thin layer of branches, then cover those branches with dirt and foliage until it's indistinguishable from the ground around it. After that, when an animal steps on the trap, the branches collapse and the animal falls into the hole."

"Oh, wow! Whoever thought that up was pretty smart," commented Rosell.

...I guess they sort of were, yeah.

I couldn't even remember how I'd learned about pit traps—they were just common knowledge in my mind—but Rosell had a point. Whoever made humanity's first pit trap really must've been pretty darn smart.

"When I really think about it, though, that doesn't seem like a very good way to hunt. It wouldn't work at all unless an animal happened to step on the trap by coincidence," Rosell muttered to himself, pressing a thumb into his furrowed brow. That was a little habit of his that made an appearance whenever he was deep in thought about something.

"You *could* put food on top of the trap to lure an animal into it? Hmm, but it would still only let you catch *one* animal in each trap, and digging a deep hole isn't easy. Hunting with a bow still sounds faster... You'd have to come up with something easier to build or something that could catch lots of animals at once to make it practical..."

Rosell mumbled on and on to himself, voicing every idea he came up with the moment it popped into his head. This continued for a while until Rietz spoke up again.

"Once you've thought up a trap that satisfies you, I'd like you to try drawing a design for it. I have paper and a writing utensil prepared for you."

Rosell blinked and replied, "I can't draw, though."

"Even a simple sketch will suffice. I believe it will be much easier to understand your design with one to look at."

"That makes sense. Okay, then, I'll draw it after I'm done thinking," Rosell agreed, then immediately dropped back into his pondering pose and started mumbling again. The kid could certainly focus, that was for sure. It was always really hard to get him to listen to you when he went into that mode.

"Do you really think he'll manage to make a trap?" I asked Rietz.

"I can't say for sure, but I *am* quite curious what results he'll produce after putting all his knowledge into making something. I think there's a very real chance he'll surprise us."

"I could see that, yeah."

There wasn't much else we could do at that point. Rosell's challenge had begun, so we just had to watch over him.

○

While Rosell worked on his trap, I decided to do some of my own research on the types of traps that already existed in this world. I quickly picked up on one fact that explained a lot: traps just weren't a traditional method of hunting in Lamberg.

Rietz, who came from outside the region, had made all the same assumptions about hunters using traps that I had, so I could safely conclude that they *were* commonly used elsewhere. That said, while Rietz was aware of traps on the whole, he didn't have much in the way of specialized knowledge about them, so he wasn't able to teach

I WILL USE MY APPRAISAL SKILL TO RISE IN THE WORLD

me very much I didn't already know.

I eventually decided to try thinking up some traps myself, but quickly found that it was a lot harder of a thought experiment than I'd first expected. To begin with, I didn't know very much at all about the sort of animals that people usually hunted in this world. Making a decent trap without knowing about the creature you were trapping, as it turned out, was next to impossible. Rosell had all the wildlife knowledge you'd expect from a hunter's son, though, so at least he wasn't working with that sort of handicap.

Anyway, I gave up on making my own trap not too long after I started. I *was* still giving the situation thought, though, and I quickly realized that Lamberg's lack of trapping culture posed an opportunity. If Rosell came up with a good enough trap, then impressing Greg would only be the start of our potential gains—we could also send the town's ability to produce food through the roof! We'd be killing two birds with one stone!

My expectations were high as I eagerly awaited the completion of Rosell's design.

○

Finally, several weeks later...

"It's finished!" declared Rosell, brandishing a piece of paper. He sounded happier than I'd ever heard him before, and I didn't even need to ask *what* he'd finished. It had to be the plans for his trap.

"All right," replied Rietz. "Then let's take a look, shall we?"

"Yeah!" said Rosell. He was absolutely beaming as he spread out the plans for Rietz to see, which was really rare for him. I could tell he was really excited about finishing his creation.

Rietz carefully inspected the plans. It was Rosell's first attempt at drawing a blueprint, so there were plenty of places that didn't make perfect sense at a glance, and he ended up explaining them to Rietz piece by piece as he pored over the design. I decided to listen in and see what I could make of the plans as well.

Gradually, I got a picture of what sort of trap he'd put together. First off, the prey: Rosell had decided that instead of designing an all-purpose trap, he'd make something that targeted a single species. Specifically, he'd thought up a trap that would capture a type of animal called "suws" that lived in abundance in the woods near the town.

Suws looked like small wild boars, and they basically tasted like beef. Their meat reminded me less of the sort of heavily-marbled wagyu that was raised in Japan and more of the leaner beef that was imported to Japan from Australia. They also had one very distinctive trait that Rosell used to full effect for the purpose of his trap: an instinctive impulse to charge at anything that was colored yellow.

The first step was to fence off a large, wide-open area. Into the center of that area went the bait: a cloth that had been thoroughly permeated with the smell of apples, a suw's favorite food. Suws had a very keen sense of smell, and would naturally gather around the trap.

It wouldn't have been much of a trap if the fence didn't have some sort of entrance, of course, but it *also* wouldn't have been much of a trap if the suws could come and go as they pleased. The door would work sort of like how pet doors in my old world did, and its outside surface would be painted yellow. Suws would see the color, charge right at it, and push straight on through to the other side by virtue of momentum. The door was designed to only swing in one direction, so once the suws were inside, they were stuck unless they

I WILL USE MY APPRAISAL SKILL TO RISE IN THE WORLD

could somehow pull the door inward.

I thought the trap sounded quite effective, but Rietz had other ideas.

"There's one thing I'm concerned about," he explained. "Just how durable will the door have to be? If it's too brittle, we'll run the risk of the suws breaking it, but if it's too solid, there's a chance they'll hurt themselves on it, fall unconscious, and block the entrance."

"Suws are hard-headed, so it takes a lot to knock one out," countered Rosell. "I think that using a solid, durable door is the right choice."

"I see," said Rietz with a nod. "Next, how will you deal with the suws once you've captured them?"

"There'll be a human-sized door built into the fence, so if there are only a few suws inside, you can just walk in and take care of them yourself. Suws are timid, so as long as you're not wearing yellow, they probably won't charge you. I think they'd be easy prey if they didn't have anywhere to run. If there are too many trapped inside, though, you'll have to pick them off from outside the fence with a bow, so it'd be a good idea to add a simple platform for people to stand on."

"Hmm..." Rietz mumbled, lapsing into thought for a moment before speaking up once more. "Shall we try building one, then? We can start with a small-scale trap, making the fence just large enough to trap two or three suws. We won't have to make a platform that way, so it won't cost much in the way of resources, and there'll be no need to report the project to Lord Raven until we produce results. When we do, we can ask him for permission to construct a larger-scale trap. Does that sound acceptable, Master Ars?"

"Yeah, let's go with that plan."

AS A REINCARNATED ARISTOCRAT

Man, who knew he'd manage to come up with this well-thought-out trap? He's one hell of a five-year-old, that's for sure!

Thinking back on it, Rosell had an A-ranked aptitude in Weaponry. I'd never really considered it before, but from a certain perspective, traps *sort of* felt like they could fall under that category. It certainly explained a lot if they did.

Anyway, our plan was set: we'd create a usable version of Rosell's trap! I tasked a few of my family's servants with the actual construction. As far as materials went, the fence would be made from wood. It was a fairly simple design, all things considered: wooden posts driven into the ground with planks attached between them. We made sure to use planks that were nice and sturdy, just in case a suw decided to try to break through, and we added a small hole into one of them that would let us look inside.

For this first trial run, we made the enclosure about fifty square feet in total. That would fit three suws no problem, but if the trap worked a little better than planned, and even more charged in, there was a danger they'd collide with the suws already trapped inside. That didn't seem like a fundamental design problem, though—it only really applied to the test trap, and would naturally stop being a factor when we made a larger, more practical version.

We decided to make the door from a thin iron plate. We couldn't make it too thick or it wouldn't swing open properly, and we couldn't make it too thin or the suws would be able to break it down. Frankly, I had no idea what the right balance between the two extremes was, and I figured that aspect would take some experimentation to get just right. If we screwed it up, we could always make another door and try again!

We ended up heading into town to procure the yellow paint we needed to color the door. It was easy to imagine that each charging

I WILL USE MY APPRAISAL SKILL TO RISE IN THE WORLD

suw would scrape off some of the paint in the process, so we made sure to apply a pretty heavy layer of the stuff. The price of paint varied wildly depending on its color, but luckily enough, yellow was one of the cheaper ones, so we didn't have to shell out much for it.

That just left the bait: a piece of cloth made to smell like apples. That would be easy to make, thankfully. They grew plenty of apples down in the village, so we just had to juice a few of them and get the cloth nice and soaked.

In the end, the construction process for our first trap took three days in total, from start to finish. We set it up in the very center of the woods that were just outside the town of Lamberg.

"D-Do you think it'll work?" Rosell asked anxiously as he looked over the finished trap.

"There's only one way to find out," I replied. "But, I mean, this sort of thing always ends up being a process of trial and error. It doesn't matter if it doesn't quite work perfectly at first so long as you keep improving every iteration!"

"I-It doesn't?" Rosell asked, seeming a little relieved to hear it. For someone as pessimistic as him, I guess it *would* be surprisingly reassuring to know that it was all right if he failed.

All that was left was to leave the trap behind and let it do its thing.

○

The next morning, Rosell, Rietz, and I all went out to check on the trap.

"I believe we've caught something," Rietz said the moment the trap came into view.

I gave it a closer look and quickly realized what had tipped him off: the paint on the door was slightly scratched. That had to be a sign that a suw had charged through it.

Rietz went over to the hole in the wall, peeked inside, and said, "There are two of them inside. It looks like they're asleep."

Rosell blinked and replied, "Huh? R-Really?"

"So it worked?" I added excitedly.

We all clustered around the hole to peek inside. It wasn't low enough for me and Rosell to look through on our own, so Rietz lifted each of us in turn to take a look. Lo and behold, two suws were sleeping within, just like he'd claimed. Part of me was impressed that the critters had the nerve to fall asleep in such a dangerous situation.

Next, Rietz gave the door a close inspection and said, "I see no problems here. I believe this design should stand up to quite a fair amount of abuse."

In other words, our shot in the dark when it came to the door's durability had actually hit the mark.

"D-Does that mean we can make a bigger one next?" Rosell asked.

"I don't see why not," replied Rietz. "If it works this well, it should make suw hunting quite a bit more efficient for everyone. It might even make Greg see you in a whole new light, don't you think?"

"M-My dad? Really?" asked Rosell. We hadn't actually brought up the possibility that his father might appreciate him more if his trap turned out well. I figured that mentioning that part would put a ton of pressure on him, so I'd decided to keep it to myself.

"Well then," said Rietz. "Let's get to making a full-sized trap. I was thinking we could ask the local hunters to aid in the construction effort this time around."

I WILL USE MY APPRAISAL SKILL TO RISE IN THE WORLD

"Good idea," I replied. "By the way, what are we going to do with the suws we caught today?"

"We can knock them unconscious and bring them back to the estate," said Rietz. "I'm sure the cooks know how to butcher a suw, so we can have them for lunch. Speaking of which, you should eat with us, Rosell! I'm certain that a suw you caught yourself will taste especially delicious."

Rietz went into the trap, knocked out the suws, and carried them back to the estate, where we did indeed end up having them for lunch. Rosell devoured his portion gleefully.

○

The next day, we gathered all the local hunters in the town's meeting hall to explain the plan we wanted them to help with. I was hoping they'd give us the okay and help build the new trap without raising too much fuss.

"A trap to catch suws, eh?" said Greg after Rietz finished explaining the trap's function, using a diagram he'd drawn for reference. That drawing, of course, was a more refined version of Rosell's original blueprint. "Yeah, I see how this works...and it's not a bad idea. If it's as effective as you say, then it could make our suw hunts a hell of a lot easier. You've got as good a head on your shoulders as folks claim, Master Ars! Can't believe you thought this up on your own!"

Greg sounded rather impressed, but I shook my head and replied, "Actually, *I* wasn't the one who thought it up at all. Rosell came up with the design."

"*What*?!" Greg recoiled in shock, then looked over at Rosell. "You're pulling my leg. *Rosell* designed this device? Impossible!"

AS A REINCARNATED ARISTOCRAT

"If you'll recall, the last time we spoke, I told you that Rosell has immense talent. I'd encourage you to take this as proof of how intelligent your son really is. Every aspect of this trap's design was Rosell's work—I didn't so much as lift a finger to help."

Greg gaped at his son and asked, "I-Is that true, Rosell?"

Rosell nodded, which prompted the reply, "And it actually *works*? You're *positive*?"

The moment he learned that Rosell had created the trap, Greg started questioning its quality. He was having a really hard time accepting the fact that his son *wasn't* a total waste of space.

"We've already conducted a small-scale test of the trap, which proved highly effective. A large-scale version is likely to work just as well," Rietz explained.

"So essentially, we were hoping that all of you would help us build it," I said. "Are you interested? Needless to say, the suws captured in the trap will be yours to keep, and you're free to take note of the trap's design and build your own in the future."

As soon as I finished my explanation, the hunters started volunteering to help. In the end, the only one of them who *didn't* immediately raise his hand was Greg, who still seemed stubbornly reluctant to be a party to our plan. Finally, though, he gave in and raised his hand as well.

"All of you are willing, then? Perfect! In that case, we'll begin construction tomorrow. We'll be setting the trap up in the woods nearby. I'll show you the location, so please gather here first thing tomorrow morning."

Everyone showed up the next morning, as promised, and we began construction of the full-scale trap. We decided to place it in the same central location where we'd built the small-scale test trap, disassembling that one and building the new one in its place.

I WILL USE MY APPRAISAL SKILL TO RISE IN THE WORLD

This time around, we made the enclosure about seven times larger than the test version. There were a few trees inside the area we'd be fencing off, which would make dealing with the trapped suws a challenge, so we chopped most of them down, repurposing them as materials for the fence.

We'd have to build the viewing platform that we omitted from the test trap's design as well. Its design was incredibly simple, and it would be about a dozen feet tall. A tower like that wouldn't be of much use in battle, but for our purposes, it was more than sufficient.

From start to finish, the trap's construction took six days. It wasn't an incredibly large-scale project, and we had a lot more workers available to help out than we'd had the first time, so it wasn't all that much harder to build than the test trap had been, in the end.

"And you're *sure* this thing can trap a suw?" asked Greg, casting a skeptical glance at the newly-finished trap.

"It's larger than the one we made as a test, but the basic principles of its design are identical. It will work, rest assured," replied Rietz. However, Greg looked unconvinced. Only time would dispel his doubts.

Just like last time, we left the trap alone for a day to let it work its magic. When we gathered up again to check on our catch, Rosell showed up with massive bags under his eyes. I assumed he'd been so anxious about whether or not the trap would work, he hadn't been able to sleep a wink the night before. He hadn't seemed nearly that nervous when we checked on the first trap, but of course, Greg hadn't been along to witness his results at the time. That *had* to have turned the pressure up to eleven.

It only took a quick glance at the door to tell that we had a catch on our hands. Once again, the yellow paint was conspicuously scratched. It was quite a bit more damaged than it had been the first time around, in fact, which most likely meant that we had trapped even more suws.

"I believe this was a success," said Rietz, who'd probably noticed the same signs I had. He walked up to the trap and glanced in the peephole in the wall. "There are three...no, *four* suws trapped inside."

"S-Seriously?" asked Greg incredulously.

"L-Lemme take a look!" shouted one of the other hunters. All of them gathered around and took turns peering through the hole.

"I'll be damned, he's right! There really *are* four of 'em in there!"

"It *actually* worked!"

The hunters began whooping and hollering in celebration. I took a look inside as well, and there were indeed four suws within the trap. They were awake this time, licking the apple-scented cloth. Rosell took his turn to look after me, then let out a long sigh of relief when he finally saw the suws for himself.

"Just think of how much effort this'll save us!" said one of the hunters. "No more chasing suws all over the woods!"

"Little buggers can really run, so if you miss your first shot, it's all over," said another of them. "And they're small, too, so they're not exactly easy targets."

"They'll be a snap to hunt when they're penned in like this, though! Gotta say, Greg, I was worried your youngest wouldn't measure up to his brothers, but looks like he's something special after all!"

All the hunters were over the moon at the thought of the trap's potential, and the compliments kept pouring in one after another. Rosell wasn't used to *any* amount of praise, much less overwhelming praise from all sides, and was clearly bewildered. Greg, meanwhile, was bewildered in a whole different way, but he eventually walked over to Rosell and rested a hand on his head.

"You did good, kid," said Greg, tussling his son's hair.

Rosell's eyes widened with shock. Then he nodded, said "Thanks!" and cracked the biggest grin I'd ever seen on him.

○

The local hunters began putting Rosell's trap into practical use immediately. As a direct result, they started bringing in suws far more consistently than ever before, and suw meat quickly became something of a staple food in Lamberg.

Since suws were so challenging to hunt using traditional means, their meat had always been considered a luxury up until that point. As such, Rosell's innovation sent waves through the village's culinary culture. It wasn't long before the villagers started using suw jerky to barter, which meant that foods from other territories they hadn't been able to get their hands on quickly grew much more readily available.

Like we'd hoped, the praise that Rosell received from his father began to chip away at his deep-seated spirit of pessimism. *My* father was quite pleased with the development as well, so he summoned Rosell and his father to our estate to receive a reward for Rosell's innovation.

"For your contributions to Lamberg's prosperity, I hereby grant you a reward of five gold coins," said my father, passing the money to Rosell. That was a rather considerable sum of cash, so Greg's eyes widened in shock.

Incidentally, Charlotte happened to be present at the time, and I caught her muttering, "That's worth twelve mes..." under her breath. I blinked, then quickly crunched the numbers. I'd paid five silver coins for Charlotte, and each gold coin was worth ten silver, meaning...

Yeah, the actual answer's definitely *ten. I should probably make sure Charlotte gets at least a basic education before this gets out of hand.*

Surprisingly, though, Rosell himself didn't seem all that happy to receive the gold. If anything, he looked conflicted. He'd been over the moon when Greg praised him for his work, too—so what made this so different? Five gold coins was *a lot* of money, after all, and pretty much anyone would be happy to receive a sudden, unexpected windfall. I was so curious that when my father's little reward ceremony concluded, I went over to Rosell and asked him about it directly.

"Oh, I just wasn't sure if, well...I really deserve it," explained Rosell.

"Of course you do!" I replied. "You made something truly incredible, Rosell! It's only natural for you to be rewarded for it!"

"B-But, I mean...now that all the hunters in the villages are using traps, they might hunt down all of the suws in the woods! If that happens, then it'll be my fault that nobody gets to eat them anymore..."

"Oh..."

That's...a pretty good point, actually. If they keep hunting suws at this rate, they might totally wipe out the local population.

It was a simple fact—obvious, even—but my exuberance at our success had blinded me to it. Rosell, on the other hand, was thinking ahead and keeping his mind focused on the long-term picture.

"I c-can't let that happen, right? Not after the lord gave me this much money... I have to do something, *anything*... But would the hunters listen to me if I asked them to release a few suws from each

I WILL USE MY APPRAISAL SKILL TO RISE IN THE WORLD

catch? What sort of hunter would let their prey get away on purpose? Maybe I could ask them to let young suws go…? Oh, but if their parents get killed, then the children will probably die off on their own… Maybe I should make a new trap that catches a different sort of animal? Or maybe I can come up with an even better solution…"

Rosell was back in mumble mode, focusing intently on overhunting countermeasures. The fact that he was envisioning future disasters and coming up with plans to prevent them when most people would be celebrating their accomplishments was probably a sign that his pessimistic nature hadn't *really* changed overall.

On the other hand, that exchange made me remember that, sometimes, a little pessimism could actually be a good thing. I was convinced: Rosell could turn out to be an excellent tactician just the way he was.

Interlude: Rosell's Postscript

My name is Rosell Kischa, and I'm the son of a hunter. I never thought I'd be anything more until I met Ars, the son of a local nobleman, and my life changed dramatically. Suddenly, I was going over to Ars's estate day after day, just to study. He told me that I had talent when he invited me over for the first time, and I'm still not really sure what he meant by that, but I actually enjoyed studying quite a bit and didn't mind playing along.

Ars is around the same age as me, but we're worlds apart in terms of maturity. Why, Ars is practically an adult. He isn't a scaredy-cat like me, and the way he talks sounds real adult-like somehow, too. He also has the power to see other people's strong points, which makes Mister Rietz and the other adults really respect him.

I think Ars's power is amazing, too, but I'm also a little scared by it. What if he can actually see more than just people's strong points? What if he can see all of the secrets I keep stowed away deep within my heart? What if he knows that I've been secretly taking his books back home with me to read after our study sessions end…?

I would spend *all* of my time reading if I could, but books are far too precious to lend out to a child like me. Taking them in se-

I WILL USE MY APPRAISAL SKILL TO RISE IN THE WORLD

cret is my only choice. I don't actually have any other secrets, but if Ars *can* read my mind, then that one secret is enough to get me in serious trouble.

There's only one thing to do—I have to learn as much as I can about Ars's power! And the quickest way to go about that is to ask him directly.

"My power lets me see people's talents, names, and sex," Ars explains without a second's hesitation. "It doesn't let me read minds or anything like that."

"Oh, okay," I reply, immediately relieved. It's still an incredible power, but I guess it's not incredible in *that* sort of way.

"If you're worried about the books you've been smuggling home, I already know all about it. I didn't have to read your mind to figure *that* out," he continues.

"Eek!"

"Don't worry, I don't mind at all! I just hope you'll tell me before you borrow them in the future. It's only polite."

I feel hesitant, but ask, "So if I ask to borrow books, you'll actually let me?"

"Yes, of course," replies Ars.

"Th-Thank you! I'll be sure to ask you next time, I promise!"

And so, I've received formal permission to borrow Ars's books. He really is a good guy. He lets me read his books, and he's taught me all sorts of things, so I'm starting to grow quite fond of him. I even kind of hope that I'll be able to repay him for everything he's done for me.

Ars says I can become an incredible tactician someday. I'm still not convinced, but maybe I'll focus on studying to prove him right.

Chapter 4

Three more years came and went, and before I knew it, I'd turned nine. Throughout that time I'd grown quite a bit taller...and stronger as well.

The potential issue of suw overhunting was resolved fairly easily in the end. We went to my father to ask him to intervene, and he imposed limits on the hunting of suws that would ensure the local population remained stable. The punishment for violating the regulation was rather harsh, so the local hunters all took great care to not step out of line. On the less punitive side of things, Rosell *did* manage to invent several new traps that were designed to capture other types of animals. As a result, the suw limitations didn't actually do much damage to the hunters' bottom lines.

Anyway, the hunting situation aside, all sorts of things had changed over the past three years. The biggest cause of those changes was the fact that recently, my father had fallen ill with concerning frequency. He developed a chronic cough that came and went for no apparent reason, usually accompanied by a fever.

Unfortunately, I didn't have any sort of advanced medical knowledge from my past life, so I was unable to help diagnose his sickness. To be fair, even if I *were* a trained medical professional, there was no guarantee that the illnesses of this new world matched modern Japan's. I knew that plenty of illnesses were caused by viruses and bacteria, and there was absolutely no guarantee that the viruses and bacteria in this world would be the same as those on Earth. If anything, it'd be weird if they *were* the same.

In any case, what really mattered was that my father was afflicted with a mysterious and unidentifiable illness. Nobody knew whether it was the sort of sickness that would pass with time, or if it was one that would kill him if it wasn't treated properly. The one thing we knew for certain was that several months had passed since his illness began, and he'd been in very poor condition ever since. Whatever he was suffering from, it definitely wasn't benign.

I tried to insist that my father stay in our estate and conserve his strength, but he was hell-bent on going out into battle regardless of my advice. I even offered to sortie in his place, but unsurprisingly, he wasn't about to send a nine-year-old out onto the battlefield. Eventually, I concluded that there would simply be no persuading him, and switched gears to convincing him to at least take Rietz along with him. Rietz was the one person I trusted above all others, and I knew that with him around, my father would be safe even in the event of an emergency.

In consequence, of course, when Rietz was out at war, I was left without a tutor. Conflict was becoming more and more common in Missian by the day, and before long, Rietz was away more frequently than he was at home. We'd hardly even had any time to spend together at all in recent months.

I hadn't neglected my search for talented new recruits over those three years, and I *had* found and hired several promising individuals, but it had been quite a long time since I came across anyone truly outstanding. I was starting to get the feeling that I'd picked out

I WILL USE MY APPRAISAL SKILL TO RISE IN THE WORLD

all the talent there was to find in Canarre, so moving on to a new city seemed prudent.

The problem, of course, was that traveling farther away was dangerous. The odds of getting attacked by bandits along the way were concerningly high. I'd have to bolster my personal guard before I could even consider making that sort of trek, but all of our capable fighters had been sent off into battle, Rietz included.

In short, long-distance travel was going to have to wait until peace was restored to the land. I really wished that would happen sooner rather than later, but I had no misconceptions about how likely *that* was.

○

One chilly winter's day, I found myself in the estate's dining hall, warming myself by the fireplace. Winter in Lamberg didn't set in as swiftly or brutally as it did in other parts of the world, but it was still cold enough that the extra warmth of the fire was greatly appreciated.

A side effect of the cold rolling in was that fewer skirmishes broke out in the area. Nobody wanted to be out fighting in a frigid field, after all, and as a result, my father and Rietz were around more frequently. My father was at home on that particular day, so we even managed to eat a meal together.

We weren't alone, either. My siblings, Kreiz and Wren, both ate alongside us—though they also finished their meals in unison, said their thanks, and leaped up from the table well before the rest of us did. It felt like the two of them had been babies just yesterday, but they'd grown up before I knew it, and were talking and running around with reckless abandon in no time at all.

AS A REINCARNATED ARISTOCRAT

Kids sure do grow up fast, huh?

Despite being twins, the two of them didn't look exactly alike. Kreiz had my father's golden hair, while Wren's hair was black, like mine. Their faces were *fairly* similar, but you could still tell them apart very easily even without taking their hair into account.

I guess that's just how it goes with fraternal twins.

"Let's play, Big Brother!"

"Let's plaaay!"

My siblings tugged at my sleeves, eager to drag me into their games, but I had something I had to discuss with our father.

"Sorry, but you'll have to play with Rietz for now," I said, attempting to punt the problem onto his plate instead.

"Aww!"

"C'mon, we wanna play with *you*, Big Brother!"

"Let's plaaay!"

"Agh, okay, okay! I have to go speak with Father now, but I'll play with you afterward, I promise! Just wait patiently until then, okay?"

That finally convinced them to run off and harass Rietz until I was ready for them.

Turns out that suddenly having to deal with a pair of siblings is pretty tough! Who knew?

After they left, I moved on to the topic of conversation I'd been planning to bring up.

"How have you been feeling lately, Father?" I asked, approaching him.

"I'm perfectly..." my father began, then descended into a series of hacking coughs. "...Perfectly fine, thank you."

"That's a little hard to believe after a cough like that," I replied sheepishly.

I WILL USE MY APPRAISAL SKILL TO RISE IN THE WORLD

"It's just a cough. There's no need to worry," said my father, before succumbing to another hacking fit. It felt like his condition had been deteriorating as of late. Perhaps the cold was to blame?

"Umm, Father? As I've said before, I really do think you would be better off not marching into battle..."

"And as *I've* said before, that isn't an option. Or do you expect me to tell Lord Lumeire that I can't sortie while Missian burns around us because I have the sniffles?"

When my father referred to "Lord Lumeire," he meant Lumeire Pyres, the Count of Canarre and my father's liege lord. He wasn't exaggerating about Missian burning around us, either. The duchy really was teetering upon the brink of utter chaos.

Almost precisely one year ago, the Duke of Missian had collapsed. He'd barely managed to cling to life, but his illness had sent him into a coma that he had yet to wake from. He'd left a letter to be opened should he be indisposed that named his younger son his successor, but said letter's authenticity was quickly called into question. The duke's older son was especially loud about his suspicions and accused his brother of forging the letter outright.

Frankly, I wasn't entirely convinced that the elder brother was wrong about the letter being a forgery. Although he'd been considered inferior to his younger brother for most of his life, he'd recently found great success on the battlefield and racked up a surprising number of accomplishments. Where once the duke's vassals feared the day that his eldest son held the duchy's reins, now they seemed downright optimistic.

Thus, when the younger brother was named the duke's successor, the elder found himself with an ample supply of nobles who harbored their own doubts and were willing to back him up. However, there were also plenty of nobles who firmly believed that the note was written in the duke's hand and allied themselves with the younger brother.

And so, in no time at all, the duchy was split in two. The precise situation that everyone feared had come to pass. War was unlikely to break out in earnest while the duke still lived, but the instant he passed away, a major conflict was all but inevitable.

Lumeire, the Count of Canarre, had chosen to ally himself with the elder brother. In contrast, the Count of Perreina, the county to the east, had chosen to back the younger brother. The resulting tension between the two counties had caused no small number of border skirmishes.

To make matters worse, the duchy that Canarre shared a border with, Seitz, was ready and willing to take advantage of the chaos in Missian. They had already started interfering much more proactively in Canarre's affairs. The situation could hardly have been any more perilous, and while House Louvent's military force wasn't especially large, we *did* have an unusually well-trained crop of soldiers. With a track record like my father's, it was inevitable that he'd be sent into battle time and time again.

"In that case, I'm perfectly willing to sortie in your—"

"Not on your life!" my father roared, cutting me off. "I've told you a thousand times, Ars. A boy who has yet to see his first battle has no business commanding an army!"

I had thirty years of life experience in another world, but I knew perfectly well that none of it was worth a damn when it came to knowing how to handle a real-life battle. My father was right. I couldn't look him in the eye and declare that everything would turn out well if he left me in charge.

I desperately wished that I could prove myself—that I could

show him that, even at the age of nine, I was capable of taking to the field—but I knew that it was simply beyond me. And so, all I could do was clam up and turn around, ready to depart from the dining room.

"Wait, Ars," said my father. "There's something I forgot to tell you."

I turned back around to face him and asked, "What is it?"

"It seems a letter from your fiancée has arrived. I've entrusted it to Rietz, so feel free to read it when you can spare a moment."

"Oh, from my fiancée?" I replied, then paused.

Hmm? Wait...fiancée? Surely I must have misheard him? A fiancée would be a woman I'm engaged to be married to, right?

"Umm, Father...? I think I might be misunderstanding something. Did you just say it was from my *fiancée*?"

"Oh, did I never tell you? That's right. You have a fiancée," said my father, blithely turning my whole world upside down.

I have...a fiancée...?

I shook my head. Really, this wasn't *that* shocking a development, was it? I was a noble, after all! A lord's son being engaged at an early age was perfectly reasonable! The fact that my father *hadn't said so much as a single word about it* up to that point, on the other hand, was significantly less reasonable and more than a little shocking!

"So, wait," I said. "I'm *actually* engaged? And you just...never told me? *Why?*"

"It slipped my mind," replied my father.

How does your son's engagement, of all things, "slip your mind"?!

My father might have looked like a shrewd and cunning individual, but every once in a while, he exposed the fact that he had a dangerously careless side to him.

I WILL USE MY APPRAISAL SKILL TO RISE IN THE WORLD

"Your fiancée is the daughter of the Lord of Torbequista, a region of Canarre," explained my father, before being interrupted by another coughing fit. After the attack subsided, he continued. "That lord, Hammond Pleide, is an old friend of mine. Around a decade ago—a year before you were born—Hammond had his third child. He already had two boys, who were six and four, but the third turned out to be his first daughter, so we vowed that if I ever had a son, he and Hammond's daughter would be wed."

My father's explanation, punctuated by the occasional cough, didn't turn out to be the complicated political affair that I was expecting. Of course, my father *was* an upstart as far as nobles went. Our bloodline was far from extensive or prestigious, so expanding our circle of relatives was quite important.

Needless to say, that lack of an extended family tree would remain a problem after I inherited my father's title. Taking that into consideration, being engaged to a genuine, by-birth noble wasn't all that bad a deal for me. Marrying the person you fell in love with out of a pure desire to be together was considered the norm in my old world, and I couldn't deny that part of me still fantasized about walking that path myself, but I supposed I'd just have to give up on that sort of romanticized, well, romance.

In any case, Rietz was supposedly in possession of the letter, so giving it a read seemed like the logical next step to take. Thus, I went on my way to seek him out.

○

I eventually found Rietz in the study. Rosell, Charlotte, and the twins were all there as well. Charlotte was keeping the twins company while Rietz and Rosell were busy hitting the books. I'd tasked

Charlotte to join them in their studies recently, considering her apparent lack of any sort of basic education. Judging by what I'd heard, though, her memory left much to be desired.

"Good morning to you, Master Ars."

"Good morning, Ars."

"Oh, Master Ars. Morning."

The moment I stepped into the room, Rietz, Rosell, and Charlotte greeted me in turn, and I returned the gesture. All three of them had changed substantially over the last three years.

To begin with, Rietz was now eighteen, and the somewhat childish roundness of his features had completely vanished. He looked every bit the adult he was. I mean, by Japanese standards, eighteen was still quite young, but Rietz had been through so many battles and seen so many of the horrors of war that there wasn't so much of a trace of childishness left in him. He'd grown taller, too, and had to be nearing the 6'3" mark.

His experience in battle had done wonders for him as well. At the moment, his stats looked like this:

| LEA: 95/99 |
| VAL: 89/90 |
| INT: 95/99 |
| POL: 90/100 |

Every single one of them had gone up, and all of them except for Valor were in the nineties.

Rosell, meanwhile, was eight, and still very much a kid. He'd grown quite a bit as well, though, and was probably somewhere around 4'3". His face was as youthful as ever, but I'd noticed he was developing something of a persistent glare, possibly thanks to

I WILL USE MY APPRAISAL SKILL TO RISE IN THE WORLD

how much of his time he'd spent with his brow furrowed in deep thought.

In sharp contrast to his appearance, his personality was as adult-like as could be. Every once in a while, he'd bust out some pearl of wisdom that even made the actual adults nearby nod in admiration! His stats looked like this:

> LEA: 40/88
> VAL: 15/32
> INT: 88/109
> POL: 50/95

The gains his Intelligence had made were remarkable, but that aside, only his Politics had made any real advances. I wasn't exactly surprised, though—he'd done precisely no martial training over the past three years, and he hadn't been out commanding troops on the battlefield, either. I made a mental note to look into having Rosell get some experience with martial arts sometime in the future.

Last, but certainly not least, was Charlotte, who was now fifteen. She'd still looked like a child back when we first met, but she'd gone through a growth spurt since then, and had blossomed into a fully-fledged woman. Her growth in the chest area was particularly impressive—she was, in a word, stacked.

That fact made it really hard to know how to react when she got it into her head to hug me out of nowhere. I had no clue *why* she did it, and given my meager experience with women, I didn't know what to make of it in a ton of other ways as well. I'd known Charlotte for three years, yet the inner workings of her mind were still completely opaque to me. The one thing I could say with relative confidence thanks to my siblings was that she liked little kids.

AS A REINCARNATED ARISTOCRAT

As for her stats...

> LEA: 78/92
> VAL: 103/116
> INT: 44/45
> POL: 36/40

...she'd made some impressive progress in some respects, and less in others. Her Leadership score had gradually grown as she went through battle after battle, but her Valor, oddly enough, had remained more or less stagnant. It had only gone up by two points over a full three years.

I still didn't have a clear grasp of what dictated the growth rates for people's stats. I'd seen cases where people gained three whole points in a single day, but also cases like Charlotte's where it took three years for two measly points. I *did* have a theory in Charlotte's case, though: she hadn't grown in that respect because she had no *desire* to improve.

I'd gotten the impression that Charlotte was already totally satisfied with the current level of her magic, so she wasn't making any efforts in particular to polish her skills. To be fair, her current stats *were* already outlandishly high, so I couldn't really blame her for feeling like she'd reached her peak. I just also couldn't help but wonder how infernally powerful her magic would become if she were to completely max out her Valor, and sort of wished she'd put a bit more effort into raising it. Part of me hoped that a mage as powerful as her would show up someday and spark some friendly competition between the two of them.

"Rietz, did my father give you a letter?" I asked.

I WILL USE MY APPRAISAL SKILL TO RISE IN THE WORLD

"You mean the one from your fiancée? He did, yes," replied Rietz, pulling a letter from his breast pocket and handing it to me.

"A-Ars, you have a *fiancée*...? What's she like?" asked Rosell.

"I've never met her, so I don't know. I only found out about her a moment ago," I explained. "Actually, I don't even know her name yet."

"You don't? That sort of thing actually happens?" asked Rosell, sounding a little shocked.

"You've got a fiancée, Master Ars?" asked Charlotte. "But I thought that was why you bought *me*! You were gonna marry me, right?"

"Wrong!" I snapped. "Where in the world did you get *that* idea?!"

"Oh, okay, I see. You bought me to make me your mistress!"

"*Absolutely not!*"

Charlotte snickered at me. Apparently, she'd just been making fun of me this time around. She had a bad habit of saying completely outlandish stuff in total earnest every once in a while, so I always had a really hard time figuring out when I had to take her seriously.

I took a look at the letter. A name was printed on the front of the envelope: Licia Pleide.

I guess that must be my fiancée's name. I'll have to make note of that.

I opened the letter and gave it a read. The first thing I noticed was that her handwriting was clean and elegant. As for the letter's content, it started with a simple-enough greeting, then moved to talk about her recent affairs—how she'd taken up flower gardening as a hobby, and was pleased with how beautiful her garden was turning out to be. Finally, it concluded with the words, "As we promised, I intend to pay you a personal visit in very short order. I look forward to your hospitality."

Considering I'd only learned of her existence a matter of minutes ago, it probably went without saying that I'd made no such promise. I had to assume that either my father had done so in my name, or my fiancée had dreamed it up herself. Considering recent events, the former seemed far more likely...but perhaps that was just wishful thinking on my part. I'd have a *lot* of apprehensions about marrying a girl who could dream up a promise like that and convince herself it had actually happened.

Another worrisome detail was the fact that she'd written that she planned to visit "in very short order," but *hadn't* given any indication as to when exactly that would be. She probably assumed that I'd been fully briefed on the matter, so she didn't think that level of specificity was necessary.

Incidentally, in my new world, each year consisted of three hundred and sixty days, which were split up across twelve months. Each month was precisely thirty days long, so all things considered, the system was pretty similar to the one we had back on Earth. I'd never learned why things were split up that way, though.

On Earth, of course, one year indicated one revolution around the sun, but I didn't even know if this world was a proper globe, much less how the solar system may or may not be part of how it functioned. There *was* a sun-like object in the sky during the day, plus moon-like and star-like ones at night, so it seemed *pretty* likely that things worked the same way here as they had in my old world.

Anyway, that day in particular was the third day of the sixth month. That was one aspect in which the new system confused me—winter spanned from the fifth month to the seventh month here. Spring went from the eighth month to the tenth, summer was the eleventh to the first, and fall was the second to the fourth. My birthday, by the way, was on the eighth day of the eighth month. But of course, all of that was pretty off-topic.

I WILL USE MY APPRAISAL SKILL TO RISE IN THE WORLD

Steering back to my original point, my best guess was that "in very short order" probably meant she'd be showing up somewhere from the seventh day of the month to the ninth or so. That was just blind guesswork, however, and if I wanted a clear answer, my only choice was to ask my father.

"What did the letter say, Master Ars?" asked Rietz.

"Apparently, the girl I'm engaged to will be paying us a visit soon," I replied. "Have you heard anything about that?"

"Huh?" Rietz blinked. "No, I'm afraid I haven't. If that's true, though, then it's a matter of grave importance! Hosting a guest like her would require us to make numerous preparations, and we've done nothing of the sort! Do you know precisely when she'll be arriving?"

"No, I don't. I don't remember signing off on this visit, either, though I suppose you've already guessed that yourself."

"Well then, I suppose you'll have to ask Lord Raven for the details," said Rietz, arriving at the same conclusion that I'd reached.

I went back to the dining hall, but by the time I arrived, my father had already left. The next most likely place for him to be was his room, where he'd been spending a lot of time lately recuperating from his illness. Sure enough, I found him there, and asked him about the surprise visit.

"Oh... Come to think of it, I believe I might have agreed to something along those lines, yes," admitted my father. "It was quite a long time ago, though... Hammond said that the two of you should meet while you're still young, and I...*think* I probably agreed? You have to understand, Ars, that I was fairly far into my cups at the time. I hardly remember the conversation at all."

"But you *did* agree to it, then," I sighed. "When exactly is she supposed to arrive?"

"Let me see...I believe it was the sixth...the sixth day of the sixth month? No, the *fourth* day! That's it—the fourth day of the sixth month. Yes, I'm certain of it."

The fourth day? But, wait, that's...

"Th-That's *tomorrow*!"

"Yes, it is," my father blithely replied.

"H-How can you be so calm about this?! And why did you never think to tell me anything?!" I pressed.

My father glanced away sheepishly, scratched his chin, and then turned back to me with a profoundly serious expression on his face and replied, "Ars. I need you to listen, and listen well."

"A-All right," I replied nervously.

"Even the greatest of men make mistakes every once in a while."

"..."

I instantly regretted interpreting his expression as "serious" in any capacity. I was, frankly, appalled.

"Rietz!" I shouted, turning to my ever-capable retainer, who had accompanied me to my father's chamber. "Prepare the household to receive guests immediately!"

"Understood, Master Ars."

○

Getting ready to host an ambiguous number of guests with only a single day to prepare was—not to put too fine a point on it—an absolute goddamn nightmare. Thus, the entire estate was thrown into a state of chaos.

In the worst-case scenario, our preparations would prove woefully insufficient, my fiancée would be scandalized, and my engagement itself would be put into jeopardy. Forgetting about her visit

I WILL USE MY APPRAISAL SKILL TO RISE IN THE WORLD

was nothing short of an insult, and there was absolutely no way I could be honest with her about what had happened. I *had* to make it look like we'd been preparing for days, yet I had almost no time at all to make that happen.

I ended up enlisting several villagers who happened to be free that day to help out with our last-minute preparations. Not only did we have to get the inside of the estate ready, but the exterior had also gone a little too long without a solid touch-up, so it needed a thorough cleaning as well.

We worked at a frantic pace, and all of us were so stressed that we were basically at a loss, with the sole exception of Rietz the quintessential superhuman. *He* kept his cool the whole time, doling out clear and precise orders to everyone around him even as he accomplished his own tasks at a blinding pace. After working with him for so many years, none of my family's other employees dared to look down on him for being a Malkan anymore, so they allowed him to take the lead without complaint.

As a final touch of hospitality, I decided to prepare a bouquet to present to my fiancée upon her arrival. Her letter had made it clear to me that she was a big fan of flowers, so I hoped the gesture would go over well. She'd written that she was especially fond of a type of flower called miramis blossoms. It seemed she appreciated the fact that they bloomed in winter, a season normally bereft of greenery.

If I were to compare them to an Earth flower, miramis blossoms looked an awful lot like lycoris flowers, a species of spider lily, except with white petals. We had some blooming in our estate's garden, conveniently enough. I remembered hearing that lycoris flowers were poisonous and considered symbols of death in some sects of Buddhism, so I was a little biased against them. However, once I forced myself to look past those preconceptions, I had to admit that they *were* quite pretty. Miramis blossoms weren't poisonous and had no religious significance, either, so unlike lycoris, there wasn't any baggage to get in the way of their beauty.

I put together a bouquet of miramis blossoms, and even transplanted many miramis plants from the village into our estate's garden just to give her an extra-good first impression. I did have *some* doubts about my plan—after all, would someone who grew her own flowers be happy to receive even more of them?—but upon further reflection, I decided that what really mattered was me showing off the fact that I'd taken note of her interests and was trying to cater to them.

In the end, after a full day of frantic work, we'd managed to get the estate to a borderline presentable appearance. Lord Hammond was also minor nobility, ruling over a territory not much larger than that of my father's, so I *hoped* his daughter wouldn't be offended by the fact that our offerings were somewhat less than extravagant.

Rietz walked over to me as I surveyed our work. After a day like that, I could tell that even *he* was a little worn out.

"We've done all we can," he said. "Now it's up to you to make a good first impression, Master Ars... Though of course, I doubt we have anything to worry about on that front."

Thanks for piling on the pressure, Rietz.

Unfortunately, he was right. Whether or not she got a good impression of House Louvent ultimately rested on *my* shoulders. No matter how much we polished our estate's appearance, if she decided that I wasn't to her liking, then all that effort would be wasted.

Rietz seemed to have total faith in me for some reason, but to be totally honest, I had very little confidence in myself. My fiancée was

I WILL USE MY APPRAISAL SKILL TO RISE IN THE WORLD

a year older than me, according to my father, which would make her ten at the moment. I would've felt better about dealing with her if she were a little younger—ten was a tricky age for girls, to my understanding. At the age of ten, people were very much still children, but *treating* a child of ten accordingly was a very good way to get on their bad side.

I was pretty sure that kids usually tended to develop their first crush around the age of ten, as well. I'd never been the popular type, though, and I wasn't exactly a knockout in the looks department in this life, either. My appearance was perfectly mediocre.

Is this really going to go well?

I didn't have much time to plan, unfortunately, and before I could come up with a solid strategy, she arrived.

"Master Ars, Lady Licia has been sighted! She'll be here momentarily!"

The moment I got the news, I hurried outside, ready to welcome her. A golden-haired girl was standing before the gateway to our estate, accompanied by a small retinue of butlers and maids. She smiled as she watched me rush out the front door, then stepped up to introduce herself.

"It is a pleasure to meet you. My name is Licia Pleide," she said, giving me an elegant curtsey as she did so. I could tell in an instant that she'd had a noble upbringing.

As I bowed politely and introduced myself in turn, I took a closer look at Licia. The first thing that struck me was how short she was. Boys and girls weren't generally that far apart height-wise at the age of ten—if anything, girls tend to be a little on the taller side—but she was definitely shorter than me, in spite of the fact that I was a year younger and far from tall myself.

Height aside, she seemed like a calm, gentle, and beautiful girl.

I WILL USE MY APPRAISAL SKILL TO RISE IN THE WORLD

Her upturned eyes made her look kind, while her skin was pristine.

She was, of course, still a child, and had the figure to match. I'd been visualizing her as a kindhearted girl ever since I learned she was fond of flowers, and she certainly looked the part.

Still, I decided to appraise her, just for good measure. She was my fiancée, not a prospective retainer, so I wouldn't have been devastated if her stats were nothing to write home about, but if she was exceptional, then this arrangement was all the better.

> Licia Pleide
> Age: 10
> Female
> **Status:**
> LEA: 5/10
> VAL: 5/10
> INT: 45/73
> POL: 77/100
> Ambition: 80
> **Aptitudes:**
> Infantry: D
> Cavalry: D
> Archer: D
> Mage: D
> Fortification: D
> Weaponry: D
> Naval: D
> Aerial: D
> Strategy: B

Wh-What the hell *sort of stats are* those?!

AS A REINCARNATED ARISTOCRAT

Her Politics score was the first to shock me. Her Intelligence was quite high as well, to be clear, but compared to her Politics, it didn't even make me bat an eyelash. A maximum of 100! And it was already 77!

Politics was a fiddly stat to pin down. It still wasn't entirely clear to me what having a high Politics score actually meant for a person's abilities. Perhaps they were an exceptionally good communicator, an expert barterer, or a master of negotiations. If I had to put it into simple terms, I'd say that your Politics score represented your ability to express yourself. And then there was her Ambition. It was at 80...but why? Was she plotting to become the wife of a big-league lord or something?

I'd thought that she was a calm, gentle girl at first glance, but a single appraisal was all it took to shatter that impression. Sure, she was still smiling away at me, but suddenly, it looked less like the natural smile of a pleasant, kindhearted individual and more like a cold, calculated smile that was expressly engineered to give its recipient the best first impression possible. She was indeed exceptional, no doubt about it, but whether she'd prove to be the boon or bane of the Louvent household was entirely up in the air.

For all you know, maybe her Politics score represents the fact that she's naturally charismatic and just has a way with people! Maybe it's not calculated at all on her part! In any case, overthinking this probably isn't going to do me any good.

"Umm... Is something stuck to my face, perchance?" asked Licia. I'd been so stunned by the results of her appraisal that I'd ended up staring a little too obviously.

I spent a second in frenzied thought, trying to come up with a decent excuse, but then one of the maids behind her spoke up first and said, "Oh, I'm sure he's just bewitched by your beauty,

I WILL USE MY APPRAISAL SKILL TO RISE IN THE WORLD

Milady!"

Considering the circumstances, that seemed as good of a stop-gap excuse as any.

I owe you one, miss maid!

"Th-That's right!" I declared, latching onto her explanation. "I was just thinking you have the loveliest smile, that's all."

Under normal circumstances, I'd *never* have acted like that much of a pompous flirt, but desperate times called for desperate measures and I'd never known women to get upset about being complimented...not that I'd known many women, period.

"Oh, my! You flatter me," Licia said as her cheeks grew faintly flushed. It was such a natural reaction that I had a hard time believing she was just acting.

"Please, allow me to show you into the estate," I said.

"That would be lovely! Please do," replied Licia.

We walked side by side through the grounds, her maids and butlers following about five paces or so behind us.

"Lamberg truly is a wonderful place," said Licia, breaking the silence once more. I couldn't quite tell if she truly meant it, or if she was just being polite.

"Is it?" I asked.

"It is! The land here is blessed with an abundance of nature, and the village is full of life. I'm quite fond of my own homeland, Torbequista, but to be frank, I believe that this region is even more wonderful."

Once again, it really didn't seem like she was lying to me. I'd been worried that she'd be disillusioned by the fact that her fiancé lived in a random, insignificant corner of the countryside, but maybe those concerns were groundless?

"What sort of place *is* Torbequista?" I asked.

AS A REINCARNATED ARISTOCRAT

"It's out in the countryside with nature to spare, just like Lamberg, and its people are kind and caring," Licia replied. "That being said, they're somewhat less than bold, on the whole. We have very few achievements to speak of on the field of battle. I must admit that when I heard the tales of Lord Raven and the valiance of the troops he commands, I felt rather envious!"

Our idle chatter continued as we approached the estate's main building. Normally, it would only have taken a minute or so to walk there from the main gate, but between all that talk and the occasional pause to look around, it was quite a while before we finally arrived.

Licia had an exceptional talent for keeping a conversation flowing. I'd never been much of a talker, myself, so I had to give her the credit for how lively our little chat ended up being. You'd think she'd have been at least a little apprehensive about meeting her fiancé for the first time, but she certainly didn't let it show.

She asked just the right questions to pull me into the conversation, and did an excellent job of steering it toward topics that I'd have something to contribute to. Her reactions seemed genuine as well—every time she'd laugh or gasp in surprise, it struck me as totally natural. She also made sure to compliment me whenever an opportunity arose, which put me in a pretty good mood. In fact, I was ready to completely open up to her, even though it had only been about five minutes since we'd met!

If I'd been an ordinary child without memories of another lifetime, or if I hadn't had my Appraisal skill to help me out, I figure she would've had me utterly charmed beyond the point of no return over those five minutes. In the back of my mind, however, I hadn't dismissed the possibility that she was doing it on purpose...and if that was the case, then Licia was a girl I could not afford to under-

I WILL USE MY APPRAISAL SKILL TO RISE IN THE WORLD

estimate.

Rietz had a high Politics score, too, and *he* wasn't nearly this skilled at the art of conversation. He wasn't a poor conversationalist, to be clear—it just wasn't one of his most outstanding qualities.

Maybe your Politics score and your ability to communicate aren't actually as directly linked as I thought. Or maybe some other ability plays a factor, and I just haven't picked up on it yet.

As slowly as we were walking, we *did* eventually reach the main building and the field of miramis blossoms I'd had planted around it.

"Oh my, miramis blossoms! And there are so many of them! How lovely!" exclaimed Licia. "Did you plant them just for me, perchance?"

"Actually, yes," I admitted. "You mentioned that you loved them in the letter you wrote. I hope they're to your liking."

"They're beautiful," Licia mumbled as she looked out across the garden. "You did this all for me? It must have taken so much time. Thank you, truly," she said, turning to face me. Her cheeks were flushed once more, and a carefree smile spread across her face. "I am deeply moved by your generosity."

Her smile reminded me of my previous life. I'd always wanted to have a daughter just like her. I quickly reprimanded myself for the thought, though—getting all paternal on my fiancée was just plain weird on several levels! I'd have to marry her sometime in the future, after all, and we'd be expected to produce offspring. If I let myself start thinking of her in *that* light, then I could only imagine how guilty I'd feel when the time came to do the deed! Then again, that time definitely wouldn't come until she was fully grown, so maybe I was just overthinking things.

"Is something the matter?" asked Licia. I'd been staring again, though this time I genuinely *was* charmed by her smile.

Normally, I would've shook my head frantically and tried to explain my way out of it, but I'd grown past that reaction thanks to the maid from before.

"My apologies," I said. "I was just captivated by your lovely smile, Lady Licia."

"My... You certainly have a way with words, don't you, Sir Ars?" she replied, blushing once more. If I were a *real* flirt, I probably would have said something about how her smile was so striking it put the miramis blossoms around us to shame, but I didn't have the guts to do that, for better or worse. I would've literally died of embarrassment if I'd tried.

Eventually, Licia and I stepped inside the estate's main building. You needed a solid plan to entertain a guest like her, but fortunately, I had that under control! After escorting her inside, the next item in my itinerary was to formally welcome her to our home. The step *after* that was a little trickier, though. I'd planned on having lunch served, but since Licia had arrived earlier than anticipated, I was going to have to either improvise or stick to my guns and serve lunch early. That wasn't *entirely* unheard of during visits like this one, at least.

After lunch, I planned to escort Licia into the town of Lamberg for a stroll—essentially, to take her out on a date. Of course, the town was far enough from our estate that we'd have to bring an escort, so it wouldn't exactly be a private affair. We'd return to the estate after that for a moment to rest and...take a nap or something, and by that point, it would hopefully be late enough for dinner.

Speaking of dinner, I'd arranged for a performance to be staged during the meal. The Louvent household *was*, thankfully, at least somewhat prepared for unexpected last-minute visitors, so we had the means to muster entertainment at very short notice. A rather shocking number of our servants were trained musicians, so thankfully, said performance wouldn't *just* involve watching our soldiers spar with each other.

All that said, our performance plans had all been made under the assumption that we'd be entertaining *adults*. Would a kid like Licia enjoy them at all? I had no clue, so I pretty much forced the task of getting everyone ready off on Rietz. I knew I could trust him to do *something* about it, after all.

As for Licia's eventual departure, I'd prepared several gifts for her other than the miramis bouquet. I didn't actually know how long she was planning to stay, technically, but among the aristocracy, it was supposedly poor etiquette to stick around for longer than a day, so I was fairly confident she'd be off on her way tomorrow. But if I was wrong, and she decided to linger for longer, things were probably going to get pretty hectic.

I could worry about that later, though. First up was her formal greeting! And, as we stepped into my home...

"Welcome, Lady Licia," said our whole host of retainers in unison. They were gathered up inside, dressed notably more formally than they'd usually bother to be, and bowed politely as we made our entrance. The interior itself was a lot cleaner than usual, too, with miramis blossoms placed here and there as decorations and a whole host of art we usually kept in our storehouse put out on display.

Under normal circumstances, the entire household would have shown up to greet Licia, but my father was notably absent. I assumed that he was reluctant to meet with her at the moment, considering his poor health. He had a point, to be fair—there'd be hell to pay if she caught whatever he'd been afflicted with! Better safe than sorry. Less explicable, however, was Rietz's absence. Had he been called away for something urgent?

"It's a pleasure to meet all of you. It seems you've already been informed, but my name is Licia Pleide. I thank you for your most gracious hospitality," said Licia, addressing our retainers with a polite curtsy. A lot of nobles made a point of looking down on those beneath them on the social ladder, but it seemed she wasn't among that number.

"I may very well find myself permanently under your care in the future, so I would like to get to know you as soon as possible," Licia continued, proceeding to go around and personally introduce herself to each member of my household's staff, one by one. The whole household's worth of servants was there, along with House Louvent's mages, cavalry, and other highly-skilled troops.

"Your fiancée sure is pretty, Ars," said Rosell, who was present despite not fitting into any of the aforementioned categories. He was being raised to become our house's tactician, yes, but as things stood, he was nothing more than the third son of a hunter. Not that having him around was a problem, per se—despite his habit of treating me a little more casually than he probably should have, he was quite well-mannered, and probably wouldn't cause any trouble.

"Where in the world is Rietz?" I whispered back to Rosell.

"Hm? Mr. Rietz didn't think he should attend, since there's a chance that having a Malkan around would displease the lady. Didn't he tell you?"

"Ohhh..."

He's still worried about all that, huh?

Rietz's achievements in battle had won him a fair share of re-

I WILL USE MY APPRAISAL SKILL TO RISE IN THE WORLD

nown. He'd been regularly ridiculed by soldiers from the other noble houses at first, but I'd heard that fewer and fewer people dared to do so as his reputation grew. Personally, I thought that there'd be no problem with him making an appearance at this sort of function. Plus, Licia was bound to find out about him sooner or later, considering our relationship.

Hell, the odds were pretty decent that she *already* knew about Rietz! If she was going to have a problem with him, then having the two of them meet as soon as possible would be for the best in the long run. Of course, Rietz was smart enough to figure all of that out for himself, but he'd decided to hold back for the moment regardless. I could only assume he'd simply chosen to err on the side of caution.

By this point, Licia was shaking the hands of everyone present and making small talk. Her smile never faltered for a second, and she was clearly smooth-talking them just as effectively as she had me. She'd given an excellent first impression to everyone in the room, that was for sure. I had to agree with everyone, too. She really *did* seem like a nice girl, plain and simple. However, deep down, I just couldn't forget what I'd seen on her status screen.

It wasn't just her Politics score, either—her Ambition was causing me some serious unease as well. It *did* make sense that someone with a Politics score like hers might be a naturally gifted communicator, yes, but when I factored in her Ambition, the odds that the way she presented herself was deliberate and calculated skyrocketed. And if that really was the case, then I knew it would only take the slightest moment of complacency for her to seize the upper hand. I couldn't allow myself to let my guard down around her until I knew more.

"Hmm... She's pretty, and she seems nice enough at a glance, but...I dunno...she's kinda scary, too," muttered Rosell as he watched Licia do her thing.

"What makes you say that?" I asked.

"W-Well, it's hard to put into words... I guess it's that her smile seems almost fake. Or that what she's saying is sort of superficial... It's like she's buttering us all up, or something... A-Ars, you should keep your guard up around that girl. If you don't, I'm afraid she might p-poison you or something... Then she'd put me under her thumb and work me like a slave... P-Please, you *have* to keep an eye on her, no matter what!" Rosell whispered into my ear.

I was impressed by how sharp his intuition was. His analysis of the situation *had* veered off in a pretty pessimistic direction as it went along, yes, but still.

I guess my only options are to get to know her as well as I can, and to make sure not to put myself at risk until I'm certain I know what makes her tick. Not even Appraisal can tell me who a person really is deep down, so I'm on my own on this one.

"Oh, look, it's Charlotte's turn!" said Rosell.

Oh, crap!

I realized my mistake a moment too late. I'd never really taken the time to teach Charlotte about proper etiquette, and even after all this time, I still had no clue what was going on in the girl's head. There was absolutely no way of predicting what she might do, but I had a terrible feeling that it might end up being something really, *really* rude!

We should've had her sit this out, not Rietz!

Licia stepped up to Charlotte, but instead of immediately offering her a handshake like the others, she paused for a moment.

"Oh," said Licia. "Might you be Charlotte? I've heard all sorts of tales about House Louvent's master mage! They say you wield magical power like none other, and burn your enemies to ash by the score!"

I assumed that the mage's robe Charlotte was wearing had tipped Licia off to her identity. I could also practically *see* Charlotte's ego inflate on the spot as she realized that her name was making the rounds among the other noble houses.

"Yes, indeed, I *am* the one they call Charlotte," Charlotte replied in a tone positively dripping with confidence. Bordering on straight-up arrogance, really. That was *not* how a mage was meant to conduct herself in front of a noble's daughter, but I took some small solace in the fact that she hadn't bungled it up *too* horrifically, and their exchange was over…or so I thought.

"I *knew* it! I just wanted to say that, from one woman to another, I respect you ever so much! Please, do shake my hand!" exclaimed Licia, much to my bemusement. It was like watching a little kid get introduced to their favorite superhero.

Well, I suppose that could've gone much worse, I thought, a bead of cold sweat slowly dripping its way down my back. Charlotte's attitude didn't improve after the handshake, unfortunately. She wasn't usually *that* insolent when she was speaking with adults, but Licia was a child, and in Charlotte's mind, that apparently exempted her from all standards of politeness.

One of these days, I have to drill some etiquette into that girl's head.

Licia finished making the rounds and turned to face me once more.

"Umm, excuse me," she said. "Is Lord Raven not present at the moment?"

"My father's illness has taken a turn for the worse, I'm afraid," I explained. "Much as he would love to meet you, he's chosen not to do so for fear of spreading his sickness."

AS A REINCARNATED ARISTOCRAT

"Is that so...? I'm terribly concerned for him, but if he simply cannot meet with me, I will not protest. Oh, and one more question—is Rietz, the Malkan I've heard so much about, not around? I've heard all sorts of tales about his brilliance upon the battlefield, so I would love to meet with him in person."

Sounds like Rietz didn't have to worry about Licia being prejudiced. Too bad he didn't make an appearance, I guess. I'll have to let him know later.

I ended up going with the early lunch plan, after which the time finally arrived for the most nerve-wracking item on our itinerary: the date. Licia and I left the estate together on foot. I couldn't pick them out at a glance, but I knew for a fact that an escort was following us just out of sight. The idea was that having a full host of armed guards accompanying us would take the fun out of the experience, so they'd hang back and stay out of the picture unless they were needed.

To be totally honest, though, I thought it would've been better for them to just walk with us and not bother with the pretext. After all, who knew whether they'd be able to make it to us in time if something *did* go wrong? Not that I was expecting any disasters—I'd certainly never been attacked in town so far.

The real problem, in my mind, was the question of what we would do once we got to town. Lamberg wasn't exactly a tourist destination. The village had zero places to go for entertainment, and I wasn't convinced it would be even suitable for a date.

I'd seriously considered just staying at the estate and taking a leisurely walk through the flower gardens instead, but Rietz advised me against it. According to him, "Showing her that you're adored by your subjects will prove to her that you'll be an exemplary lord in the future." Whether or not that was the right angle to take with a

I WILL USE MY APPRAISAL SKILL TO RISE IN THE WORLD

kid like Licia seemed a little questionable, in my mind. Then again, she was the child of a lord herself, and had probably received a specialized education, so I decided to heed his advice. Licia had already proved to be remarkably bright, so it seemed that decision had been the right one, in retrospect.

Now the big question was whether or not I could keep her entertained. Just talking with her the whole time would've been ideal, but I wasn't the best conversationalist. Thankfully, her skill in the field seemed to make up for my lack thereof, and our conversations had proven enjoyable thus far.

Anyway, it only took us a few minutes to arrive at the village. I decided to lead her to the town square. It wasn't much of a plaza or anything, but it did have a small local marketplace set up in it. You couldn't find much of anything worthwhile there, but every once in a while, something rare or unusual would crop up, and it was the liveliest part of town by a long shot. For lack of better options, it seemed like the right place to visit first.

"Shall we head for the town square?" I suggested.

"Lead the way!" Licia replied.

I showed her to the square, as planned, but when we arrived, I quickly realized that something seemed a little off. The square was usually fairly bustling, but on that particular day, there was a bigger crowd than ever. I could hear angry shouts and bellows coming from within.

"Give us our damn money back!"

"Like hell I will! This was a done deal! You can't just back out of it, you rat bastards!"

Between the shouting and the swearing, it was clear that whatever we were witnessing was on the verge of devolving into a brawl.

Oh, for the... Of all the times for trouble to crop up in town! What should I do? Can I just ignore it? No, that's not an option—I'm the son of the lord here, so ignoring the people's problems could give Licia a terrible *impression of me!*

"What do you suppose happened?" Licia muttered. She sounded worried, so as I'd feared, I was going to have to do *something* to resolve the situation.

Seriously, there couldn't possibly have been a worse time for things to go wrong.

I'd informed the townsfolk that Licia would be coming for a visit, but I hadn't given them detailed information on my plans for the day. In retrospect, I doubted that most of them even realized that I'd be bringing her into town.

"Let's go ask," I said, then walked over to one of the townsfolk who was keeping an eye on the situation from the edge of the crowd.

"What's going on? Why the commotion?" I asked.

"Oh, if it isn't the young master!" the villager said, then furrowed his brow. "Wait...wasn't your fiancée s'pposed to be coming 'round today...? Oh! Is that her? The lovely li'l lady over there, I mean?"

Licia took that as her cue to introduce herself to the man, and she was just as polite with him as she had been with the staff at my family's estate. After they finished exchanging pleasantries, the man gestured toward the crowd.

"Right, yeah, 's a real big fuss. Pretty messy stuff, if you ask me."

"Messy how?" I probed.

The man spent a moment breaking down the situation for me. Apparently, the conflict centered around the village's local trader. His operation was fairly small-scale, but pretty much all of the village's craftsmen had no choice but to deal with him.

It all started when several craftsmen who specialized in furniture and the like came up with a new variety of home heater that they planned to sell. The heaters were to be powered by flame-aspected magistones, which the craftsmen asked the trader to acquire for them. Magistones were useful for more than just the synthesis of aqua magia—they could also be used in their raw form for a variety of purposes. Flame-aspected magistones, for instance, emitted a slight amount of heat.

The details were beyond me, but apparently, it had been discovered that stimulating flame-aspected magistones with some sort of material or another would increase the heat they released. The craftsmen had taken advantage of that quality to power their newly-invented heater. My family's estate wasn't equipped with anything of the sort, but I was certain we'd have one soon enough if they ever managed to put their design out onto the market.

However, the magistones were what caused everything to break down. The trader had ended up stocking *sound*-aspected magistones, not fire. The line of communications between the craftsmen and the traders had failed catastrophically somewhere along the way, and the trader was convinced that they'd asked for sound-aspected magistones to make what sounded to me like some sort of magical megaphone to sell to House Louvent.

The craftsmen, of course, intended nothing of the sort. They laid into the trader for his mistake, telling him that they couldn't make something that complicated even if they wanted to, that they didn't want or need his sound magistones, and that he should take a long walk off a short cliff. The trader, however, stubbornly stuck to his guns and insisted that he'd been asked for sound-aspected magistones and had held up his end of the bargain. That was when the craftsmen demanded their money back, but the trader demanded that they uphold the deal and take the magistones off his hands.

All in all, I couldn't tell who was in the wrong. *Someone* had clearly screwed the pooch, but there was no way of telling who. A member of House Louvent was supposed to be present when deals of this sort were made, just in case any trouble cropped up, but there'd been so few issues as of late that everyone involved had decided it wasn't worth bothering.

If one side had been harmed by the communications breakdown, it would've been easy enough to pin the blame on the shoulders of whoever had profited, but as things stood, both sides were liable to suffer losses. If I stormed in and announced that everyone was at fault for not bringing in an intermediary like they were supposed to, it probably would've calmed the situation down for the moment, at least—but neither side would leave satisfied, and the whole thing would inevitably explode the moment I left.

Maybe I can figure out who's at fault if I interview the people who actually made the deal... No, that would only work if the one who made the mistake was honest about it. Isn't there something I can do to put this trouble to bed without causing more issues down the road?

I lapsed into thought for a moment, but before I could come up with a decent plan, Licia leaned in and spoke to me in a hushed tone, saying, "Umm, Sir Ars? If I may offer a suggestion, I believe I have an idea that could resolve this matter with no ill will on either side."

"You do? What is it?" I asked, somewhat shocked. Could a ten-year-old like her have really figured out how to solve a situation as messy as this one? Mediating a fight did fall into the realm of politics, in a certain sense, and her Politics score was far and away above that of an average person's, so perhaps she really did have the perfect answer in mind.

"Nobody took any measures to prevent this sort of problem from occurring," she explained. "And both sides are equally to blame for that negligence. That means that you could bring the issue to a close by assigning the blame to one side or the other...but that would leave lingering animosity, and they would likely soon start fighting all over again. Even worse, they might end up distrusting House Louvent as a result!"

I nodded. Everything she'd said lined up with my own analysis of the situation.

"Unfortunately, I doubt it's possible to resolve the situation without either side suffering losses. That's why the dispute escalated. I believe that to minimize the lingering animosity between the two sides, you should step in, assign an equal degree of blame to both of them, and propose a solution that costs both sides equally!"

Minimizing the damage done and distributing it equally, huh?

It was a reasonable suggestion, to be sure. I had a feeling that both sides knew they were at least somewhat to blame for the problem, and were only disavowing their fault so vehemently because they had so much to lose.

If the trader was left with only the advance the craftsmen had paid him, he'd come out of the deal deeply in the red, and even if the traders were able to recover that advance, they still stood to miss a major business opportunity. They'd surely already bought plenty of other materials for the heaters aside from the magistones, and developing the device couldn't have been cheap, either. In that sense, not being able to produce them would mean a heavy loss for the craftsmen that recovering their advance wouldn't cover.

"I have a solution in mind," said Licia. "I believe that the trader should be made to barter off the sound magistones he mistakenly obtained, then acquire flame magistones to replace them."

"Bartering them off, huh...? Now that you mention it, it's not like sound-aspected magistones are worthless. Couldn't the trader just return the advance he was paid and sell the magistones to someone else? Why isn't he considering that option?"

"Hmm... I can't say for certain, but I presume that something about his circumstances is preventing him from doing so," replied Licia.

His circumstances? What could that be...?

I thought about it for a moment...and then an explanation finally hit me.

Thanks to the rapidly escalating conflicts cropping up all across Summerforth, the price of magistones had shot through the roof as of late. The one caveat, however, was that aqua magia made by refining low-quality magistones couldn't actually be used to cast magic. That meant that the sort of low-quality magistones the trader was likely dealing in sold at a much lower price.

Despite that fact, however, it was very likely that the trader had bought his sound magistones for significantly higher than their usual market value. The craftsmen were after flame magistones, and had likely offered a high price in exchange for it. Flame magistones, I assumed, had to have been more expensive than sound magistones. I didn't know precisely what sound magistones were used for, to be fair, but regardless, they couldn't possibly have been more valuable than a variety that could be used to power a heater at this time of year.

In spite of the high price they'd offered, though, the trader ended up under the impression they wanted *sound* magistones. In other words, he believed that they were offering to buy sound magistones from him for an excessive sum of money. I didn't know the exact price of sound magistones, and it could've been higher or lower depending on how much of it was in circulation. Regardless, if the trader thought he'd be getting that high of a payout for it, he probably hadn't bothered seeking out the best possible prices and had wound up paying slightly above the market rate for it himself. In short, he'd bought a whole pile of sound magistones that he *had* to sell for more than its market value, or else he'd face devastating losses.

"If the trader has to barter the sound magistones for flame magistones, he'll likely end up with quite a bit less of it than the craftsmen initially ordered," said Licia. "So, if the craftsmen are forced to pay the price they once agreed on, they would suffer heavy losses. With all that in mind, I think you should have them work out how much they would have paid for each pound of flame magistones initially, then have the craftsmen pay only slightly more than that for however much the trader manages to actually obtain. That should minimize the trader's losses."

"That makes sense," I replied. It felt to me like the craftsmen would be getting a sort of raw deal, in the end, but on the other hand, they could make up for it by raising the price of the heaters once they were finished. I could even promise to purchase one myself for an even higher price to sweeten the bargain. We had a fireplace in the estate, yes, but a proper heater could have made life a lot more comfortable during winter.

"Hmm…" Licia thought for a moment longer, then nodded. "That's all I can think of, I'm afraid. The rest will depend on how well you arbitrate the deal, Sir Ars."

I was convinced. Her plan was as good as I was going to get, and with that settled, I intervened in the argument, explained that both sides were in the wrong for not coming to my family in the first place, and offered Licia's proposal as a means to minimize the damages all around. Neither side was wildly enthusiastic about the plan, to be sure, but I somehow managed to convince them to accept the terms.

I didn't think anyone was really happy with how the situation turned out, in the end, but at the absolute least, nobody looked like they were about to start throwing punches anymore. It seemed likely that the conflict was well and truly settled. The negotiations, however, had taken quite a long time, and the sun was already starting to set when we finished. Licia and I had no choice but to make our way back to my family's estate.

All things considered, the date was a disastrous failure. My one solace was that Licia didn't seem particularly bothered. She'd really managed to impress me, when all was said and done—it was hard to believe that a girl of her age could come up with a way to resolve a conflict that messy, though.

I was even more convinced than ever that the friendly, appealing way she conducted herself was calculated. If she was that smart, then reading people and playing to their desires was a piece of cake, right? Hell, part of me was starting to suspect that she'd been reincarnated into this world, just like me!

"You're frowning, Sir Ars," said Licia, peeking over at my face. "Is something the matter?"

"Oh, no, not exactly!" I replied. "I was just thinking that this ended up being a pretty lousy date. I'm sorry about all the trouble."

"Lousy? No, not at all! I was very impressed by how you conducted yourself, Sir Ars!"

"Impressed? By what? All I did to help was offer your idea as a solution. I barely contributed anything at all, really."

Licia shook her head and replied, "The idea was mine, yes, but

I WILL USE MY APPRAISAL SKILL TO RISE IN THE WORLD

you're the one who convinced them to accept it. They would never have considered your proposal so readily if they didn't already have faith in you as their lord. It's clear to me now that your people adore you."

She certainly does know how to flatter a guy.

I was chagrined to realize that I'd inadvertently put myself in Licia's debt. She hadn't demanded a favor in return yet, but if I let myself get too indebted to someone with Ambition as high as hers, she was sure to use it as leverage sooner or later.

Paying her back right away was probably out of the picture, unfortunately, but even more than that, I wished that I could learn a little about what really made Licia tick deep down. I wouldn't have felt safe marrying her unless I had a decent grasp of her personality. I kept brooding over the question as we walked back to my estate. Finally, our conversation took a turn that gave me the chance I needed to start learning more about her.

"What sort of people do you find appealing, Sir Ars? Just for the sake of reference," asked Licia.

"Hmm," I said, sensing an opportunity. "I suppose I like people who don't keep secrets from me. I always appreciate spending time with people who don't hold their true opinions back and don't sugarcoat things. Life's much more enjoyable that way, in my opinion."

I wasn't expecting her to actually spill the beans just like that, of course, but I was hoping her reaction might give me some clues. I wasn't exactly lying, either—even in my previous life, I'd thought that marrying a woman who didn't mince words would have been nice.

"I see! I'll keep that in mind," replied Licia. I might have been imagining it, but it felt like she'd paused for just a split second beforehand. Unfortunately, it wasn't long enough for me to know if my response had rattled her.

AS A REINCARNATED ARISTOCRAT

Looks like dragging out Licia's true feelings isn't going to be quite that easy, I thought to myself as we made our way back to my estate.

○

We arrived home just in time for dinner, and after that, it was time for the entertainment I'd arranged. The performers had been preparing themselves while Licia and I were in town, it seemed, and their act went off without a hitch. The music was only the beginning—they also put on a magically-enhanced dance performance, which I personally thought was quite remarkable. Licia seemed to enjoy the whole event, so I figured I could call it a success overall.

After the performance, all that was left was for us to say goodnight and retire to our chambers. I'd learned over the course of the day that she was, in fact, planning to return home the following morning. It seemed my assumption on that front had been safe after all. I just had to have breakfast with her, present her with her gifts, and see her off! Whether or not she'd *like* said gifts was still up in the air, of course.

Our date was a failure, but Licia hadn't seemed particularly bothered by it. One way or another, the day had ended without any *major* problems. The only remaining issue was that I still didn't have a handle on Licia's personality or way of thinking at all. She couldn't have been *just* a plain old nice girl, considering her Politics and Ambition scores.

Meh, it's not like today will be my only chance to figure her out. I can just put the pieces together bit by bit every time I meet her, I thought as I snapped my sheets to make my bed...and just about jumped out of my skin in shock.

Somebody was under my covers. At first, I thought that one

I WILL USE MY APPRAISAL SKILL TO RISE IN THE WORLD

of my siblings was playing a prank on me, but no, it wasn't either of them. My bed's occupant had blonde hair and happened to be somewhere around ten years old. In short...

"Is something wrong, Sir Ars?"

...it was Licia!

I was so shocked, so utterly incapable of comprehending why she would be *there* of all places, that I didn't even understand what she was asking.

"Did I startle you?" Licia asked.

"Y-Yes, you certainly did," I somehow managed to reply.

"I could tell! Your eyes opened as wide as dinner plates, and you made the most *adorable* face," she said with a grin. And not the friendly, sociable grin I'd seen her put on throughout the day, either—this was the grin of a mischievous little troublemaker.

Honestly, I had *no* idea what she was doing in my room, and the wheels in my mind were spinning on overdrive to figure out what the hell I was supposed to do about it. I'd thought that all I had left to do that day was go to bed, but I couldn't have been more wrong.

"Umm," I began. "You do know this isn't your room, right, Lady Licia? Did one of our servants lead you to the wrong chamber, perhaps?"

"No, not at all! They did a splendid job and led me exactly where I was supposed to go. I simply slipped out afterward!"

I didn't lock my door, so I guess getting inside wouldn't have been much of a challenge. Who told her which room was mine, though? I guess they wouldn't have any reason to withhold the info if she claimed she just wanted to chat, but...

"And why, exactly, did you do that?" I asked.

"You're a very composed person, Sir Ars, and not particularly expressive. I just wanted to see what sort of face you make when

I WILL USE MY APPRAISAL SKILL TO RISE IN THE WORLD

you're shocked, that's all!" Licia explained. Wasn't much of an explanation, in my book, but maybe that was just me.

Part of me really wanted to ask where this side of her personality had been hiding all day, and Licia seemed to guess what I was thinking from the look on my face. She pushed herself into a sitting position on my bed.

"You told me this afternoon that you prefer being around people who speak their mind and don't keep secrets, didn't you? Well, I thought that, if that were the case, it would be nice to have a chance to talk, just the two of us. Scaring you was simply a bonus."

Hearing that explanation finally helped me calm down a little. She hadn't reacted much when I mentioned that I preferred honesty, but it seemed the statement had more of an impact on her than I'd initially thought.

"Well...I'm pleased to hear it, and I would love to chat," I replied. "I want to get to know you better, as a matter of fact."

I couldn't have asked for a better opportunity to draw out her true nature. That said, I was still very confused as to why she'd put herself in this position. The one thing I now knew beyond a shadow of a doubt was that the persona she'd projected throughout the afternoon really was just an act.

"Oh my! Now I'm all flustered," said Licia. "But as it so happens, I was hoping to get to know you better as well. For instance, I would love to know—what do you think of me?"

"...What do you mean?" I cautiously asked.

"I have a certain talent. When I speak with someone, I can more or less tell how they feel about me by carefully observing the look on their face. The first time we met, Sir Ars, you looked at me with immediate suspicion."

A "certain talent"? She can "more or less tell" what people think of

185

her? Could it be that she has a skill similar to my Appraisal?

I was shocked to realize that she had that sort of power—almost as shocked as I was to realize that she'd been fully aware of my doubts throughout the day.

"Distrusting someone you've only just met isn't all that rare, to be fair," continued Licia. "Plenty of people are wary by nature. Normally, though, I can dispel that distrust simply by speaking with them for a minute or two. You, however, spoke with me for hours on end, and even worked your way out of a difficult situation thanks to *my* advice, yet not only did your misgivings not vanish—they *deepened*, of all things! And then, at the very end, you tried to draw out my true intentions with a leading question! What is it about me that you find so suspicious, Sir Ars?"

As Licia spoke, I did my best to read her expression. She seemed somewhat agitated, and perhaps even a little frustrated. As best as I could tell, she was irritated that she hadn't managed to sway my opinion of her in the way she'd hoped.

She'd earned the trust and affection of who knows how many people with her conversational skills, which probably made my immovability all the more frustrating. That was why she'd taken the risk of overplaying her hand and revealing her true nature.

Come to think of it, maybe she went out of her way to hide in my bed and scare me to vent her frustration...

"I have a talent as well, Lady Licia. I can perceive people's abilities, aptitudes, and ambition to move up in the world," I explained.

I'd resolved to tell her all about my power. She opened up to me, so keeping quiet about myself wouldn't exactly have been fair, right? Not to mention that I was going to marry her at some point. If I was going to have to tell her eventually, I figured I might as well get it over with. I couldn't tell if she believed me, but she did look a

I WILL USE MY APPRAISAL SKILL TO RISE IN THE WORLD

little shocked, at least.

"That's how I know that you're overwhelmingly more ambitious than almost anyone else I've ever met, and that you have the political talent to back it up," I continued. "And it's also why I suspected that the way you were acting was just a front."

For a moment, Licia just sat there silently, but finally, she spoke up once more and said, "I suppose there's no room for doubt—that talent of yours is certainly real. After all, I'm rather aware of my own ambitions."

"What are they? What is it you wish to do?" I asked.

"There's only one ambition that a Summerforthian woman could possibly have: to find a man of power and status to fall for," she replied. Saying it was the only ambition possible seemed like a bit of an overstatement to me, but considering the world we lived in, she was probably more right than I knew.

"Wouldn't you be opposed to marrying a man like me, then?"

"Yes, quite. As a matter of fact, I was seriously considering breaking off our engagement prior to my departure," Licia admitted. "After what you just told me, though, I've reconsidered the matter."

"You have? Why?"

"As things stand, you are indeed nothing more than the successor to a petty lord's insignificant domain. Your power, however, changes matters. With it at your disposal, I'm confident that you will rise far beyond your current station. Thus, I've changed my mind. I *want* to marry you now, Sir Ars."

I could hardly think of a more mercenary reason to marry someone. I was the one who said that I wanted to know how she truly felt, so I'd literally asked for this, but now that I actually did know where she was coming from, I was finding it rather hard to muster a response.

"Well, I'm certainly happy to hear it. I'm in favor of our marriage as well," I finally replied. I wasn't being entirely honest—frankly, I had my fair share of worries about the whole idea. I had a feeling that Licia would be the staunchest of allies I could hope for, so long as I took care to only show her my good side. But the moment I let her catch a glimpse of my weakness, the odds were distressingly high I'd receive a dagger in the back for my trouble.

I didn't have much of a choice, though. The son of an upstart lord being engaged to marry another lord's daughter was something of a rarity, so if I didn't marry her, I might never get an opportunity like that again. Plus, on a more personal note, I actually found her scheming side a little charming.

Romance didn't seem to be in the cards for the two of us, which was a shame, but I knew there was no point in setting my expectations too high. Our parents had arranged our marriage out of a sense of friendship, and I would've been happy if the two of us just happened to fall for each other, but Licia was clearly a hardcore utilitarian type. After everything I'd seen from her, I wouldn't have been surprised to learn she had no interest in love on the whole.

"I'm relieved to hear you say so! And with that, I bid you goodnight," said Licia as she got off my bed. I'd thought she would want to chat for a little while longer, but no, she was already on her way out the door before I could even react.

I guess she's satisfied now that she knows why I suspected her.

I breathed a sigh of relief as she shut the door behind her. It had been a surprising, and somewhat harrowing, conversation, but I *had* managed to learn what sort of person she really was, so it was fruitful overall. I would've been an anxious wreck if she'd gone on her way before I pinned her personality down. I climbed into bed and pulled the covers over me, my mood considerably cheerier than

I WILL USE MY APPRAISAL SKILL TO RISE IN THE WORLD

it had been a few minutes prior.

As I drifted off to sleep, I smelled something unfamiliar. It took me a little while to realize that Licia had been hiding in that very bed just moments earlier...and that I was smelling *her*. The aroma was so pleasant that it lulled me to sleep in no time flat.

○

Licia let out a quick sigh of relief as she closed the door to Ars's room. A moment later, she smiled—not the fake smile that she wore for show in public, and not the mischievous smile she'd worn in front of Ars moments earlier. No, this was a true, natural smile.

What in the world am I so happy about? Licia asked herself. But in truth, she already knew the answer: she was happy because Ars had said that he wanted to marry her.

Between Licia's ability to perceive what others thought of her, her talent for conversation, and her natural charms, the majority of the people she'd met had quickly taken a liking to her. She was beloved by all, young and old, man and woman alike, so at some point along the way, she started taking the affection that people afforded her for granted.

That had made it more than a little difficult to cope with Ars's unrelenting suspicion. She was frustrated and irritated with him—after all, what had she done to deserve his distrust?—but at the same time, she'd somehow found herself irresistibly drawn to him. Licia had yet to figure out where those feelings of hers stemmed from, but the one thing she did know for sure was that she needed Ars to fall for her, one way or another. That, clearly, was why she'd been so incredibly happy when he said he was in favor of their marriage.

AS A REINCARNATED ARISTOCRAT

He does *want to marry me now, yes...but it doesn't seem like he's fallen in love with me just yet. He will, though, one of these days! I'll see to it that he does!*

Licia had resolved Ars's suspicions by revealing her true nature to him, but she knew it would take more than that to fully ensnare him with her charms. She wasn't naïve enough to believe that something so simple could steal a man's heart.

In fact, on some level, she'd expected him to turn on her once her secret was out. She'd made her move anyway because, in her mind, being outright hated by him would have still been better than putting up with his unstated suspicion. In that sense, the fact that she'd exited the situation without earning his animosity meant that she'd come out ahead. Licia could be quite the optimist when the circumstances called for it.

The beginning was an absolute disaster, though. At least I managed to fool him, I suppose...

"The beginning," of course, meant the part where she'd been caught in Ars's bed. She'd told him that she'd wanted to see him in a state of surprise, but that was an outright lie. The simple truth of the matter was that the moment she'd fully registered the fact that it was his bed, she'd been afflicted with an irresistible urge to crawl right into it. She'd known it was an awful idea, too, but she just couldn't stop herself.

When Ars had walked into the room while she was still under the covers, Licia had nearly drowned in her own cold sweat. She'd barely had the time to come up with an excuse before he tried to climb into bed himself. The part where she said that the look of shock on his face was adorable, incidentally, had been entirely true.

Licia thought back to the smell of Ars's bed, as well as the look on his face when he'd realized she was in it, and found herself grin-

I WILL USE MY APPRAISAL SKILL TO RISE IN THE WORLD

ning all over again. In the end, on the way back to her room for the night, she smiled the entire time.

○

The next morning, Licia ate breakfast with us, I presented her with her gifts, and then she went off on her way back to Torbequista. She gave me the brightest smile I'd ever seen when I handed her gifts to her—natural and cheerful enough that I just couldn't imagine it was an act. Knowing her, though, even if she was genuinely pleased, the choice to show that fact off had almost certainly been deliberate.

A few days later, I received a letter from her. It was a simple enough report, thanking me for my hospitality and informing me that she was taking good care of the flowers I'd given her. Etiquette dictated that I send a reply, so I wrote up a response and sent it off to her at the first opportunity.

It wasn't long before I started receiving letter after letter from her at a remarkably fast pace. They were never about anything important, either. Just childish reports on her daily affairs and idle grumbling, for the most part. I couldn't simply ignore them, however—again, etiquette and all—so I sent a reply each and every time. However, it wasn't long at all before I ran out of things to write about. Forcing myself to fill up a letter every time quickly became a major source of stress in my life.

Why is *she sending all these letters, anyway? Is she testing the extent of my vocabulary? Or maybe the answer's surprisingly simple, and she just honestly enjoys hearing from me...? No, that's absurd. It's* definitely *not that.*

Aside from my ongoing correspondence with Licia, nothing in particular had changed in my life. I hadn't found any exceptional people to recruit as of late, but regardless, I was already running up against the limitations of a small noble house's resources. House Louvent simply didn't have the funding to employ many more retainers.

Thus, a year and a half passed without any major incident... until one day, my father collapsed.

Chapter 5

It was the fourth day of the third month. Autumn was upon us, and I had just turned eleven.

The news of my father's collapse came as a major shock. As of a few months prior, he'd stopped coughing entirely. We were all convinced he'd finally overcome his illness. But then one day, while he was training with his troops in the early morning, he simply fell to the ground, still as the dead. He hadn't actually dropped dead on the spot, thankfully, but he *did* lose consciousness, and with no clear explanation why. He was carried into the estate, and a doctor who lived in Lamberg was immediately called in to treat him.

"Is my father all right? Can you help him?" I asked after the doctor finished his inspection. We were sitting beside the bed where my father was resting.

"His life isn't in danger, as things stand," the doctor began, then hesitated before continuing. "But he has a high fever, it would seem. Hmm… Lord Raven was in poor health until recently, yes? I was relieved to hear he'd shaken off the malady, but I'm afraid to say that, well…"

The look on the doctor's face was all I needed to know that he wasn't about to deliver good news.

"Has my father's illness returned?"

AS A REINCARNATED ARISTOCRAT

"I believe so," replied the doctor. "And I now believe I know what he suffers from: a rather rare illness known as gley syndrome. The sickness itself is something of a mystery, though, I'm afraid. We have yet to determine what causes it, but a small mercy is that we *do* know it isn't contagious. Its victims are likely to think themselves afflicted with a common cold, but with symptoms that persist for far longer than usual before suddenly receding. Shortly thereafter, though, the disease manifests once more in the form of a wide variety of symptoms—a high fever, a loss of appetite, vomiting, diarrhea, a propensity to fall victim to other illnesses...and, ultimately, death."

I'd never heard of a disease by that name, and I couldn't remember any sickness from my old world with similar symptoms. I was never exactly an expert as far as diseases were concerned, of course, so the fact that I didn't *know* of any like it didn't mean there hadn't been one out there somewhere.

"Can gley syndrome be cured?" I asked.

The doctor shook his head and replied, "Not with any medicine we know of. The only option is to wait and pray the patient overcomes the disease. In most cases, though, I'm afraid they pass away within a year of the first sign of symptoms. Lord Raven is exceptionally hale and hearty, and I believe that the odds are high he'll survive longer than the average patient, but nevertheless..."

Death.

I was struck dumb. Was my father going to die? The thought alone sent my mind spiraling into turmoil. I knew it would happen someday, but surely this was far, *far* too soon?

"What's important now is for Lord Raven to get plenty of rest and allow his body the time it needs to heal, the same as one would for any other illness. So long as he does, there's still a chance he'll

I WILL USE MY APPRAISAL SKILL TO RISE IN THE WORLD

pull through," said the doctor. "I'm aware that he's a driven man, but you *must not* allow him to exert himself under any circumstances. Keep him at rest in bed, no matter what. I can't guarantee he'll survive even if you do, but at least then he'll stand a fighting chance."

After that, the doctor taught us some recipes for healthy food that would keep my father's energy levels up, boiled some herbs into a medicinal concoction for him, and then took his leave.

So if he gets plenty of rest, my father might still recover? No, not might. He will *recover, I'm sure of it! He's stronger and healthier than anyone I've ever known! There's no way a plain old disease would do him in!*

The fighting in Missian had grown less fierce of late, as well, which helped me stay optimistic. Lord Amador, the Duke of Missian who'd been on death's door just recently, had miraculously recovered, so his sons had ceased warring with each other. It turned out, incidentally, that the duke really *had* named the younger of the two his successor, but in light of the conflict that arose while he was indisposed, he'd decided to withdraw that decision and reconsider the matter. Apparently, he intended to consult at length with his vassals and his sons themselves before settling the question of his successor for good.

As far as I was concerned, though, what really mattered was that thanks to the duke's recovery, House Louvent had been called into battle far less frequently in recent months. As long as he didn't have to fight, I was sure that my father would let himself get the rest he needed. Or at least, I desperately hoped he would...until the worst news imaginable arrived the evening of the very same day my father had collapsed: the Duke of Missian had been assassinated. The timing couldn't possibly have been any worse.

AS A REINCARNATED ARISTOCRAT

The next day, my father finally awoke. Seeing him conscious was a relief, to be sure, but it was obvious he was far from healthy. He seemed tired, listless, and his fever had yet to break. I was worried that telling him how serious his illness was would be shocking enough to worsen his condition, so I decided to keep the fact that it could kill him a secret for the moment, and instead just emphasized that he needed rest above all else. He actually obeyed, for once, which felt like a sign of how badly the disease was hitting him.

"I believe we'd be better off refraining from informing Lord Raven about recent developments," Rietz said later, when we were out of my father's earshot.

"Agreed."

We were discussing the matter of the duke's assassination, and decided that telling my father about it would be best left for another day. The last thing I wanted was to make him worry about the duchy's politics and exacerbate his illness.

"While we're at it...what do you think will happen to House Louvent from here on out?" I asked. We were in the study at the time, incidentally. I'd called Rietz and Rosell in to discuss our options. Rietz's expertise went without saying, and Rosell's Intelligence had grown to a total score of 89, so I figured that his opinions would be valuable as well.

"Hmm," said Rosell. "I think it's only a matter of time before war breaks out, to start."

"I was worried you'd say that," I replied with a grimace.

"Well, yeah, it's sort of obvious. I mean, the duke kicked the bucket without naming a successor, right? *Of course* that would mean war."

"What do you think, Rietz? Do you see it that way as well?" I asked, turning his way.

I WILL USE MY APPRAISAL SKILL TO RISE IN THE WORLD

"I do, yes. War is all but inevitable."

Figures. The duke sure did die at the best possible moment, assuming his goal was to cause a war of succession.

"The operative question, as I see it, is not *whether* a war will break out, but *when*," Rietz continued. "Since the duke was murdered, it seems quite possible that both of his sons will claim that the other was the mastermind behind the plot. If they do, then it's entirely possible that the fighting will begin all but immediately."

"That makes sense...but while we're on the subject, who sent an assassin after the duke? And why now, of all times?"

"The assassin was captured, from what I've gathered, but he took his own life before they could get any answers out of him. The mastermind remains a mystery," Rietz explained.

"Do you think it was one of the brothers?"

"I dunno about that," said Rosell. "The succession slate was just wiped clean, as far as they're concerned, so having their dad bumped off *now* seems, well, pointless. I guess it *is* possible that the duke had already reached a decision and opened up to someone about it, though. If the son who *wasn't* chosen caught wind of that, it would've given them a motive."

Rosell paused for a moment to think, then continued. "It's also possible that the assassin got sent out from another duchy. It *was* pretty obvious that the duke's death would throw Missian into chaos, after all. Then again, it's not exactly easy for a foreign assassin to slip across the border, make it all the way to the capital, and off the duke himself, so maybe that's not so likely after all."

Sounds like the perpetrator may not have been one of the brothers... Of course, it's not like we'll ever know for sure, what with the assassin dead and all.

"No amount of thinking will allow us to track down the culprit," said Rietz. "And honestly, we simply don't have enough information to do anything about the situation at present, so I propose we drop the subject. The real question we ought to consider is what we'll do when war *does* break out. I certainly don't imagine Lord Raven will be marching into battle for the foreseeable future, considering the state he's in."

I'd told Rietz and Rosell everything I knew about my father's diagnosis, so they were both taking the grave state of his health into account.

"Could you lead our troops, Rietz?" I asked.

"N-No, that would be unthinkable! While it's true that House Louvent's soldiers and servants are more accepting of me than they used to be, fighting alongside your men and *leading* them are two entirely different things. I'm afraid you're the only one who can fill that void, Master Ars. The soldiers have sworn their allegiance to House Louvent, so their morale would suffer greatly if a member of the house wasn't there to fight by their side."

Morale, huh? That's tricky, yeah—I guess I really will have to take to the field until my father recovers.

I wasn't at all certain that I'd be able to fill his shoes properly, but if I didn't rise to the occasion, my father would have to, and that would mean his inevitable death. Thus, I had no other choice.

"Of course, I imagine that a summons from the Count of Canarre will precede any real fighting," Rietz clarified. "I'm sure he'll call a meeting soon to discuss the future of the county and decide on a course of action."

I hesitated, then asked, "And my father is in no condition to attend, right?"

"Correct. Even if all he would have to do is talk, the trip alone would strain him considerably. I believe it best he doesn't attend."

I WILL USE MY APPRAISAL SKILL TO RISE IN THE WORLD

"Hmm," I said, considering my options. "It feels like it wouldn't be right for me to *not* attend the meeting as a representative of House Louvent...but I've never done anything like this before. Can I really manage it...? Agh, it's like a mountain of problems just got dumped on my head out of nowhere! And everything was so quiet and peaceful up until just yesterday!" I moaned, clutching at my head in despair.

"G-Good luck with that, I guess!"

"Rosell..." I groaned, shooting him a glare. "You realize this is *your* problem too, right?"

"U-Umm, Master Ars?" said Rietz. "I promise that I will do everything in my power to assist you. That goes for you too, Rosell—you owe it to him to help out!"

Thankfully, Rosell nodded in agreement.

"Oh, and another thing—do you think it would be best for us to refrain from telling my father about the duke's death at all?"

"I believe so, yes," said Rietz. "Learning that the duke has passed is sure to drive your father to push himself past his limits despite his illness. If we want him to remain in convalescence like the doctor recommended, then we'll have to keep that news from him. Of course," he added with a wince, "if he *does* ever find out, I imagine he'll be *quite* upset."

"That's a small price to pay, in my book."

My father was terrifying when he got mad, sure, but I couldn't afford to let him scare me into spilling the beans this time around.

"First things first," I continued, "we'll probably have some time before the count's summons arrives. Before that happens, I'll have to spend all the time I possibly can training in swordsmanship and the art of warfare."

"Agreed, and I would be more than happy to serve as your instructor," said Rietz.

Thus, a period of intense, diligent study and training began for me. Eleven days passed by in that manner before finally, a letter arrived from the Count of Canarre requesting Lord Louvent's immediate presence at Castle Canarre. I set out at once with Rietz, Charlotte, and a few of my father's older retainers accompanying me.

I had my apprehensions about bringing Charlotte along, truth be told, but from what I'd gathered, her achievements on the battlefield and her unplaceable personality had resulted in the other houses considering her something of a terror. I was pinning my hopes on the possibility that showing the other houses that she obeyed my commands would help me earn some respect.

I hadn't sent a letter in reply, by the way, so the count and his people had no idea that *I* would be the one in attendance. The letter had emphasized the urgency of the meeting and requested House Louvent's presence as soon as conceivably possible, so I'd left without wasting any time.

We arrived at the city of Canarre and made our way through the gateway, into the section of the city guarded by its curtain walls, and finally to the gateway of the castle itself. A gatekeeper called out to us as we approached.

"Halt! You stand before Castle Canarre, residence of the count himself! None may enter without a letter of summons!"

Well, that's a problem—I definitely don't have one. What's going on here?

"Lord Raven was a familiar face to the guards, and he was always allowed to come and go as he pleased," Rietz whispered into my ear. "I'm afraid, however, that it might prove more complicated in your case..."

I WILL USE MY APPRAISAL SKILL TO RISE IN THE WORLD

"Oh. Well, that puts me in a bind," I sighed. "So what, we won't be able to get inside?"

"No, I believe it should be possible," said Rietz. "Charlotte's name is quite widely known, as is mine, to a lesser extent. This particular guard does not seem to recognize us, but if we ask him to summon one of the count's senior retainers to identify us, I believe we should be allowed inside."

I nodded to Rietz, then turned back to the guard and declared, "I am Ars Louvent, eldest son and heir to House Louvent! As my father, Lord Raven Louvent, is currently indisposed, I have arrived to answer Count Lumeire Pyres's summons in his place. If you doubt my identity, I would ask that you send word of my arrival to the castle and call one of the count's senior retainers to confirm the matter. Though they may not know me, I am certain they will know some among my retainers."

The guard frowned as he listened to my little speech. He seemed more than a bit bewildered, presumably by the fact that I looked like a child, and clearly wasn't sure what to do. Thankfully for the both of us, a more senior soldier arrived soon after to handle the situation. The gatekeeper explained the circumstances to him, and the older soldier turned to check our identities...only for his eyes to immediately widen in shock.

"G-Gods above! That's the Blue Reaper of Lamberg!" he shouted, his eyes glued to Charlotte.

"I wish they'd stop calling me that. It's such an *ugly* nickname," Charlotte muttered, pouting all the while.

No kidding! When did she pick up a brutal-sounding title like that? I wondered. That was certainly the first I'd heard of it.

"A-And the Malkan!" the soldier shouted, turning to Rietz next. "He's the Bloodthirsty Demon of Lamberg!"

AS A REINCARNATED ARISTOCRAT

I gave Rietz a look and asked, "'Bloodthirsty'?"

Rietz glanced away awkwardly and replied, "I, umm...don't *recall* doing anything vicious enough to earn *that* moniker...but, well, bloodshed is inevitable on the battlefield. People talk...and some titles are granted regardless of the bearer's will."

Thankfully, their reputations were indeed enough to confirm my identity as House Louvent's scion, so we were led up to the castle.

Castle Canarre was ancient, but as far as fortresses went, it was actually on the smaller side of things. When I heard the word "castle," I'd pictured a gorgeous, lavishly decorated palace, but this was anything but. The middle-aged man who met us at the entrance, however, was at least dressed in what I could tell was a fine and expensive set of clothing. I assumed he was one of Count Pyres's retainers, and likely a high-ranking one at that.

The soldier who had led us inside told us to wait for a moment, then walked over to speak with the man. A short exchange later, the middle-aged man jumped in shock, then ran over to us in a fluster and asked, "Is it true?! Lord Raven has fallen ill?!"

"It is, yes," I replied. "And you are...?"

"Oh, pardon my rudeness! It is an honor to make your acquaintance, Master Ars Louvent. I am Menas Renard, retainer to House Pyres," he explained, confirming my expectations. I gave him an appraisal, just for good measure.

I WILL USE MY APPRAISAL SKILL TO RISE IN THE WORLD

> Menas Renard
> Age: 40
> Male
> **Status:**
> LEA: 71/71
> VAL: 70/70
> INT: 75/77
> POL: 78/78
> Ambition: 25
> **Aptitudes:**
> Infantry: B
> Cavalry: B
> Archer: A
> Mage: C
> Fortification: B
> Weaponry: D
> Naval: D
> Aerial: D
> Strategy: B

His scores were nothing to scoff at. None of his attributes stood head and shoulders above the rest, but on the other hand, all of them sat at very respectable values. Most of his battle-related Aptitudes were ranked at B or above, even.

"It seems you've already been informed, but my name is Ars Louvent," I said. "I've come here in my father's stead. The individuals behind me are my retainers, who accompanied me to ensure my safety."

"Yes, yes, I'm well acquainted with them! We've fought side by side on the battlefield, haven't we?" said Menas.

"Quite," said Rietz with a nod, while Charlotte cocked her head in confusion. Apparently, he wasn't ringing any bells on her end. Menas didn't have a particularly memorable face, so I couldn't exactly blame her for forgetting him. It was still incredibly rude, of course, but at least I wouldn't hold it against her.

Menas, fortunately, didn't seem to be offended by Charlotte's attitude as he turned back to me and said, "It's hard to believe that Lord Raven could possibly be bedridden... What sort of sickness is he suffering from?"

"According to the doctor who diagnosed him, he most likely has gley syndrome," I replied.

"G-Gley syndrome?! B-But, wait—wouldn't that mean he's in no condition to go into battle?!" exclaimed Menas. Apparently, the man was fairly well-versed in obscure diseases.

"Yes, it does," I confirmed. "The doctor gave us strict orders to ensure he stays in bed for the time being."

"Oh no, *oh no*," Menas muttered. "Of *all* the times! This is a grave blow, *oh*, what a disaster... I just know lord Lumeire will be beside himself..."

He was even more despondent than I'd expected, but he shook his head and rallied himself back to attention, then continued, "I-In any case, I shall show you to Lord Lumeire at once! The other lords have yet to arrive, so the plan is to only assemble once everyone is present. However, I would appreciate it if you would meet with the count in advance for good measure."

"All right," I agreed, then followed Menas into the castle. We walked for some time, then arrived at an extravagant door. I assumed that the count was waiting beyond it.

"Would you be willing to wait here a moment?" asked Menas.

I WILL USE MY APPRAISAL SKILL TO RISE IN THE WORLD

"Of course," I replied with a nod.

Menas stepped inside and shut the door behind him. A few seconds passed, then...

"*What*?! Is this true?!"

...a bellow rang out from within the chamber. Shortly thereafter, Menas emerged in a fluster and beckoned us inside. The moment I stepped through the door, a bearded man rushed directly over to me.

"So you're Ars?!" the man shouted. "Is it true that Raven's deathly ill and bedridden?!"

"Y-Yes, it is," I stammered. The man's sheer intensity had me a little taken aback.

"Oh! My apologies," the bearded man said. "I am Lumeire Pyres, lord of this castle and Count of Canarre. We've met once before, Ars, when you were just a lad! You've certainly grown a head or two taller since then, though. Do you remember me?"

"I do, yes," I replied. It was quite a long time ago, so my memory was hazy, but I *did* indeed recall his face. It wasn't quite one of my earliest memories, but it was certainly up there. I knew that I'd appraised him, but I couldn't remember how exactly his stats had looked—just that they were reasonably impressive. And so, I decided to appraise him again to jog my memory.

AS A REINCARNATED ARISTOCRAT

> Lumeire Pyres
> Age: 44
> Male
> **Status:**
> LEA: 67/68
> VAL: 86/86
> INT: 56/56
> POL: 72/73
> Ambition: 31
> **Aptitudes:**
> Infantry: B
> Cavalry: C
> Archer: C
> Mage: D
> Fortification: D
> Weaponry: D
> Naval: D
> Aerial: B
> Strategy: D

His Valor was quite high, while the rest of his stats were all reasonable enough. I couldn't quite call him a model ruler based on his stats alone, however.

"There's no doubt, then, that your father has gley syndrome...?" he asked, though he didn't sound very hopeful. "To tell you the truth, my own sister passed away from the very same disease. I know all too well how terrible a malady it is, and I know that Raven must be kept at rest, no matter what happens..."

A relative of his had gley syndrome?

I WILL USE MY APPRAISAL SKILL TO RISE IN THE WORLD

The doctor had told me it was a rare illness, so I'd been surprised to hear that Menas was already familiar with it. But suddenly, it all made sense.

"But look at you!" Lumeire exclaimed, his attitude shifting dramatically and a grin spreading across his face. "Barely a child of ten, yet you're already going out into the world in your father's place! You're a true-born lord, lad, no mistaking it! Now then—the others have yet to arrive, so we'll have to wait for them before we begin in earnest. Menas, show Ars and his people to their room."

"Yes, M'lord!" Menas replied, then turned to me. "Follow me, please."

Menas guided us to a room that had been prepared for us. It was surprisingly large, and furnished with a couch, chairs, and even a bed. Clearly, we were meant to feel at home.

"I'm guessing the count plans to discuss which of the brothers we'll side with in the oncoming war," I speculated when we were alone again.

"I'd think so, yes," said Rietz. "And I imagine that Lord Lumeire has already chosen a side. Most likely, he called us here to inform us of his decision."

My best guess was that he'd choose to side with the older brother. There was a slight chance he'd ask his lords for their opinions, but I wouldn't have anything of substance to contribute if he did. With the information at my disposal, I didn't have any good reason to choose one brother over the other.

A short while later, Menas returned to the room and declared, "The other lords have arrived, and Lord Lumeire requests your presence. Please follow me."

"Understood," I replied.

Once again, Menas led us through the castle's hallways. We eventually emerged in the great hall. A circular table had been set up in its center, at which two men were already seated. I could only assume they were Canarre's other local lords, which would make the people standing at attention behind them their retainers.

Canarre was split up into four territories: Lamberg, Torbequista, Coumeire, and Canarre, the county's namesake. In terms of the territories' size and population, Canarre was overwhelmingly the largest, followed by Torbequista, Coumeire, and finally, Lamberg. It seemed natural to me that the count would directly govern the largest and most populated region, and it really was the largest by far. While Lamberg *was* smaller than the other two, they weren't all *that* much larger.

"It is an honor to meet both of you!" I said, addressing the two lords at the table. "My name is Ars Louvent, and I have come here on behalf of Raven Louvent, the Lord of Lamberg."

"A pleasure," said one of the other lords, a man with blond hair. "I am Hammond Pleide, Lord of Torbequista, and I'm to understand that you were an exemplary host to my daughter some time ago. She returned from her visit in the highest of spirits."

So this is Licia's father, I thought to myself. *I can see the resemblance.*

"I'm pleased to learn she was satisfied with what little hospitality we could offer," I replied.

"Is it true, then, that Raven's bedridden?" asked Hammond. "I'd have sworn that man could ride through hell itself and emerge no worse for the wear, if you'd asked me a week ago. Then again, knowing him, he'll beat that illness back and return to us in no time flat. I'm not concerned."

Despite his protest to the contrary, I got the impression that Hammond really *was* worried about my father. Of course, he also knew my father well enough to not even consider the possibility that the likes of a mere disease could finish him off.

"I believe we've yet to meet, young man," said the second lord, who looked like he was on the cusp of qualifying as elderly. He spoke in a slow, somewhat stilted tone. "I am known as Krall Orslow, and I serve as lord of Coumeire. It pains me indeed to learn that Raven could not attend today."

My assumption had proven true: the two men before me were indeed both lords of Canarre. I was just about to appraise both of them, but before I had the chance, I was distracted by Lumeire's arrival in the chamber. The two lords stood and bowed to him, so I quickly imitated the gesture.

"Rise," said Lumeire. I raised my head, then followed Lumeire and the other lords' example once more and took a seat.

"You have my thanks for coming here on such short notice," Lumeire began. "As I'm sure you've already guessed, I've called you here on account of the duke's assassination and the possibility of war between his elder son, Lord Couran, and his younger son, Lord Vasmarque. I wish to take this chance to make my stance on the matter clear."

That was exactly what I'd expected him to do, and I was proven right once more as Lumeire declared that he intended to support Couran, the elder brother. I stuck to my plan and endorsed his decision without objection. The other lords did the same.

"Good," said Lumeire. "I've nothing else to discuss with you at this moment. Return to your lands and prepare your troops for battle. That is all."

Wait, it is? That's it?

I couldn't believe he'd called us to the county seat for a meeting that barely lasted a matter of minutes. Upon further reflection, though, this *was* a decision that would carry no small amount of weight going forward, so perhaps that was why he felt the need to give the news in person. The three of us all signaled our understanding, and with that, the meeting came to an end.

We ended up staying the night in the castle. I had the chance to appraise Hammond and Krall during our stay, incidentally, and neither of them struck me as particularly remarkable. The next day soon dawned, and as we finished our travel preparations and made our way out of the castle, a voice called out to me.

"Ars! A moment, if you would."

It was Hammond.

"Yes? What is it?" I asked, walking over to him.

"I was hoping to ask you about my daughter, as it so happens," he explained. "She's been in a rather foul mood as of late. I've been told that you exchange letters with her quite frequently, and I was hoping you might know what has soured her so."

Licia's been in a bad mood?

Unfortunately, I didn't have the foggiest idea why that could be. None of the letters she'd sent lately had seemed particularly unusual at all.

Actually…wait a second. I read her letters, yes, and their contents seemed perfectly unremarkable, but…when was the last time I replied to one of them?

I pondered the question…and came to the inescapable conclusion that it had been *quite* a long time since I'd last sent a letter back to her. I'd *intended* to write to her, of course, but then my father collapsed, the duke was assassinated, and pretty much everything went to hell in a handbasket all at once. In the thick of all that, I'd totally forgotten to keep corresponding with my fiancée.

Okay, I'll admit, that was pretty rude of me. But surely Licia knows

I WILL USE MY APPRAISAL SKILL TO RISE IN THE WORLD

everything that's been going on lately, right? A few missed letters can't *have been enough to make her that upset...right? Unless she's been enjoying our little pen-pal situation more than I'd expected, in which case, well, yeah. I guess that would probably put her in a pretty bad mood.*

I confessed to Hammond that I'd forgotten to reply to her letters, and his face lit up in newfound understanding.

"Ahhh, yes, that *would* do it. You would hardly believe how excited my daughter is for your letters, each and every time. I understand circumstances have been keeping you busy as of late, but I'd greatly appreciate it if you'd send one her way."

That settled it—if she'd been looking forward to my letters *that* much, I was the culprit.

"Understood," I replied sheepishly. "I'll write to her the moment I get home."

"Please do," Hammond said, then bid me farewell.

With that, we left the castle and hurried off to Lamberg.

○

I got home to find a letter from Licia waiting for me. Its contents were short and to the point: "It has been quite some time since I last received any correspondence from you, Sir Ars. Has something happened? Or have I done something to offend you? If so, I would appreciate it if you would tell me what it was."

It was like she'd written the letter specifically to make me feel as guilty as possible. Actually, considering the way Licia operated, she really might've written it with that specific intent in mind. Knowing I was playing into her hands didn't make me feel any less terrible, though.

AS A REINCARNATED ARISTOCRAT

I wrote up a reply immediately: "You've done nothing wrong, Lady Licia. The simple truth is that between my father's collapse and the assassination of the duke, I was distracted, so writing back to you slipped my mind. The fault is entirely mine, and I apologize."

After that, I gathered Rosell and Rietz up in the study to discuss our plans.

"I think the count has the right idea," I began. "Our top priorities right now should be making sure we have enough troops, and getting them as well-equipped as possible."

"Our army's equipment is certainly something we can address," said Rietz. "But I'm afraid that recruiting more soldiers will be less than feasible under current circumstances. We can ensure that our current troops are as well trained as possible, of course, but it will be difficult to truly strengthen our forces without the ability to bolster numbers."

"Right, that makes sense," I replied with a nod.

"If war breaks out before Lord Raven recovers," Rietz continued, "I'm certain you will wind up leading our men into battle, Master Ars. As such, I believe it is of utmost importance that you learn to command the troops and allow them to acclimate to your lead. Our numbers may not be sufficient for it, but I still believe that leading the men in a mock battle would be a solid course of action."

A mock battle? That means that unlike the real deal, nobody will die if I screw up.

I *definitely* liked the sound of that, and I figured it would make for a good experience in all sorts of ways. Hopefully, having a few mock battles under my belt would keep me from panicking when it came time for the real deal.

"Do you have any ideas, Rosell?" I asked, turning to my other top advisor.

I WILL USE MY APPRAISAL SKILL TO RISE IN THE WORLD

"Hmm... You said the count's planning on backing the older brother, right? Does it look like he has any shot at winning?"

"It's hard to say with the information we have right now."

"Gotcha," said Rosell. "I hate to say it, but that means we're in a really bad place. If an upstart house like the Louvents end up on the losing side of this war, they could easily get crushed. We need to make sure we end up on the winning side, no matter *what* happens."

"That makes sense too," I sighed. "Still, we can't exactly defy the count's orders, can we?"

"If it becomes clear that the older brother's a lost cause, we'd either have to persuade the count to switch sides...or think about betraying him and jumping ship on our own."

"Betraying the count...?"

Man, that's brutal. I guess I might have to start thinking like a feudal warlord if I plan on surviving much longer, though.

"Right now, our biggest problem is that we don't have enough information," Rosell continued. "We can't make plans or talk strategy without a proper understanding of the circumstances. We have to start doing anything and everything we can to learn about the current state of Missian, and we need to do it *now*."

"Okay, but what *specifically* should we do?" I asked.

Rosell paused, then answered, "Ask someone to gather info for us, I guess? We could have a soldier do it."

"Do you actually think that would work?"

"Hmm..."

Rosell and I fell into thought, which Rietz took as a sign to offer his input. "As a matter of fact, a perfect option for gathering information *is* available to us: a band of mercenaries who call themselves the Shadows. They specialize in shadow magic, information-gathering, and espionage. They would get us exactly the information we need if we paid their fee...but their services don't come cheap."

"Mercenaries..." I muttered. "Hiring them without consulting my father would probably be a step too far. Let's consider that after he's recovered enough to discuss the matter."

"Understood," said Rietz.

Still, simply learning that there was a band of mercenaries who specialized in that sort of thing was a win. Rosell was right, after all—information was, without question, our most important resource.

"We can't hire mercenaries yet," I continued. "However, we *can* at least pick out a few of our soldiers who seem suited for the role and send them out across Missian. It's better than doing nothing, at least."

"Very well—I'll see to it," Rietz replied.

With our immediate course of action set in place, we brought the day's discussion to a close. We had two priorities going forward: engaging in mock battles, and setting up the rudimentary framework of an information network.

Thus, a couple of weeks passed by...and then, once again, the situation suddenly and dramatically changed.

○

I'd spent the past weeks honing my command skills via mock battles and picking out soldiers who seemed naturally suited to spycraft. The former, frankly, hadn't been going so well. I'd studied my fair share of tactics, but it turned out that knowing the theory of battle and applying it to real, live soldiers under my command were two very different things. From my perspective, a nearly insurmountable

I WILL USE MY APPRAISAL SKILL TO RISE IN THE WORLD

barrier stood between me and the leadership skills I was expected to have, that barrier being my inability to set foot on the battlefield without immediately shrinking back in terror.

Even knowing that we were only practicing and that nobody was out for blood, seeing a crowd of soldiers brandishing their blades and charging toward me scared the living daylights out of me, and it was really hard to stay calm and issue orders to your men when you were abjectly terrified. If I was *that* bad off in a mock battle, I could only imagine the disgrace I'd make of myself when the time came to actually go to war. I was *deeply* concerned about my future as a military leader.

Choosing spies, meanwhile, had unfortunately proven rather difficult as well. Appraisal wasn't nearly as useful for the task as one might expect. There was no "Spy" Aptitude, for one thing, and I could only guess which of the base stats would be most useful for that sort of information-gathering work.

It made a certain amount of intuitive sense to me that people with high Valor and Intelligence would make good spies, so I tried to search for candidates with solid scores in both of those stats. We couldn't just pick some soldiers out of the crowd and send them off into the world with a smile and wave, of course, so Rietz was busy training them for their new positions. He'd done his fair share of spy work back when he was a mercenary, it seemed, so he had enough specialized knowledge to at least get them started.

Then, the fifth day of the fourth month arrived.

"I've waited long enough. It's time for me to resume my duties!"

"You can't! Please, just rest!"

"Grr!"

My father had regained a considerable amount of strength, which was a good thing, but his ever-intensifying insistence that he get back to work was significantly less promising. *We* understood that he'd put himself at risk of a relapse if he got right back to it, but *he* had never been the type to sit still for long. We'd managed to keep him from doing anything risky so far, but I was very worried that we were nearing the limits of his patience.

At long last, I managed to convince him to stay in bed, then walked over to my own room. We'd staged another mock battle the day before, and I was still feeling the exhaustion from that ordeal. I'd decided to spend the day resting up and regaining my strength, and was looking forward to a nice, long nap...until I noticed Rietz charging toward me.

"Master Ars!" he shouted, sounding panicked.

"What is it?" I replied. "In case you've forgotten, I'm planning to rest today."

"I'm aware, yes," gasped Rietz. "However, I've just received news that you *must* hear!"

"What news?"

"Seitz has mobilized an army—and they march upon Canarre!"

"Th-They *what* now?!"

Suddenly, I was just as worried as Rietz. Seitz was the duchy to the immediate west of Missian, and the County of Canarre was right on the provincial border. It suddenly hit me: I'd been so preoccupied with the conflict between the brothers that I'd completely forgotten we had *other* potential enemies to deal with! The duke was dead, and the duchy's major powers were actively splintering into warring factions, so it was the *perfect* moment for another duchy to step in and snatch up as much territory as they could get their hands on!

"They say the enemy is heading for Coumeire," Rietz explained. "They're due to arrive within four days, and a letter from the count

I WILL USE MY APPRAISAL SKILL TO RISE IN THE WORLD

has arrived ordering us to dispatch our forces at once!"

Coumeire was situated right on the border, while Lamberg was on the opposite side of the county, meaning we lived further away from Seitz than any other territory. That was only a small comfort, though. If Seitz was going to invade the other territories, it was only a matter of time before they'd advance upon Lamberg as well. Even if the count *hadn't* ordered us into action, we would've had no choice but to ride to Coumeire's aid.

My father had recovered considerably, but he was still in no state to ride into battle. In other words, my first stint as commander would be arriving *considerably* earlier than I'd expected. I was still terrified of mock battles, and yet there I was, staring down the imminent prospect of fighting on a real battlefield. The moment the reality of the situation sunk in, my heart started pounding so fast that I thought I might drop dead on the spot. I was beyond nervous, but I did my best to keep a straight face so Rietz wouldn't realize it.

"Understood," I said. "We'll sortie at once. I'll take command of our troops."

Rietz hesitated for a moment, then nodded and said, "Very well."

He clearly knew just as well as I did that I wasn't up to the task, but with circumstances as they were, he couldn't argue against the decision. I could only imagine how conflicted he felt.

The two of us made our way to the training grounds to inform our troops. Rietz explained everything he knew about the enemy forces on the way, but really, it wasn't much. The count's letter hadn't even specified how many of them there were. If they'd sent a massive force, then all of Canarre's armies combined probably wouldn't even be able to slow them down, but Seitz had its own fair share of internal strife, so I was hopeful that we weren't looking at that sort of all-out invasion. If they *did* hit us with everything they had, then we'd stand no chance of victory and would have no choice but to call for reinforcements. As for whether or not they'd actually come, I couldn't say.

We arrived at the training grounds and informed the soldiers that we'd be marching into battle. The grounds immediately descended into a flurry of activity: some of our men armed themselves, while others ran off to gather up the soldiers who weren't on duty at the moment. Charlotte was one of the latter, and arrived at the training grounds in a half-asleep daze. I guess she'd been out like a light until somebody showed up to get her.

When everyone had finally arrived, I stood before our troops. I thought that I had to say *something* to them to raise their morale before we marched for the front. The second I looked out across their faces, though, the crushing reality of what I was about to do sank in once more, and my anxiety returned in full force. I had to pause for a moment, take a few deep breaths to calm myself down, then finally address the troops in as loud of a voice as I could muster.

"Today, we go to war to protect our homeland of Canarre! I—"

"Hold!"

My speech had started out well enough, but before I could say more than a few words, a booming voice echoed across the grounds, cutting me off. I knew that voice like the back of my hand—it was my father's, and I turned to look at him in shock. He stormed toward me, his expression more intimidating than any I'd ever seen on his face.

"You're not ready for this, Ars," my father bluntly stated.

"F-Father," was all I could muster.

"I knew you were hiding something from me," he muttered, looking me right in the eye. "And I suspected that something had

I WILL USE MY APPRAISAL SKILL TO RISE IN THE WORLD

happened to the duke. I've stayed quiet until now because I know that resting will keep me alive...and I thought that stepping up to work in my place would be a chance for you to grow...but I can't allow you to go to war in my stead, least of all when the very existence of Canarre hangs in the balance. *I* will go."

The look on my father's face told me that he wasn't going to change his mind, no matter what anyone said to him. He was absolutely determined to take to the battlefield. I was horrified by the thought, however. If my father went into battle *now,* and if his condition worsened, there was no coming back! He would die!

"But Father, you're ill!" I said, making one last attempt to appeal to his reason. "You *can't* go to war!"

"I've shaken off the worst of it. I'm no longer unable to swing a sword," my father replied.

"But what if you relapse? You realize you could die, don't you?"

"I won't. And even if I do, I could ask for nothing more than to die protecting Canarre—protecting Lamberg and its people."

What can I say to change his mind?! The man's absolutely hell-bent on marching off to war!

His condition *had* improved, clearly, and it *was* possible he could survive a campaign, but it was equally possible that his condition could deteriorate at any moment. The more mysterious the sickness, the more cautious you had to be. I had to do something, *anything* to convince him to stay home.

My father decided to keep me from leading our army because he didn't think I was up to the task...and he was right. Still, I had to find a way to make him think otherwise, no matter what it took.

At that point, Rietz stepped up to the two of us and said, "Lord Raven, you should know that Master Ars—"

"Silence!" my father roared. Rietz's mouth snapped shut.

AS A REINCARNATED ARISTOCRAT

"Father," I said, doing my best to finish his thought, "I've been fighting mock battles to prepare myself. I'll admit that I'm still lacking in many regards, but I swear to you that I will lead our men to glory!"

"And did you fight well in those 'mock battles' of yours?" my father asked. "I hardly need to ask—of course you didn't. I don't even need to see you in action to know that. You don't have the face of a warrior yet, Ars."

I fell silent once more upon hearing those words.

What does "the face of a warrior" even mean? Is it something that only seasoned veterans like him understand?

Seconds passed in silence before my father spoke up again.

"That's right...in my sickness, I almost forgot. If you're so convinced you can go to war, Ars, I shall test you, here and now. Gullar!" my father barked, shouting out the name of one of his soldiers. "Is the man in the jail still alive?"

Gullar, one of the older men in the force, snapped to attention and replied, "Y-Yes, he is, more or less. We didn't think it right to execute him without your express orders."

"We'll do it now. Bring him here."

"Y-Yes, Sir!" Gullar exclaimed as he sprinted off toward the jail.

What in the world is my father up to? What sort of test is this?

Eventually, Gullar returned to the training grounds with a man in tow. The mysterious individual was wearing manacles and absolutely filthy clothing, and he sported a scraggly, unkempt beard.

"Who is he?" I asked.

"His name is Barramorda," answered my father. "And he is a devil in human skin who murdered, assaulted, and burgled his way through the town of Lamberg until we captured him shortly before I fell ill. I intended to keep him imprisoned long enough to arrange

I WILL USE MY APPRAISAL SKILL TO RISE IN THE WORLD

his execution, but thanks to that damnable disease, he slipped my mind...so I'll do it now. And *you,* Ars, will watch."

"And that is to be my test?"

"It is. You are to watch impassively. To remain calm and composed. Should you avert your eyes, or close them, or tremble, or double over with nausea, or show even the slightest *speck* of distress—you fail. To go to war is to see men die by the dozens, and if that disturbs you, then you are not ready to take to the field. A leader's ability to stay composed is worth far more than their ability to fight," my father declared, then gestured toward Barramorda. "If you can watch this man die and not bat an eyelash, then I shall acknowledge that you are a man full grown. I will entrust my army to you and rest quietly within our home, awaiting your return."

I gritted my teeth.

To watch a man die...and remain completely composed? Can I do this? Could I ever even be capable of it?

I had never seen a battlefield. I had never seen someone die. I'd looked up pictures of corpses once in my last life out of idle curiosity, and just that was enough to make me fall violently ill and swear to never seek that sort of imagery out again. I had no idea if I'd be able to watch a man be executed right in front of me and keep my cool.

As I mulled over the question, though, my father and his men were already preparing to carry out the execution. A wooden block was brought out into the field and Barramorda's head was pressed up against it, forcing him to his knees. He struggled violently, very literally fighting for his life, but several of my father's soldiers held him firmly in place as another with an axe stepped up to the block.

"Barramorda!" shouted my father. "You stand convicted of crimes most foul, and I, Raven Louvent, lord of these lands, do hereby sentence you to death!"

With that final word, the soldier with the axe raised it up high, then brought it down upon Barramorda's neck, severing his head with a single stroke. The head fell to the ground, rolling across the dirt as a jet of crimson blood gushed forth from the stump.

I watched it happen...and was shaken to the very core of my being. I felt my heart pound wildly within my chest, but I couldn't let my father see that, so I kept my face perfectly expressionless, staring fixedly at Barramorda's severed head until it rolled to a stop... facing me. The cold, lifeless eyes stared directly into mine...and I just couldn't hold it back anymore as a wave of intense nausea overwhelmed me. I didn't vomit, but I *did* retch.

"You have failed," my father coldly declared. "There's no shame in that. Everyone reacts that way the first time. I did as well, in fact. However, if this is enough to make you lose your composure, then you are unfit to lead our troops into battle. I shall go."

I clenched my fists, staring at the ground, and my father continued, "You've always been a precocious child, Ars, and you've grown up fast, but you are still a child. It is far too soon for you to go to war... Come now, don't worry so much. I won't die, of that I swear."

I wanted to shout, *You're wrong! I'm no child! I'm a fully grown man inside, dammit!* But I couldn't. I'd been raised in a country at peace, and when it came to witnessing death, I really was no better off than a child.

I couldn't argue with him or stop him.

My father rode off to battle...and I was left behind at our estate to simply sit and wait for news. Rietz would occasionally send me letters from the front, updating me on how the war was progressing, so I wasn't *completely* out of the loop, at least.

I WILL USE MY APPRAISAL SKILL TO RISE IN THE WORLD

The Seitz army turned out to not be so large that defeating them was *entirely* off the table, but they still had five soldiers to every one of Canarre's men. Everyone knew they were in for a long, drawn-out conflict, and as expected, the early stages were harsh on our side. In the end, though, the enemy was beaten back thanks in no small part to the daring exploits of House Louvent's army, spearheaded by my father.

The war dragged on for about four months, and my father returned home on the twelfth day of the eighth month, a mere four days after my twelfth birthday. He seemed perfectly fine when he returned to Lamberg, but five days later, his illness returned with a vengeance.

My father ended up bedridden more often than not, developed a seemingly ceaseless cough, and soon lost his appetite entirely. Not eating took a toll and he quickly wasted away, growing thinner and frailer with each passing day. Finally, one month after his illness returned, his doctor came to us with grave news: my father no longer had any hope of recovery. There was no telling precisely when, but someday soon, he would die.

It was my fault. If I'd been capable enough to lead our army in his stead, if I'd been strong enough to convince him I was ready, then my father would have spent those four months recuperating in our estate. Perhaps then his illness would never have returned. I did everything I could, going out to call on another doctor for a second opinion, and then a third, but they all said the same thing. Still, though, I didn't stop searching.

I had memories of my previous life, and they might have kept me from ever seeing my father as my *true* father. Nevertheless, I knew very well that if it weren't for him, I wouldn't be alive. I would never have been born again, needless to say, but I also never would have been able to lead the life I'd led. My comfortable, strife-free existence was all thanks to him, so I just *couldn't* allow him to die thanks to my inadequacy.

"Another failure?" I muttered to myself.

It was the second day of the eleventh month, so summer was just beginning. I'd brought another doctor in from the next county over, but once again, I was told that my father was beyond saving.

"Maybe we should go to a bigger town. I'm thinking we should try Arcantez, the capital of Missian, next. There *has* to be a doctor there who can help."

I hadn't been sending our retainers out to look for doctors. No, that was a task I only entrusted to myself. Anyone who studied medicine would need a high Intelligence, so me being there meant that we could easily weed out the professionals from the quacks.

"Master Ars," Rietz began, then paused. He looked incredibly conflicted.

"What is it?" I asked.

"Arcantez is an extremely long journey from here. A round trip will take twenty days at the bare minimum, and when we consider how long it will take to find a doctor, the trip may last even longer."

"I see," I said with a nod. "Still, I'm willing to go a little out of my way if it'll help my father recover. I'd be worried about leaving the estate undefended in our absence, though, so you'll have to stay behind this time. I can take Rosell's brothers and Charlotte along as guards—I'm sure they'll keep me safe."

"That's not what I meant! If you're away for too long, then… well…" Rietz trailed off again.

"What is it? Something that's hard to say?" I asked. "Go on. Don't hold back now."

I WILL USE MY APPRAISAL SKILL TO RISE IN THE WORLD

After a brief pause, Rietz finally spoke up once more. "If your search keeps you away for too long, then when the time comes, you may not be there to hear Lord Raven's last words."

It felt like my heart had just leaped into my throat. It wasn't that the thought had never crossed my mind—I just hadn't been allowing myself to consider it. My father had already wasted away so much that I hardly even recognized him. The pall of death hung heavily over his face, and even when he pulled himself to consciousness, he could barely speak. It would hardly have been a surprise if he passed away the very next day.

"Are you telling me...to give up?" I finally replied.

Rietz didn't answer directly. Instead, he said, "I believe that if you're not by Lord Raven's side when the time comes, you will regret it for the rest of your life. Think carefully, Master Ars, before you go out to search for another doctor."

I gritted my teeth. The way Rietz had phrased it was so *calm,* so goddamn *composed* that it enraged me. It wasn't his fault, though. He was simply looking at the situation objectively and telling me what he believed I needed to hear most. If anyone was at fault, it was *me* for refusing to look reality in the eye. I knew it...but I still couldn't suppress my fury. At the rate things were going, I was going to say something awful to Rietz, so I spun around and left the room without speaking another word.

"Master Ars!"

I figured I'd go spend some time in my room to cool my head, but on the way there, one of our estate's caretakers called out to me. Specifically, the one who was in charge of nursing my father.

"What is it?" I asked.

"Lord Raven has stirred!" said the servant. "He's more lucid than he's been in months...and he says that he wishes to speak to you!"

AS A REINCARNATED ARISTOCRAT

I was already heading for his room the moment I heard that he was awake and talking. I entered through the door to his chamber and found him in bed, alone.

"You called for me, Father?"

"You've arrived, Ars? Good, good," said my father. I was struck by how clear his voice was. He'd barely been able to talk at all these days, so it felt like it had been ages since I'd heard him speak like this.

My father was as emaciated as ever, but his eyes were clear and full of life. As recently as yesterday he'd had the eyes of a corpse, even when he *was* conscious, but no, *this* was the father I used to know—the father with a gaze so strong and full of purpose, he could make lesser men flinch with a mere glance.

"It's rather warm, isn't it?" my father observed. "What's the date today?"

"The second day of the eleventh month," I replied. "I can fan you if you're too hot."

"That won't be necessary. Summer already, though? It feels like it was springtime just yesterday. I must have slept a long, long time."

"You did," I said. "And honestly, it's been hectic without you around! We'll be in trouble if you don't get better soon, you know?"

"Yes, I know, I know. An illness like this can't keep me down—I'll shake it off by tomorrow," my father chuckled, then fell silent. A few seconds passed before he spoke up again. "There's so much that I still wanted to tell you, Ars."

"I'll listen to anything you have to say to me, Father," I replied. "I want to hear it all."

"I'll spare you the trivial small talk, at least. Now's not the time for that. No, I want to tell you the story of my life," he said, looking up at the ceiling. "I was not born here in Lamberg. I came from a tiny farming hamlet in a remote corner of Missian. The lord who ruled over that land was an avaricious miser of a man who bled his people nearly to death with taxes. We lived in poverty through no fault of our own. I couldn't stand that sort of life, and around the time I turned ten, I chose to run away from home and leave the whole village behind to seek my fortune in the city."

"By some twist of fate, the Duke of Missian had chosen that day to pay the town a visit. Our lord held some measure of seniority within Missian's nobility, and he had invited the duke to a party, or something of the sort. I forget the details—it was all so long ago. Vague and scattered as my memories are, though, there's just one thing I remember clearly."

"What is it?" I asked.

"The sight of the duke, riding through town atop a pure white steed with a host of fully-armored soldiers following in his wake. It shook me to the core, Ars. Until that moment, the only nobles I knew were the corrupt monsters who ground my family into the dirt. I never imagined that one of *them* could be so magnificent... so *noble,* in the truest sense of the word. The moment I saw him, I knew what I wanted in life. I wanted to be a man like him—a man who could stand at the head of a vast army and lead them to glory."

My father's gaze grew distant as he spun his yarn. I knew he'd been born a farmer, but I'd never heard anything else about what led him to his current station.

"I taught myself to wield a blade, became a soldier, and fought like a man possessed. Eventually, Lord Lumeire recognized my achievements and appointed me a lord of my own domain."

"Do you still want to become a duke, Father?"

I WILL USE MY APPRAISAL SKILL TO RISE IN THE WORLD

"Heh... I gave up on that dream around the time I married your mother and fathered you, Ars. I may be a petty lord, but compared to the life I used to live, what I have now might as well be heaven. I'm satisfied," he concluded before descending into another coughing fit.

"Are you all right?!" I asked in a panic.

My father coughed a few more times, then finally caught his breath, sighed, and said with much chagrin, "It seems I've spoken too much. Ars...I leave the rest to you."

I couldn't bring myself to reply, but my father kept speaking anyway. "This land of Lamberg, and everything within its borders, is a treasure. It is my life's work. My retainers, my people, my wife, Wren, Kreiz... All of them mean the world to me, and I'm entrusting them to you now. It pains me to place this burden upon your shoulders while you're still a child, but I have no choice. Ars—your power to see people's potential is something special. I know you have what it takes to use it well...and to lead House Louvent down the right path."

"Father..."

"I know how you think, and I know you feel responsible for what's become of me, but the fault does not rest with you. This is the path that I chose for myself. Now it's up to you to stand tall and carry on the Louvent name. Do you understand?"

I didn't know what to say. Answering him would have felt like admitting that he truly was on his deathbed.

"Say something, Ars. Please...put my mind at ease."

"I..." I paused, more conflicted than I'd ever been before, but finally nodded. "I do."

"Good. Then I leave the rest...to you..."

My father closed his eyes and fell into a deep, peaceful slumber. He showed no signs of waking as two days passed...and on the third, he drew his final breath.

○

"From this day onward, I, Ars, shall succeed my father Raven as the head of House Louvent!"

I did as my father told me. I stood tall and proud, declaring that I would carry on his legacy for all of his retainers to hear.

My father had spent a lifetime building House Louvent from the ground up. Hard times were upon us, so an insignificant noble family like ours would surely struggle to survive. Thus, I had to be strong. I had to wield my power to the fullest, to help my people and my land stand firm, and to protect everything that my father held dear. I was resolved to see it done.

A few days after my father passed, word arrived that the eldest son of the late Duke of Missian, one Couran Salemakhia, had mustered an army. From that day forward, I would lead House Louvent through a turbulent era of war and bloodshed.

Chapter 6

The news of Couran's mobilization arrived all too soon after my father's death. Couran had issued a manifesto on the same day he called his troops to arms, a copy of which had made its way to even a small noble house like ours.

The manifesto was, in short, a screed written solely to attack Couran's younger brother, Vasmarque. He pinned the assassination of their father on Vasmarque, to start, offering nothing in the way of concrete evidence to back up the claim, then took the opportunity to list each and every one of Vasmarque's faults in what struck me as excessive detail. He claimed vehemently that his brother was unworthy of the title of duke, and that only he could serve as his father's successor.

He also reproached Vasmarque for stubbornly maintaining control of Arcantez, the current capital of Missian. It seemed Couran had demanded that his brother turn the capital over to him time after time, but his requests had always fallen upon deaf ears. Now he'd had enough, so he intended to storm the capital by force if that was what it took.

That last detail was particularly interesting to me because I'd had no idea that Arcantez was under Vasmarque's control. The city was the capital of Missian in both name and practice, boasting the largest population of any city in the duchy. That, of course, meant that it had a correspondingly sizable local garrison.

There were only three cities in all of Missian that came close to rivaling Arcantez in scale. The closest to Lamberg was a city in the west called Maasa, and there were also similarly-sized cities in the south and the east called Semplar and Velshdt, respectively. Arcantez, by the way, was situated in central Missian.

Couran currently held control of Semplar, a coastal city. Access to sea routes made it a thriving trade hub and one of the most prosperous cities in all of Missian. That, in turn, meant the local government had the funds to hire mercenaries, so despite its lesser population, it gave Couran access to at least as many soldiers as Arcantez did to his brother.

That just left the question of who the counts ruling over Maasa and Velshdt would side with. I knew nothing about said counts, so I couldn't even begin to guess where their loyalties rested. I needed to figure out what direction Couran was likely to march in, and to do that, I needed information.

One day, Rietz came to me with a report and said, "Lord Ars? A letter from Lord Lumeire has arrived. I suspect it is a summons requesting your presence at Castle Canarre."

I read the letter and found that Rietz had predicted its contents perfectly before replying, "You were right. I wonder what he wants to discuss..."

"I presume strategy for the oncoming conflict," Rietz speculated. "It's also possible he's received orders from Lord Couran that he wishes to relay to us."

"Hmm. Do you think Canarre's forces are going to be dragged into the mud this time around?"

"A good question," said Rietz. "I imagine that depends on how

I WILL USE MY APPRAISAL SKILL TO RISE IN THE WORLD

the situation unfolds. There's no telling who the counts of western Missian will choose to support, after all. If the Count of Maasa ends up fighting for Lord Vasmarque, the situation may prove perilous."

A very small portion of Canarre's northeastern border was shared with the County of Maasa. Maasa boasted an army several times the size of Canarre's, so if open conflict between the two counties broke out, we would have very little chance of winning a straight-up fight. Word had it that Perreina, the county immediately east of Canarre, would be backing Vasmarque, so if Maasa chose his side as well, Canarre would have essentially no choice but to jump aboard their bandwagon and abandon Couran's cause.

"I guess we'll learn a little more about what's going on once we make it to Castle Canarre," I sighed. "Oh, and this will be my first formal duty as the Lord of Lamberg, too."

"It will, yes. Though, seeing as you've been to the castle as the lord's proxy already, it doesn't quite feel like your first time, does it?" noted Rietz with a smile.

"Yes, true enough," I agreed. Although, that said, the last time I went to Canarre was for a far simpler meeting than I knew we'd be having this time around. Considering how complicated the talks were likely to get, this still felt like my first *real* job.

"Oh, that's right!" I exclaimed as a thought struck me. "While we're already out and about, would we be able to make contact with those mercenaries you mentioned, Rietz? 'The Shadows,' was it?"

Now that my father was no longer with us, the question of whether or not to hire mercenaries fell entirely upon my shoulders. We were still training some of our own soldiers in the art of information-gathering, but that process had proven as time-consuming as expected, and I wanted to get our network up and running as soon as possible. Information would be absolutely vital to our decision-making process going forward—no matter how high of an Intelligence someone had, they could never make the right call without a full grasp of the situation.

"It should be possible to make contact with them in Canarre, yes," said Rietz. "However, they aren't motivated exclusively by money, so I can't guarantee we'll be able to actually retain their services."

"Mercenaries who aren't motivated by money? How is that a thing?" I asked, arching an eyebrow.

"It's rare, but every once in a while, you'll find a band that works for some higher purpose. The leader of the Shadows is something of an eccentric, so I can't say for sure what standards they follow."

"I see. Well, if we *can* hire them, I'd certainly like to, so please arrange a meeting with their leader for after we're finished in the castle."

"Understood."

I set about choosing who would accompany us on the trip. I decided to bring along Rietz, Charlotte, and the other retainers who'd accompanied me last time, as well as Rosell. It seemed possible I was in for a genuine war council, and while I wasn't expecting Rosell to *contribute* to the discussion at his age, I did think it would make for a good experience, and help him learn to be a better tactician.

Once my party had gathered, we immediately set out for Castle Canarre. The trip went smoothly this time, and we arrived without incident. Unlike our first visit, the gatekeeper recognized me immediately and led us straight into the castle.

"Thank you for coming, Ars. It is truly a shame what happened to Raven... He will be dearly missed," Lumeire sighed as soon as he saw me, his expression grave. "Much as it pains me to admit, though, I do not have the time to grieve his death. We shall begin our war council as soon as Lord Krall and Lord Hammond arrive."

I WILL USE MY APPRAISAL SKILL TO RISE IN THE WORLD

"Understood," I replied.

The other two lords of Canarre showed up soon after, and we gathered around the same round table as last time. Lumeire kicked off the meeting by addressing the three of us.

"I have something important to say before we begin our council. Recently, Raven Louvent, the Lord of Lamberg, lost his life to a terrible illness. He was a dauntless man whose accomplishments on the battlefield put his peers to shame…"

The other two lords didn't seem very surprised by the news. They must have learned of my father's death through other sources, so they simply sat there, listening in somber silence.

"Tragic though his passing may be, now is not the time to mourn Raven's death. We shall honor his name by fighting for the future of Canarre to our last breaths, as he did to his!" Lumeire declared, then motioned for me to stand. "As I'm sure you are aware, Ars here has inherited his father's title and succeeded him as the head of House Louvent. Though he may be a child in body, I assure you that he is equal to us adults in spirit, and is worthy of his new station."

I should probably say something now, right? I thought for a moment before speaking up.

"I am Ars, the new Lord of Lamberg. Young though I might be, I shall dedicate my body and soul to seeing my duties fulfilled."

It was a perfectly generic greeting—perhaps a touch *too* generic—but I figured that was better than going overboard and making a terrible impression. Everyone present politely applauded my mini-speech, and I sat back down once they were finished.

"Now then," said Lumeire. "Let us begin our council of war. I would like to open the floor to *anyone* here who has a comment on the current state of our county. I will not chide you for stating or asking the obvious, so hold nothing back."

So our retainers are allowed to speak? Not just us?

I glanced back at Rietz and the others. Rietz met my gaze and gave me a quick nod, hoping to communicate that if he had anything to say, he would do so. Rosell, incidentally, was hiding behind Rietz at the time, so I wrote him off as a non-participant.

"To start," Lumeire continued, "a summary of the current state of affairs seems in order. Menas, if you'd be so kind."

"Very well, M'lord," said Menas, the retainer I'd met during my last visit. "To begin with, you should all know that Lord Couran and House Pyres have been communicating extensively behind closed doors. Some of you may worry that Lord Couran's decision to raise an army was foolhardy, but I assure you, he has every intention of winning the war he has chosen to wage. He has negotiated the aid of four of the western counties, Maasa included, as well as all five of the southern counties, for a total of nine counties' worth of forces to add to his. In addition, he has contracted the services of the most famed band of mercenaries in all of Rofeille, the Maitraw Company. With a force that large, Lord Couran's victory is all but assured."

So Lord Couran's been hard at work behind the scenes...though I guess that's not really a surprise. Apparently, he's not so inept after all.

I felt like it was an exaggeration to say that his victory was assured, though. In my view, nothing was a sure bet in war, and his younger brother most certainly hadn't wasted the past several months.

"Only one western county, Perreina, rebuked Lord Couran's overtures," Menas continued. "The county is entirely surrounded by Lord Couran's allies, yet they have still refused to disavow their allegiance to Lord Vasmarque. I have come to the conclusion that we have no choice but to either bring Perreina to our side through more underhanded tactics, or otherwise crush them in battle."

The County of Perreina was situated just east of Canarre, and it had been some time since any internal strife had been reported from the area. Due to that, bringing them to our side via backroom dealings seemed far less likely than simply defeating them in battle.

"Though winning their allegiance through peaceful means may prove difficult, the losses we would sustain waging war on the county would be costly. That's why we have decided to prioritize methods of bringing them over to us that do not involve an outright invasion. If any of you can propose such a means, now would be the time to do so."

Oh, so the invasion's plan B after all? That's not what I expected.

Unfortunately, though, I was absolutely clueless as far as ways to bring them to our side went. After all, I knew next to nothing about the county's current state. I glanced back at Rietz just in time to see him raise his hand.

"You have an idea? Speak, then," said Lumeire. A few others in the room scowled at the sight of Rietz, a Malkan, daring to take the floor, but Lumeire himself showed no signs of that sort of contempt. Apparently, he wasn't one for prejudice.

"I believe that it will be exceedingly difficult to bring Perreina to our side without sufficient information on their dealings," said Rietz. "To that end, I would propose that our first priority be determining *why* the Count of Perreina has chosen not to side with Lord Couran despite his county's adverse circumstances."

"A sound argument," said Lumeire with a nod. "But how, specifically, do you propose we obtain this information?"

Is he going to bring up the Shadows?

We hadn't even made contact with them yet, so promising their help felt like a risk to me. Then again, if we *did* get them under contract, then Lumeire would probably be quite impressed with us.

Rietz surprised me, though, by instead mumbling to himself, "A good question... We'll have to come up with a means, yes," then shooting me a wink.

Oh—is he telling me to bring the mercenaries up myself? Maybe he thinks that if I make the proposal, it'll make me look good in front of this council.

Frankly, I was a little embarrassed that he'd set the stage for me that blatantly, but there wasn't any sense in wasting the opportunity he'd created.

"Why don't we hire mercenaries to gather that information for us?" I suggested. "As it so happens, I'm aware of a band that would suit the particulars of this mission perfectly."

"Mercenaries," Lumeire repeated thoughtfully. "While I *do* have individuals trained in spycraft under my employ, I'm afraid to say that none of them are by any means experts. Are these mercenaries of yours skilled?"

I glanced at Rietz, and he nodded back to me. If *he* thought they had what it took, then I felt confident assuming that they weren't a band of clowns, at the very least.

"They are," I replied confidently.

"Very well, then," said Lumeire. "In that case, I shall leave the acquisition of information on Perreina's internal affairs to you. That said, should you fail to retain the services of these mercenaries, or should you determine that they are unworthy of trust, I would ask that you report back to me immediately. Failure is no sin, but *silent* failure could be the death of us all."

"Understood," I replied with a nod.

Looks like Lumeire's pretty good at handling underlings, I thought to myself at the same time. I'd had my fair share of subordinates at

I WILL USE MY APPRAISAL SKILL TO RISE IN THE WORLD

work in my previous life, and the worst-case scenario was always one of them screwing up and failing to admit it to me.

The war conference came to a temporary halt soon after, so I left the castle to make contact with the Shadows.

"U-Ugggh," moaned Rosell, clutching at his head as he walked beside me. "I couldn't *say* anything, I couldn't *ask* anything..."

"You must have been *really* nervous, huh?" I said.

"O-Of course I was!" snapped Rosell. "That room was *full* of the sort of people I usually only see in my nightmares!"

Some of the retainers in the room had very obviously been quite battle-hardened. I mean, it was a *war* council, after all. I had to admit, their grizzly beards and stern expressions *had* been pretty intimidating, but House Louvent had its fair share of people like that as well, so I didn't know what he meant.

Maybe he just can't handle that many of them in a room at once.

"Anyway, I couldn't focus on the meeting at all thanks to *them*," Rosell spat. "What'd they decide on in the end?"

I quickly explained that we were going to meet with the Shadows, and a profound look appeared on Rosell's face.

"Hmm... So everything went more or less how I expected it to, then... Ugh, but I bet the mercenaries are going to be terrifying, too... M-Maybe they'll even kidnap me and try to sell me..."

"That's not going to happen. Relax, Rosell. Even if the negotiations go south, we'll have Rietz and Charlotte there to protect us."

Rosell's pathological negativity had *slightly* improved since he was little, but he was still a hardcore pessimist at heart.

I turned to Rietz and asked, "So, where should we go to meet with the Shadows?"

"They're based outside of the walls, in a bar called the Tremps. I'll lead the way."

"Please do."

Rietz led us through the streets until suddenly, a familiar-sounding voice rang out behind us.

"Lord Ars! Please, wait just a moment!"

I turned around and saw a golden-haired girl of around my age running toward us. I realized why I recognized that voice—because it belonged to none other than my fiancée, Licia.

"Lady Licia!" I exclaimed, taken aback. "This is a shock! Did Lord Hammond bring you along with him?"

"He did," said Licia. "Though not without putting up a fight. I just had to come along and see you, so I put my foot down! *He* put *his* foot down in regards to the council, though, so I had to wait back in our chambers until the meeting concluded."

"No wonder I didn't see you there," I replied. "Speaking of which, it's good to see you again."

We'd written more times than I could count, but this was our first time seeing each other in person in a year or so. We'd managed to get together once since the day we first met, but ever since then, we'd had no direct contact. Licia had clearly grown a lot over that past year, too—she was taller, and her figure was beginning to fill out. She was thirteen, and very clearly going through a growth spurt, so it wasn't much of a surprise that she looked so different.

"Yes, it's been far too long!" said Licia. "You've grown quite dashing since we last met, Lord Ars."

"It feels as though I've hardly grown at all compared to you, Lady Licia. You've become astonishingly beautiful."

"My!" Licia exclaimed with a blush, then got right down to business. "By the way, Lord Ars, I'm told you intend to meet with a band of mercenaries called the Shadows?"

"That's right," I replied. "But wait, who told you that?"

I WILL USE MY APPRAISAL SKILL TO RISE IN THE WORLD

"I *may* have been listening in on your conference, truth be told," Licia admitted. "But more importantly, if you plan to meet with the mercenaries now, perhaps you'd be willing to take me along? I believe I might be helpful."

I paused to consider her offer. Licia *was* an accomplished negotiator, and she could indeed be quite helpful when it came to bargaining with the mercenaries. On the other hand, though, a mercenary band's base had to be dangerous, right? I had absolute faith in my guards, of course, but I still had some apprehensions about bringing her to such a seedy place.

"Lady Licia," I said, "I'm afraid that the Shadows' base is likely quite a dangerous place."

"That's perfectly all right!" she replied immediately. "I've already received permission from my father to accompany you. Does that make a difference?"

Hammond actually gave her the okay?

I mulled it over once more. If her father was down for it, I didn't see any reason *not* to take her along, and I'd have felt a little bad turning her down after she went out of her way to ask him. Just in case, though, I asked Rietz for his opinion.

"I doubt it would be an issue," he replied. "Our destination isn't *that* dangerous, really. If it were, I wouldn't be taking you with me either, Lord Ars."

"Fair enough. All right, then, Lady Licia—shall we? Just be sure not to stray too far from the rest of us."

"Thank you, Lord Ars!" Licia exclaimed with a grin.

We resumed our walk, now with an extra party member in tow, and eventually reached a surprisingly large building with a sign reading "Tremps" hung out front.

"Come to think of it, Rietz," I asked as I surveyed the building, "how did you find out about the Shadows in the first place?"

"Well," said Rietz. "You know I used to work as a mercenary myself, of course. The band I belonged to traveled across Missian, and at one point I ended up here in Canarre. I got to know the Shadows after the leader of my mercenary band hired them for a job."

"A band of mercenaries hired *another* band of mercenaries?"

"They did, yes. The Shadows are in a different line of work than we were, after all. They deal in information, espionage, assassination, and the like. *We,* on the other hand, specialized in traditional warfare. For a band like ours, fighting for the losing side of a war meant sustaining heavy casualties and often not getting paid on top of it. In the worst case, we could have been wiped out. That was why we hired the Shadows to gather information on the state of conflicts and sabotage our enemies. They were quite helpful, frankly."

"Interesting! I didn't know there was that much variation among mercenary bands."

"Of course, my band *was* wiped out in the end," Rietz added with a shrug. "Our leader got too greedy for his own good, and that was that…"

Rietz seemed to sink into his own memories. Considering how many of his friends and allies must have died, I couldn't imagine they were particularly pleasant experiences. I decided not to pry any deeper as our group walked into the Tremps.

I could immediately tell that it was a popular bar. The place was bustling, and despite its vast size, there were hardly any empty seats. It was only midday, so I could only imagine how packed it would be come nightfall.

"This place is as busy as ever," Rietz commented.

Guess it's always been this way.

I WILL USE MY APPRAISAL SKILL TO RISE IN THE WORLD

"The Shadows introduced me to the bar's owner back in the day, so I'll try talking to him first."

Rietz picked out the owner and walked over to him, and the rest of us followed along. As we slipped through the crowd, I noticed that we were drawing quite a lot of attention. It wasn't every day you saw a Malkan as well-dressed as Rietz, Charlotte's choice of clothing made the fact that she was a mage rather obvious, and Licia and I were very clearly nobility from our attire alone. In retrospect, we weren't exactly dressed with subtlety in mind.

"These stares are getting on my nerves," muttered Charlotte. "Can I burn them?"

Can she what?!

Charlotte's striking features were attracting the attention of the local men, which she clearly did *not* appreciate.

"Of course you can't!" I whispered back. "A few stares won't kill us, so just bear with it. Unless things get violent, I mean—*then* you can burn them."

"Fiiine," groaned Charlotte. "Ugggh, what a drag…"

I was kind of taken aback. She was always so mild-mannered back at my estate, so I'd never seen this belligerent side of hers before.

Maybe I just caught her in a bad mood?

In any case, although we got plenty of attention, nobody seemed interested in giving us a hard time, so we reached the owner unmolested.

"It's been a while, Alex," said Rietz to the owner. He looked to be middle-aged, with a muscular build and a rather impressive beard.

Alex gave Rietz a skeptical look and replied, "A Malkan…oh, *you*. Rietz, was it? You were with the Kraiment Mercenaries, weren't you?"

"Yes, that's right," said Rietz with a nod.

"Thought you were dead. Heard that most of you got done in, actually, and that the few who made it out with their hides intact went their separate ways."

"The Kraiment Mercenaries *did* disband, yes, but as you can see, I'm very much alive," said Rietz. "At the moment, I serve as a retainer to House Louvent."

"A retainer? House Louvent? That's the lord down in Lamberg, eh? How the hell'd you... Wait," Alex paused. "I've heard whispers of a Malkan boy down in Lamberg who fights like a demon on his lord's behalf. That's you?"

"Most likely, yes," Rietz admitted.

"Well, that sure clears things up. If I remember you right, then those rumors might not've been all folktale after all. You were one of the tougher Kraiments, weren't you?" Alex asked as he glanced over Rietz's shoulder. "That kid behind you the new Louvent lordling? I heard word the old one bit it and his kid took up the mantle."

"My name is Ars Louvent," I said, jumping in to assert myself a little. "I am indeed the head of House Louvent, as well as Rietz's employer."

"Well, good to make your acquaintance. Name's Alex Tremps, and I'm the owner of this boozehole," Alex said with a perfunctory bow. "So, tell me, what brings you lot here?"

"We have a job for the Shadows," said Rietz.

"Ohhh, *them*," said Alex. He looked a little flustered.

"Is something wrong?"

"Nah, not exactly. Thing is, the leader of the Shadows who took on jobs for the Kraiments? Bloke retired about two years ago."

"What?!" Rietz shouted in shock. "But the man *lived* for his

I WILL USE MY APPRAISAL SKILL TO RISE IN THE WORLD

work! Did an injury do him in?"

"The opposite—a wife. Said he couldn't afford to stay in such a risky line of business anymore, and that was that."

"I see," Rietz said with a frown. "That puts us in a difficult position…"

"Oh, well, the boss moved on, but the Shadows are still around," Alex clarified. "'Course, a fair chunk of the old guard split after he left. It's a whole new operation these days."

"And what do you make of these new Shadows?" Rietz asked. "Are they capable?"

"They put the old Shadows to shame," Alex replied with a sly grin.

"They put them to shame…?" repeated Rietz. It sounded like he could hardly believe his ears. "But…the old Shadows were legendary! And yet, this new crew is somehow even *more* skilled?"

"Believe it or not," said Alex. "The new boss has a real gift for the work, and a talent for spreading the wealth, skill-wise. The rest of them've improved by leaps and bounds. I haven't gotten word of them failing a single job since the old boss handed over the reins."

"That's astonishing," said Rietz.

"Thing is, though, this new boss is even more *off* than the old one. Nobody knows how the hell the Shadows decide what jobs they take these days. There's no guarantee they'll take you on as clients unless you meet them and ask."

"Then that's what we'll do," said Rietz. "Can you introduce us to this new boss of theirs?"

"I'll introduce you to whoever you want me to, so long as you've got the coin to pay for the privilege. It'll have to be later, though. After dark, understand?"

"Does the new boss only show up here at night?"

AS A REINCARNATED ARISTOCRAT

"Nah, the boss is already here. It's just that the Shadows only take on new work at night. Don't ask *me* to explain it, but one way or another, I won't be taking you to the boss until night falls. Feel free to search on your own, though, if you're up for wasting your time," Alex said with a shrug.

Considering how crowded this place is, yeah, that probably would be a hopeless endeavor…if I didn't have my Appraisal skill to save the day, that is!

Alex said that the Shadows' boss had a gift, and I was certain that meant that they'd have to have high enough stats to catch my attention. They *had* to have a much higher Valor than the average person, if nothing else! The fact that they wouldn't take any jobs until night meant that searching for the boss wasn't really a productive use of time, but I didn't have anything better to do, so I decided I might as well look around in the meantime.

"All right," I said to Alex. "We'll wait here until night falls, then."

"Suit yourself. Order some drinks and a bite to eat while you're at it, if you feel like doing me a favor. You look a bit short for the hard stuff, but I've got some less boozy drinks in the back, if that'd suit your fancy."

"It would, thank you," I replied, then paid for both the introduction and some drinks and fruits I took the opportunity to order from him. After that, we found a table, took a seat, and waited for night to fall.

As we waited, I started appraising the bar's clientele one by one, keeping a close eye out for the leader of the Shadows. The place was packed, and I appraised absolutely everyone I could find, but nobody had a status screen that screamed "leader of a band of clandestine mercenaries" to me.

Maybe I'm wrong about spies having high Valor.

I WILL USE MY APPRAISAL SKILL TO RISE IN THE WORLD

Unfortunately, Appraisal didn't have an Aptitude for information-gathering listed. I was starting to tire myself out with all that staring, too, so for the moment, I decided to give up on my hunt. Instead, I called out to a nearby waitress and asked for a glass of water—I was feeling a little thirsty, after all.

"Water? Coming right up!" said the waitress. Water was readily available in the Canarre region, so the price was negligible.

Come to think of it, I never appraised that waitress, did I?

She was still young—probably only a year or two older than me—and her black hair was tied up in a ponytail. Her looks weren't outstanding or anything, but I certainly would've called her attractive, at least.

I mean, let's be real—she couldn't possibly be the Shadows' leader.

I almost didn't bother appraising her, but figured, hey, what did I have to lose? And so, I gave it a shot.

I WILL USE MY APPRAISAL SKILL TO RISE IN THE WORLD

> Mazak Finde
> Age: 22
> Male
> **Status:**
> LEA: 33/44
> VAL: 91/92
> INT: 87/90
> POL: 22/23
> Ambition: 45
> **Aptitudes:**
> Infantry: A
> Cavalry: C
> Archer: S
> Mage: A
> Fortification: C
> Weaponry: A
> Naval: D
> Aerial: C
> Strategy: B

My jaw dropped.

She's—I mean, he's a boy?! And twenty-two years old, at that?! He's a full-grown adult! And man, just look at those stats! So his name is Mazak? Or at least, that's his name unless my skill's bugging out for whatever reason.

I appraised Rietz, just to check, and his stats were the same as ever, so I was fairly confident my skill wasn't on the fritz. Then, I appraised the waitress...I mean, the *waiter* one more time...and his stats were exactly the same as they'd been the first time. Apparently, they were legit.

Could it be...? Could this Mazak person be the leader of the Shadows?

He was the only person with the stats for it in the building, and considering said stats, I was positive that at the absolute least, he wasn't just an ordinary waiter. It'd have been one thing if he had high stat *caps,* but the fact that his current stats were almost maxed out made his abnormality plain as day. He'd been through some sort of training, no doubt about it.

Assuming his stats were real, then Mazak had become the leader of the Shadows when he was only eighteen or nineteen. When I really thought about it, the Shadows were all about spywork, and what could be better for making your target let their guard down than looking like a teenage girl?

He was no teenage girl, though—he was a man of twenty-two, shockingly enough. Did he come from a line of people who were naturally short and girly, or was it some sort of medical condition? I had a feeling that his stats probably wouldn't have been that high if he had a developmental disorder, so I was inclined to suspect the former.

"Umm...did you want to order something else?" Mazak asked, looking a little uncomfortable. It seemed I'd been staring a little too openly.

I figured that I probably shouldn't ask him if he was the leader of the Shadows straight-up. They didn't take jobs during the daytime, for whatever reason, and it seemed he was fully immersed in his role as a waitress, so I had a funny feeling that if I jumped the gun, he wouldn't take on the job at all. I might even turn him against me entirely if I revealed his identity and damaged his pride!

I WILL USE MY APPRAISAL SKILL TO RISE IN THE WORLD

Leaving a bad first impression was the last thing I wanted to do, so I settled on not saying anything about his true identity.

"No, I'm fine, thanks," I replied.

"Oh? I'll be right back with your water, then," he said. He came back with a glass moments later, then went on his way. It was incredible—he *really* came across as a young girl, from his voice to the tiniest mannerisms. Even if he himself revealed his true identity, without evidence, it'd just come across as a bad joke.

"I see you've taken quite a keen interest in that girl, Lord Ars," said Licia with a smile that didn't reach her eyes. She seemed a little miffed, actually. I guess the way I'd been staring at Mazak had gotten on her nerves.

I decided to tell the truth about why I'd been watching him. No point letting Licia stew over it, after all.

"I'm fairly certain that 'she' is the leader of the Shadows," I whispered, quietly enough that nobody outside our table would hear me. Everybody *at* my table, meanwhile, gaped at me in disbelief.

"You realize that she's a girl who can't be much older than me, don't you?" asked Licia.

"Actually, *he's* a twenty-two-year-old man."

"What?!" all of my companions shouted in unison.

"Shhhhhh!" I quickly hushed them.

We're probably fine—nothing too *weird about people shouting in surprise! I'm sure nobody heard the first part!*

"Y-You're joking, right?" said Rosell. "How could she *possibly* be anything other than a girl?"

"I'm positive," I replied. "There's no doubt about it."

Licia looked a little thoughtful and said, "I'm sure a person like that could be the leader of the Shadows…but a twenty-two-year-old man? *That* strains credulity…"

AS A REINCARNATED ARISTOCRAT

I couldn't blame her. I'd seen the appraisal results with my own two eyes, yet even *I'd* second-guessed them.

"I believe it," said Rietz. "I've never known Lord Ars to be wrong about such matters. Though that said, I *didn't* know he had the power to reveal an individual's sex."

No surprise that Rietz would trust me. He's known me the longest, and he's seen time and time again how accurate my Appraisal skill is.

"If that's the boss, then why don't we go ask him about the job right now? I'm getting sick of waiting," said Charlotte. I quickly explained that if we jumped the gun he might not take the job at all, so she agreed to wait a little longer, though she made it clear she wasn't very happy about it.

A little while later, nature called, and I got up to use the restroom. Rietz reflexively stood up to escort me, but since the bar wasn't particularly rowdy and it would've been embarrassing to have someone following me to the toilet, I told him he didn't have to bother.

I bet he's going to keep his eyes glued to the restroom's entrance anyway, but eh, that beats the alternative.

I stepped into the restroom. This world *did* have decent enough water infrastructure, all things considered, so the toilets weren't as unhygienic as one might assume. I finished my business, turned to leave…and nearly dropped dead of a heart attack.

"All right, kid, let's chat. How'd you figure out I'm the Shadows' boss?" asked Mazak, who was standing literally right in front of me.

When did he get there? I didn't notice him at all!

When he was acting like a waitress, he'd seemed like a bright, cheerful girl, but now he was staring fixedly at me, completely expressionless. He looked so calm and analytical that I was astonished. How could a single person give off two impressions so wildly differ-

I WILL USE MY APPRAISAL SKILL TO RISE IN THE WORLD

ent just by changing the look on his face?

"'S the first time I've been busted, you know?" said Mazak.

As it so happened, though, I had an extremely similar question on my mind: *How did he know that I knew who he was?*

I decided to play dumb and asked, "What are you talking about?"

"Nuh-uh, that's not gonna fly. I'm sure you thought you were whispering quietly enough, but I heard every single word you people said. You're Ars Louvent, freshly-minted Lord of Lamberg, and you came here to hire me for a job. Then, *somehow,* you figured out that I was the boss, a man, and twenty-two. Feel like denying any of that?"

Mazak had been quite a ways away from our table while we had that discussion. If he'd managed to eavesdrop anyway, then his hearing was remarkably sensitive. Of course, he probably wouldn't have been able to get by as a spy if it weren't. All that said, he'd let one interesting fact slip: if he didn't know how I knew his identity, then he hadn't overheard our *entire* conversation.

"It wasn't easy to get in here without anyone noticing, y'know?" said Mazak. "Some weird asshole was watching the restroom like a hawk, so I had to take a back route that only the staff know about. I didn't go to all that trouble for nothing, so you're *going to* tell me how you figured me out, one way or another."

I guess Rietz really was watching out for me after all! Mazak got the better of him, but I can't blame him for not accounting for a secret passage.

"Why are you so curious about how I figured you out?" I asked.

"Hiding your identity's kind of a big deal in my line of work, and I've got a lot of confidence in my skills. If somebody takes me down a peg, then I've gotta figure out how they pulled it off. Or what, you think I'd just let you piss all over my work and walk away? Spill your guts, kid. Where'd I screw up?"

"You didn't," I replied after a moment's hesitation. "Your act was perfect."

"Then how'd you know?"

I'd hit my limit—I *had* to fess up. I could tell that if I kept giving him the runaround, he was probably going to get violent with me, so I told him about my Appraisal skill.

"The power to see other people's abilities...?" Mazak repeated disbelievingly.

"That's right. You possess abilities far exceeding the average person's, so I knew you were likely the Shadows' leader. Incidentally, my power also lets me see your name, sex, and age. Mazak Finde, I presume?"

Mazak gasped. His eyes widened for just a moment, but then he shut them and sneered, "Sorry, but that's a swing and a miss. I gave up *that* name ages ago. I go by Pham these days."

He changed his name? Interesting—then it looks like my skill doesn't update that information. It must only tell me their birth name.

"Gotta say, though," he continued. "That skill makes you the natural enemy of folks in my line of work."

"It does?"

"Better believe it. Like I said, you can't get by in this field unless you can conceal your identity. That makes the way I look real convenient—nobody ever suspects the little girl in the room to be rooting around for their deepest secrets, y'know? That's why I never let anyone other than my most trusted allies in on my identity. I don't even let my clients see my real face. Alex and the rest of the Shadows are the only ones who know who I am."

Part of me *really* wanted to ask, "Then what do you do with

I WILL USE MY APPRAISAL SKILL TO RISE IN THE WORLD

people like me who figure your identity out?" However, I kept my lips firmly shut. It had just hit me how risky of a position I was in, and I'd already pushed my luck pretty far.

"I've only got two options for someone with a dangerous power like yours: bring 'em over to my side, or make sure they never get the chance to work against me, if you catch my drift. You got a preference?"

My heart skipped a beat out of sheer terror, then started gradually pounding faster and faster. If I chose the wrong answer, things could get *very* nasty, *very* quickly.

"I think it goes without saying that I'd rather be on your side," I replied. "By the way, you know I'm the head of House Louvent, don't you? I've already told my retainers your identity, and if anything happens to me here, you won't just be making enemies of my people—even the count might hunt you down. I'm sure you'd rather not get chased out of this city, right?"

"Any town works for me," Pham snorted dismissively.

"It can't be that easy to pick up and move your whole operation, can it?"

"It's a pain at first, I'll give you that, but nothing we can't handle."

"And what if my retainers followed you? What if they were willing to chase you to the far ends of the continent to kill you for what you did to me?"

"I'd do them in before they got the chance."

"I don't know about that. My retainers are pretty strong."

Pham paused for just a moment...then cracked up.

"Hah hah hah! Oh, don't piss yourself, kid. I can hear your heart beating up a storm, y'know? Guess you *are* just a brat, though. Dunno what I was expecting."

AS A REINCARNATED ARISTOCRAT

Rats! I thought I was keeping a straight face, too. How are you supposed to fool somebody into thinking you're calm when they can literally hear your heartbeat?!

"I was *kidding*," Pham continued. "I'm not planning on making you disappear, don't worry. I happen to *like* unique sorts, and though I wasn't lying about your power being dangerous, it makes you as unique as it gets. I'd never turn down a job from someone like you. Plus, working for nobles tends to mean repeat commissions if we pull off the job, and *that* means spreading my identity around would bite you in the ass just as hard as it would me."

I let out a sigh of relief.

Oh, thank goodness, he was just kidding. I seriously thought that I was about to get murdered.

"You can tell me about the job once night falls," said Pham. "Just sit tight until then."

"Understood," I replied.

Pham struck me as a little dangerous—maybe more than a little, actually—so part of me was seriously considering backing out of this whole plan. However, after everything we'd just been through, giving up on hiring him and making a break for it felt like a surefire way to make a lifelong enemy out of him. I wasn't particularly interested in having to watch my back for assassins at all hours, so it seemed I'd have to see this through.

Pham turned to leave the restroom...just in time for Rietz to burst through the door.

"Lord Ars!" he shouted a moment before his gaze fell upon Pham.

Rietz didn't hesitate for a second—he'd drawn and swung his sword before I even knew what was happening. Pham, however, was just as fast, pulling a knife from his breast pocket and intercepting

I WILL USE MY APPRAISAL SKILL TO RISE IN THE WORLD

the swing.

"Wait, Rietz! Stop!" I shouted. "He's on our side!"

"Huh? Is that so? My apologies," Rietz said, lowering his sword.

"Okay, kid, I've gotta hand it to you," said Pham. "You were right—I *would* rather have you and your people on my side. I'm not gonna say I *couldn't* kill this guy, but I can tell he wouldn't make it easy."

With that final remark, Pham left the bathroom.

Rietz, meanwhile, turned to me and asked, "Are you sure you're all right, Lord Ars?"

"Yes, I'm fine, really!" I reassured him.

"I'm relieved to hear it. I was keeping watch, yet I didn't notice anything was wrong at all! There must be another entrance," Rietz commented, glancing around the bathroom. "In any case, you were right, not that I ever doubted you. He *must* be the current leader of the Shadows, considering how easily he blocked my strike."

It seemed that Pham's skills had impressed Rietz already.

The two of us left the bathroom and returned to our table. A short while later, Pham emerged back onto the floor, once again in full waitress mode. I was flabbergasted—how could a person change how they came off *that* dramatically at the drop of a hat? Once again, I was half-convinced that he really *was* a totally different person.

Time passed by, and finally, night fell. It wasn't long before Alex walked on over to our table.

"Thanks for waiting. I'll take you to see Pham, the boss of the Shadows, now."

We got up and followed Alex up a staircase, passing by the second floor and emerging on the third. He then unlocked a door and ushered us inside.

"Pham, your guests are... Huh? You going around showing your face off to clients these days?"

"No point in hiding it," replied Pham from inside. "They already figured me out."

"What...?" Alex blinked in confusion, unable to process what he'd just heard. "They figured you... What? You mean they saw you at work and picked you out as the Shadows' leader?"

"That's exactly what they did," said Pham. "The boy, specifically. He's got a weird power up his sleeve, it seems. Picked me out of the crowd at a glance."

"I'll be damned," muttered Alex, seeming downright shocked.

I guess somebody seeing through Pham's disguise was way beyond his expectations. Can't blame him, though, considering how good of a disguise it is. I sure wouldn't have been able to tell without a helping hand, myself!

"S-So Ars *was* right?" marveled Rosell. "She really *was* the leader of the Shadows?"

"And 'she' really *is* also actually a he, I assume," added Licia, who'd apparently still been skeptical on that front. Even after his true identity had been revealed, it was hard to see Pham as anything other than a girl. His natural voice was a *little* lower than the one he'd used while posing as a waitress, but it didn't exactly scream "man" to me.

"Yeah, I'm a man. No question about it," said Pham. Even after hearing it straight from the horse's mouth, Licia didn't seem totally convinced, but selling her on that point was pretty low on my list of priorities. I honestly couldn't have cared less whether he was a man or a woman.

"I don't dress like this for kicks, either," Pham added. "Young girls are the most universally underestimated people in this whole

I WILL USE MY APPRAISAL SKILL TO RISE IN THE WORLD

damn world. Being able to drop into the role at a moment's notice makes my job a hell of a lot easier, so I work here to practice."

I wondered why he'd bother with the whole waitress act...

He had it down pat, in my book, but I had a funny feeling that Pham himself still felt there was room for improvement. Either that, or he refused to stop practicing even though the act was perfect to make sure he never lost his touch.

"So, let's talk business, yeah? What'll the Shadows be getting done for you?"

"Huh? Does that mean you've already decided to take the job?" I asked, bewildered.

"That's right. Like I said—you've got a pretty unique power, and I like that. Working for you sounds like a good time."

I was still a bit stunned, but I quickly explained the details of the job to Pham. He crossed his arms when I finished and replied, "Hmm... The reason why Perreina isn't giving in and joining your little alliance, eh...?"

"Can you figure it out?"

"Stupid question. *Of course* we can. Turning up info like that's our bread and butter. I'd bet we'll have an answer for you in no time."

"You will? Really?"

"Give us a week and you'll see for yourself."

That's even faster than I was expecting. I thought it'd take at least a month!

"I'll cut you a deal, since this is our first job for you," said Pham. "One gold for the job with a three silver advance."

Three silver? That's cheaper than I was expecting, too!

I had more than enough money on hand to hire him on the spot. I'd been prepared to do some haggling if his price had been outrageous, but it seemed that wouldn't be necessary after all. I handed over the three silver without hesitation.

"Thanks for the business," Pham said as the coins clinked into his palm. "Shouldn't take more than a week, like I said. But for safety's sake, let's say the deadline's two weeks from now. Come back then, at night, and you'll have your answer."

With that, our negotiations with Pham and the Shadows came to a close. In the end, it had turned out to be way less of an ordeal than I'd initially expected—I was anticipating a real interrogation. All that was left for us to do was wait and believe in Pham's skills. And given the results of my appraisal and the quality of his disguise, that second part was going to be very easy.

Licia spoke up as the four of us walked out into the streets: "Well, that certainly proceeded swimmingly! I came along in the hopes that I could be of some use, but it seems I missed my chance."

She honestly sounded a little disappointed. We'd managed to hire the mercenaries we wanted, though, so I didn't see any need for her to feel sorry.

I'd better say something to cheer her up, huh?

"Still, I'm glad you came along. Having you with us made the trip far more enjoyable," I said.

"Huh? I-It did...?" Licia stammered, her cheeks flushing. She glanced away, but only a few seconds later, she looked back again, a brilliant smile on her face. "Well, it just so happens that I feel the same way! I enjoyed this excursion with you, Lord Ars."

Out of all the smiles I'd seen Licia wear, this was definitely the brightest. It was a pure, authentic smile that looked like it came from the bottom of her heart. I believed it, too—my intuition told me that this one truly wasn't faked.

Our mission concluded, we returned to stay the night at the

castle. The next morning, we set off for Lamberg once more.

○

Two weeks later, as promised, we arrived at the Tremps. This time, though, we made sure to get there after dark.

"Nice of you to show up," said Pham as we stepped into his office. I'd brought Rietz, Charlotte, and a few other guards with me this time. Rosell ended up staying in Lamberg, though.

"Did you manage to get the information we wanted?" I asked.

"'Course we did," said Pham. "But you'll have to pay your tab before you get to hear it."

I handed over the remaining seven silver coins, which Pham accepted with a smile.

"Thanks for the business."

"By the way, I've been wondering something. You're not the *only* member of the Shadows, right?" I asked.

"'Course I'm not. I'm the only one who talks to the clients, though. That's the boss's duty."

In other words, they exist, but we don't get to meet them. I guess it wouldn't really make sense to have the whole crew meet all their clients.

"All right," said Pham. "Let's get down to business, then. You wanted to know why Perreina won't jump ship to Couran's side of the war, yeah? Well, first up, a quick bit of basic searching led us to discover that the Count of Perreina, Rulrook Dolan, owes Vasmarque a great debt."

"A debt?" I repeated.

"That's right. See, Vasmarque's endorsement is what enabled House Dolan to rise all the way to the seat of count, so Rulrook owes the man his success."

I WILL USE MY APPRAISAL SKILL TO RISE IN THE WORLD

"And that's why he chose to side with him?"

"That's *part* of why, but it's not that simple. The debt's heavy, but not heavy enough to make him choose a path that's all but sure to lead to his house's downfall."

"Then he must have some other reason, right?"

"Right. So we dug a little deeper and turned up something *real* interesting," said Pham, passing me a rolled-up letter.

"What is…?"

"Just read it."

I unfurled the letter and began to read, only for my jaw to drop in shock. The letter was a solicitation from Vasmarque addressed to the Count of Perreina, requesting that he enter into an alliance. The letter included a list of the counts who had already pledged their loyalty to Vasmarque, along with their signatures and seals—in other words, all the houses on it were firmly on his side. Among their number were the counts who ruled over the eastern and northern counties, as well as a provisional entry for Perreina itself. None of that was particularly surprising, but there was one extra name on that list that was downright stunning: the County of Maasa, home to the largest city in western Missian.

"Does this really mean…?" I muttered in wonder, glancing over at Rietz, whose eyes were just as wide as mine.

"The County of Maasa has sided with Lord Vasmarque?" Rietz whispered in disbelief.

"That's right," said Pham. "And *that* means that as things stand, Vasmarque holds a *hefty* advantage. The man probably sent this letter off to the Count of Perreina because he knew that, between that advantage and the debt the count owed him, he would side with him for sure. I mean, with Maasa on Vasmarque's side, Couran's campaign's all but dead in the water. Who'd board a ship that's already sinking?"

"And this letter is genuine? How did you get it? It can't have been easy to obtain something this important," I said. I didn't have the knowledge or skills to tell whether or not the house seals on the letter were authentic, so I couldn't say with total certainty that the whole thing was a forgery.

"Trade secret," said Pham. "We can't go blabbing about how we get our hands on stuff like that, no matter how much we trust the client. That's need-to-know information, and if you're not one of us, you don't need to know. What I *can* tell you is that it was without a doubt obtained from Castle Perreina, the residence of the count."

Ugh, trade secrets? Really? Though I guess even if I did know how he got the letter, that still wouldn't necessarily prove it's real. Any number of people could be trying to deceive me in this situation.

On the other hand, if I wasn't willing to trust Pham's word, then there hadn't been any point in hiring him in the first place. Lumeire had surely had his fair share of dealings with the other counts, so I decided to see if he knew more about their seals. He seemed the best bet to determine if the letter's contents could be trusted.

"My apologies for doubting you," I said. "I hope you'll understand that this is just…rather unbelievable news."

"No skin off my back," said Pham. "That's all the info I have for you right now. You know where to find us if you have another job."

"Right. The information is greatly appreciated. You don't mind if we take this letter with us, do you?"

"All yours."

I collected the letter and we made our way out of the bar. It was time to head back to the inn we were staying in and plan our next move.

"This is going to get way out of hand, isn't it?" I speculated. "As-

I WILL USE MY APPRAISAL SKILL TO RISE IN THE WORLD

suming that letter *is* real, then Lord Couran will be rushing into this war at a major disadvantage. What are we supposed to do now...? Do you think we should deliver the letter to Lord Lumeire right away?"

"Let me think," said Rietz, who was busy re-reading the document we'd received from Pham.

"Something about this letter feels wrong," he eventually concluded.

"You don't trust Pham?"

"No, that isn't quite what I mean. I fully believe that this letter *was* stolen from Castle Perreina, but the problem is the Count of Maasa's signature and seal. I believe they may be forgeries."

"And that would mean...?"

"In short, it would mean that this letter could be a stratagem on Lord Vasmarque's part. I believe that he may have forged the Count of Maasa's signature and seal in order to pressure the Count of Perreina into committing himself to Lord Vasmarque's cause."

"Would that really work?" I asked, raising an eyebrow. "Wouldn't the Count of Perreina have seen the Count of Maasa's real signature and seal plenty of times already?"

"Perhaps, but it's far from impossible to make a forgery convincing enough to pass a cursory inspection," replied Rietz. "I've heard that there are even some forgers who make a living solely by creating seals that are indistinguishable from the real thing."

"Hmm... What makes you think it's a forgery, though?"

"The fact that the Count of Perreina was the only one who Lord Vasmarque tried to recruit," said Rietz. "That strikes me as *extremely* unnatural."

"Does it? But the Count of Perreina already owed Lord Vasmarque a favor. Wouldn't it make sense for Lord Vasmarque to go after Perreina first, since he'd know their count would have the highest odds of being receptive to the offer? Especially considering that if anyone turned the offer down, the fact that an offer was made would almost definitely get leaked."

"But would that information leak really work to Lord Vasmarque's disadvantage?" asked Rietz. "I imagine that many of the western counties have allied themselves with Lord Couran in no small part *because* they believe that the Count of Maasa has taken his side. If he really *had* chosen to support Lord Vasmarque instead, then going public with that information could easily win over other allies as well. Vasmarque would have nothing to lose from the revelation...and everything to gain."

"Hmm... That's a good point, actually. But even if the seal *is* a forgery, it seems odd that Lord Vasmarque didn't reach out to the Count of Canarre and try to convince him, too."

"Perhaps he thought that would be overplaying his hand?" suggested Rietz. "The farther the letter spreads, the more likely that someone will notice it's a forgery. A single message to the Count of Maasa is all it would take to prove its inauthenticity, after all. As such, it would make sense for Lord Vasmarque to only use this tactic on the one count who owed him a debt and was likely already deeply involved with his affairs."

"I get it..."

"Perhaps we might learn something if Lord Lumeire takes the letter directly to the Count of Maasa and asks about it...? No, that would prove nothing. After all, if the letter *is* genuine and the Count of Maasa is involved in some sort of plot, he would have no reason to be upfront about it... In any case, yes, I believe it would be in our best interests to show it to Lord Lumeire immediately."

"I thought so. In that case, let's make our way to Castle Canarre

I WILL USE MY APPRAISAL SKILL TO RISE IN THE WORLD

on the double!"

Showing up at the castle this late at night was most certainly a breach of etiquette, but considering the urgency of the situation, I figured the count would forgive us. We made our way toward Castle Canarre, which was only a short walk away from where we were staying. There was no gatekeeper stationed outside at this time of night, but there *were* guards posted on watch around the perimeter of the castle, so we were able to explain the circumstances and get them to let us inside.

Soon after we entered, Menas ran up to us in a fluster.

"Welcome, Lord Ars!" he called out. "Lord Lumeire is eagerly awaiting your news regarding the Count of Perreina!"

It seemed the guards had told him why we'd come.

"I'm sorry to come calling so late at night," I said.

"No, no, think nothing of it! Even a second's delay can make a world of difference when news of this magnitude is concerned. Come, come! I'll lead you to Lord Lumeire at once!"

Considering the fact that we'd shown up unannounced, I was surprised by how readily we were granted an audience with the count.

Maybe we just happened to arrive while he wasn't busy with anything else?

Menas guided us to Lumeire's room.

"Well met, Ars," Lumeire said as we stepped inside.

"Thank you, and my apologies for disturbing you so late at night," I replied.

"No matter. Frankly, I've done no small amount of second-guessing myself as to whether entrusting you with such an important task was a wise decision. I'm very impressed to see you return to me with information in hand so quickly."

"I'm afraid you might wish to reserve your praise until after you've heard his report, M'lord," noted Menas.

"Y-Yes, of course. There's no telling what sort of information it is, after all," Lumeire said, then cleared his throat. "So, let's hear it. What have you learned?"

"First, I'd like you to read this," I said, gesturing to Rietz. I'd given the letter to him for safekeeping, so he took it out and passed it to Lumeire.

"A letter...?" muttered Lumeire. He unfurled it and began reading. "A letter of alliance? And a list of counties pledged to Lord Vasmarque's cause, with accompanying signatures and seals... Hmph, Perreina's as well... What?! What is the meaning of this?!"

I had a funny feeling that Lumeire had just reached the Count of Maasa's signature. His jaw dropped and his eyes bulged in shock.

"H-How could this be...? The Count of Maasa, siding with Lord Vasmarque? N-No, that *can't* be... The Count of Maasa has always held lord Couran in the highest of esteem, and he's never been one for deception..."

It seemed that Lumeire was even more shocked by the count's apparent betrayal than we were. He *did* know the man personally, after all.

"I-Is this letter genuine?" he asked, turning his gaze back to me.

"It was obtained from the Count of Perreina's home, so yes, in all likelihood, it is," I explained. "However, I can't be certain that the seal and signature of the Count of Maasa are authentic."

"What do you mean?" asked Lumeire. I quickly explained our suspicions that the letter may have been part of Vasmarque's scheme to lure the Count of Perreina into an alliance.

"I see. Lord Vasmarque's always been a crafty one, and I wouldn't put this sort of scheme past him... However, the signatures and seals

I WILL USE MY APPRAISAL SKILL TO RISE IN THE WORLD

upon this document look indistinguishable from the real things, to my eyes," he said as he slowly and carefully inspected the page.

Lumeire had surely seen nobles' signatures and seals far more times than any of us, and I wasn't about to second-guess his judgment. That said, if he *was* right, then it would mean we'd have no choice but to assume the Count of Maasa was our enemy. I had to wonder what sort of action Lumeire would take if he decided that was the only explanation.

"Ahem," said Menas, who was standing off to the side and listening in on our conversation. "Might I take a look at that document?"

"Oh, that's right," said Lumeire, passing him the letter. "I'd forgotten you have a power that comes in handy at times such as these."

Menas spent a moment slowly and carefully inspecting the letter, then looked up once more.

"Hmm, yes. I believe that the signature and seal of the Count of Maasa are indeed forgeries."

"Really?!" I exclaimed.

"Yes, indeed. Wait just a moment," said Menas, who then stepped out of the room.

"Menas possesses the power to ascertain the authenticity of signatures, seals, and the like," explained Lumeire as his retainer left.

I had no idea he had that sort of ability!

My Appraisal skill allowed me to see people's status screens, but it had become increasingly clear that it did *not* allow me to tell whether or not they had special skills or abilities of their own. I was starting to appreciate that there was always a lot more to a person deep down than what little my power could tell me about them. Part of me was hopeful that my skill would evolve and start giving me that sort of info eventually, but considering the status screens hadn't changed in the slightest since the day I was born, I figured I should keep my expectations low.

Menas soon returned with a second letter in hand.

"This letter bears the genuine signature and seal of the Count of Maasa," he explained. "To be on the safe side, I suggest we compare them."

Menas placed the two letters side by side, lining the relevant sections up. The count's seal, incidentally, depicted a hexagon with a circle within it, and a five-pointed star within the circle.

"Yes, I thought as much," mumbled Menas. "The shape of the circle really *is* slightly askew…and the hexagon is slightly too small."

Honestly, I couldn't tell at all, even after he pointed the differences out. I *almost* thought I could see the discrepancies after staring at the seals for several moments longer, but I suspected I was just fooling myself.

Next, Menas brought out a ruler and started taking careful measurements of the two seals.

"Yes, yes, I knew it! The difference is slight, but it *is* there. The signatures are quite similar as well, but the count's genuine article is written in a slightly different hand than the forgery. And a forgery it is—I am now confident beyond a shadow of a doubt. The others are genuine, however, so they have likely all pledged their support to Vasmarque."

"What's truly important here is that the Count of Maasa's are fake. *That* is a relief," said Lumeire. I could tell that he *really* didn't want to end up in a conflict with the County of Maasa. "I shall report on these matters to the Count of Maasa and Lord Couran. I'm certain that between the three of us, the problem will be settled in no time. You have done exceptionally well, Ars, and I assure you that you will be rewarded accordingly in due time."

"I am honored by your praise, Lord Lumeire," I replied.

I WILL USE MY APPRAISAL SKILL TO RISE IN THE WORLD

I felt a little awkward about being complimented over my so-called accomplishment. After all, Pham was the one who'd done all the actual work, and Rietz was the one who'd introduced me to him. Then again, taking credit for your retainers' accomplishments *did* strike me as a very feudal-lord sort of thing to do.

We wound up spending the night in the castle, then returned to Lamberg the next day.

○

A few weeks passed before I received word on the plan to bring the Count of Perreina over to our side. A message finally arrived one day, informing me that the plan had succeeded and that I was to report to Castle Canarre. We set off at once, and it wasn't long before I stood face-to-face with Lumeire once more. This time, however, I ended up attending my audience with the count on my own. Lumeire, Menas, and I were the only ones present.

"Well met, Ars," said Lumeire. "Once again, allow me to congratulate you: your efforts proved instrumental in our success. Thanks to you, the Count of Perreina has agreed to side with Lord Couran."

"I am pleased beyond measure that I was able to be of service to you and Lord Couran," I replied.

"As you should be. I'm not exaggerating—your work really did make all the difference. Come to think of it, I suppose I never told you, but the Count of Perreina can provide us with a certain resource of incredible strategic significance."

"A resource...? What is it?" I asked.

"Explosive magistones. They're an incredibly rare form of ore. Perreina is the only source of the stuff in Missian, and it is one of only four in all of Summerforth. Aqua magia refined from explosive magistones allow the user to perform truly incredible, and truly destructive, feats of magic."

That was certainly the first I'd heard of Perreina having such an incredible resource. For a moment, I thought that having their count on our side could prove incredibly advantageous, but then it occurred to me that Perreina had been committed to Vasmarque's side for quite a long time before they'd defected. In the worst case, Vasmarque may have already secured himself a considerable supply of magistones.

"Unfortunately, the Count of Perreina has informed us that Lord Vasmarque continues to help himself to the magistone reserves," sighed Lumeire, immediately confirming my suspicions. "They've set up checkpoints along the border and are stopping anyone who attempts to cross with magistones on hand, but it seems the smugglers are one step ahead of Perreina's border guards, as they continue to deliver a large quantity of magistones into Lord Vasmarque's clutches. I can't say with confidence that we have the upper hand in that respect."

"Still," continued Lumeire in a brighter tone. "We're *far* better off than we were when the Count of Perreina was trapped under Lord Vasmarque's thumb. The tide is turning in our favor, of that I'm certain! But enough talk—I'm sure you're anxious to see your reward. Menas!"

"Yes, M'lord!"

Lumeire gave Menas a wave, prompting him to step out of the room, then return moments later with two boxes loaded onto a small cart. The boxes themselves were quite different in size, with one of them quite small and the other notably large.

"You'll find three hundred gold coins within, altogether," said

I WILL USE MY APPRAISAL SKILL TO RISE IN THE WORLD

Lumeire. "Consider it your reward for a job well done."

"Th-Three *hundred* gold coins?"

I had expected him to reward me in gold, yes, but three hundred was far beyond my wildest expectations. I'd been anticipating closer to *fifty*.

"Indeed," Lumeire replied with a nod. "Lord Couran contributed his own coin to your reward. I'm ashamed to admit it, but my pockets aren't particularly deep these days, and his money accounts for the bulk of it. The small box is my contribution—fifty gold coins in total. The remaining two hundred and fifty in the large box are your reward from Lord Couran."

That explained it. I hadn't anticipated Couran personally rewarding me as well. It made sense that he had money to spare, though, considering he ruled over Semplar. Two hundred and fifty gold was probably chump change to him.

"My sincerest thanks," I said as I accepted the boxes. I took the cart as well, though I had a feeling they were going to be a nightmare to transport regardless.

"There's one more thing I ought to tell you," continued Lumeire. "Lord Couran wishes to meet you in person."

"Huh? Wait, seriously?" I replied in shock. I'd helped him out, sure, but there was a world's worth of difference between Couran's social standing and my own.

Broadly speaking, the status of a lord was determined by the worth of the land they ruled over. Noble ranks and the status they granted used to be a far more strict affair, supposedly, but in the current day and age, they practically felt like a formality compared to the practical power that a lord wielded.

Semplar, the territory that Couran ruled over, was one of the most affluent regions in all of Missian. Plus, being the son of the late duke gave him no small amount of pull. His influence was overwhelmingly greater than that of a petty lord like me, and it was a shock that he would bother going out of his way to meet with me. It seemed likely that something unusual was playing out behind the scenes.

"Truth be told," said Lumeire, "I mentioned you in conversation with Lord Couran and he took quite an interest in you. Raven told me about your talent to perceive the talents of others some time ago. Well, really, he boasted to me about how you were the one who recruited Rietz and Charlotte. The moment I mentioned your capabilities to Lord Couran, he told me that he'd be most interested in meeting you."

So that's where this is coming from—it's all about my skill.

I had to admit, Appraisal *was* an incredibly useful ability to have. It was no surprise that someone in Couran's position would take an interest in it.

"Plans have been made to throw a party in celebration of Perreina's recruitment," Lumeire continued. "Perreina spent long enough sworn to the other side's service that there's still some lingering doubt among our allies regarding their allegiance, and the idea is that a social gathering will help dispel that skepticism. Serious stuff, I assure you. In any case, I want *you* to attend that party as well. This isn't an order, and you're welcome to refuse...but I trust you'd never even consider that an option, would you?"

"I certainly wouldn't," I replied immediately. "I would be honored to attend."

I'd been wanting to appraise Couran for quite a long time, so a party seemed like the perfect chance to not only see him, but also all the other nobles he'd forged alliances with. Knowing how capable the people on my side were could prove invaluable in the long run,

I WILL USE MY APPRAISAL SKILL TO RISE IN THE WORLD

so I couldn't let a chance that good slip past me.

"Excellent," said Lumeire. "I'll inform Lord Couran at once. And again, Ars, what you've done for us is truly commendable. I expect great things from you."

"Thank you, Lord Lumeire. I intend to do my utmost to support Lord Couran."

We left the castle soon after, reward money in tow.

"All right!" I said. "Back to Lamberg, then?"

"Just a moment, please," said Rietz.

"What is it?"

"About the Shadows—we wound up hiring them to dig into the Perreina situation for us, yes, but have you forgotten our initial goal? Weren't we going to ask them to supply us with information on the overall state of Missian?"

A long, awkward silence followed.

"Oh. Right."

I really had completely forgotten. Getting information on the Count of Perreina was never our primary goal in the first place! Our initial plan was to make contact with the Shadows; Perreina was just an afterthought!

"Good point, yeah. And now that you mention it, we do have plenty of funds on hand! How about we make our way to the Tremps and commission some spies?"

"I think that would be an excellent idea," said Rietz.

That said, what am I actually going to ask them to, well, do?

I could definitely get information on our allies from Lumeire, and I'd be able to look into their stats at the party I'd just been invited to, so asking about them seemed like a waste. Information on our enemies, on the other hand, would obviously prove useful, and the best place to dig up info on them was their base of operations:

Arcantez.

The security at Castle Arcantez would be tight, of course, and infiltrating it for the sake of gathering information might be a challenge, even for the Shadows. That said, they wouldn't necessarily have to get into the castle itself to find useful information. Simply gathering intel in the castle town could potentially prove incredibly helpful. As for how long we'd commission them for, I figured I'd set the contract to last as long as the war lasted.

"I'm thinking we should ask them to go to Arcantez and keep gathering as much useful information as they can manage until the war ends," I said, summing up my thought process to Rietz.

"Yes, that sounds prudent to me," said Rietz. "I should note, however, that setting the duration of the contract to the duration of the war means we'll likely be charged a very hefty sum."

"Fortunately for us, we just received a very hefty sum as a reward," I replied.

With a solid plan in mind, we headed off to the Shadows' bar.

"About the mission," said Charlotte as we arrived at our destination. "Why not just hire them to kill 'Vasmarque' or whatever his name is and be done with it?"

I did a double-take.

That certainly came out of nowhere!

"I, uh, think assassination might be a little out of the question," I replied. "I'm sure his security's as airtight as it gets. I guess it *would* bring the war to an end right away, though..."

"I recommend against it," said Rietz. "An assassination of that magnitude is the sort of decision you shouldn't be making. We have no idea what Lord Couran intends to do with his brother when the war is over, after all. Enemies or not, they *are* siblings, and he may plan to imprison Lord Vasmarque rather than kill him. I don't

I WILL USE MY APPRAISAL SKILL TO RISE IN THE WORLD

believe we should take such a drastic step unless Lord Couran specifically requests that we do so."

"Oh, *come on*," moaned Charlotte. "I thought that if you beat the enemy general, you could win the war in one fell swoop! That's what they told *me*, anyway."

If I had to hazard a guess, I'd say my father was the one who put that particular idea in her head. I guess it's not exactly wrong. Definitely too drastic of a measure for the current circumstances, though.

The three of us walked into the bar. Night had already fallen, so Pham was nowhere to be found on the first floor. We explained to Alex that we were here to hire the Shadows, and a short while later, he led us up to Pham's office.

"Didn't expect to see you again so soon, Ars Louvent," said Pham with a subtle grin as we walked through the door. I quickly explained the details of our request, trying not to let his shockingly girly looks distract me.

"'Useful information,' eh? Anything more specific you'd want out of us?" he asked when I finished.

"Let's see... Information on the size of our enemy's forces, their tactics, their overall strategy, the strengths and weaknesses of their nobles, information that could give us a diplomatic edge—really, I'd want you to report anything and everything you come across and believe could be significant."

"Arcantez... That city's a real pain in the ass to work out of. You should know that this is gonna cost you, and if you wanna keep us working for you until the war's over, we're talking a span of years, potentially. What do you say to five gold a month?"

"Making it sixty gold a year? I can pay that," I replied immediately. His offer wasn't far off from the price I'd anticipated, so I didn't bother haggling.

"Not quite done yet, though," added Pham. "I'll be asking for a bit extra on top of that for any particularly important info we dig up."

"A bonus, huh? How will we determine your specific payment for those?"

"We'll just have to talk it out when the time comes."

"I see. No objections there."

"All right, then—consider it a done deal," said Pham. "I'll take the first month's payment upfront, then I'll send a subordinate of mine to report to you on a monthly basis. He'll stop by here every month with a letter from me, collecting our payment for the next month in exchange."

"Understood. But if that's how we're doing this, I'd like to meet this subordinate of yours ahead of time," I replied.

"Fair enough," said Pham with a shrug. "In that case, come back tomorrow."

"I'll do just that," I replied, then gave him his five gold. And with that, our negotiations came to an end.

We left the Tremps, stayed overnight at an inn, and went right back to the bar again the next night to meet Pham's subordinate.

"My name is Ben, and it's nice to meet you," said a man who I could only describe as the most unremarkable individual I'd ever met. His face had no noteworthy or particularly distinguishing features. His voice was utterly unmemorable. In fact, I had a feeling that I'd forget what he'd looked like by the next *day*, let alone the next month.

Well, if I can't remember his face, I'll just have to remember his stat block!

Thus, I gave Ben a quick appraisal.

I WILL USE MY APPRAISAL SKILL TO RISE IN THE WORLD

> Alexandros Vermandolt
> Age: 29
> Male
> **Status:**
> LEA: 33/88
> VAL: 78/80
> INT: 77/78
> POL: 45/66
> Ambition: 3
> **Aptitudes:**
> Infantry: A
> Cavalry: B
> Archer: A
> Mage: B
> Fortification: C
> Weaponry: C
> Naval: C
> Aerial: C
> Strategy: B

His status screen turned out to be *full* of surprises. I'd more or less expected Ben to be a pseudonym, but I *hadn't* expected his real name to be such a mouthful, to start. That would make life easier for me. Even if I forgot his face entirely, a single appraisal would let me know it was him in an instant.

Equally surprising, though, were his stats. His Leadership cap was incredibly high—high enough that he probably could've become a general if he'd applied himself to the task. I knew this wasn't the time to go headhunting, but under any other circumstance, I definitely would've taken a shot at recruiting him to be one of my retainers.

Then again, if good stats were all I was looking for, I would've tried to recruit Pham to be one of my retainers as well. That thought raised a question in my mind: did mercenaries ever become retainers of a noble household in this world? I imagined it was *possible,* at least, and if having the Shadows formally enter my employ was an option, I'd definitely want to pursue it.

Maybe if I keep climbing the social ladder, it'll end up being a possibility someday.

I introduced myself to "Ben" and then, as that left us with nothing else in particular to discuss with him or Pham, we took our leave shortly thereafter.

○

A few days had passed since I received Lumeire's reward. It was the fifteenth day of the twelfth month, at the height of summer.

Lamberg's climate was pleasant enough in the winter, but summers were almost unbearably hot. This world lacked air conditioning, too, so I spent each and every day wishing that fall would hurry up and arrive already.

"Lord Ars?" said one of my estate's caretakers. "A letter from Lord Lumeire has arrived for you."

That didn't come as a surprise. I'd been anticipating correspondence from Lumeire, and I had a pretty good guess as to what it was: an invitation to the party he'd mentioned the last time we spoke. Sure enough, I opened the letter to find it was precisely that. The party was scheduled to take place on the thirtieth of that same month, and it would spill over into the first of the month after. The

I WILL USE MY APPRAISAL SKILL TO RISE IN THE WORLD

new year *was* celebrated in this world, and the party had been deliberately timed to commemorate the occasion. That, more than likely, meant that I could look forward to a rather lavish affair.

The party would be held at Castle Perreina, and the invitation specified that I would not be allowed to bring guests. I wasn't offended, considering that under normal circumstances, I myself probably wouldn't have been of high enough status to get invited. And besides, even if they couldn't attend the party, Rietz and the others would most definitely be coming to Perreina as my escorts. I would've liked to ring in the new year with them, if possible, but sadly, we'd have to put a rain check on that this year.

The journey to Perreina would take about three days on horseback. I decided to give us five, just to be on the safe side, so we departed for Perreina on the morning of the twenty-fifth. This time, I was riding a horse that I'd claimed as my own. It had a red coat, was on the smaller side, and was very well-behaved and easy to handle.

Unfortunately, horseback riding was also far more tiring than I'd expected it to be, and it was, again, the height of summer. I'd never ridden a horse for days on end before, either, so by the time we reached Perreina, I was a haggard mess. We arrived on the twenty-ninth, slightly later than I'd initially anticipated.

Perreina was another walled city, much like Canarre, though slightly larger. Also, like Canarre, it featured a sprawling exterior city that rested outside the curtain walls. We quickly found an inn and bedded down for a long rest. If we'd arrived just one day later, I would've ended up attending the party in a state of exhaustion. But thankfully, leaving early had bought me a full day to rest up and recuperate.

That day passed by rather quickly, though, and before I knew it, the evening of the thirtieth had arrived. It was time for the party, so Rietz and the others escorted me to the castle's front gate.

"I'll be off, then!" I said with a wave.

"Best of luck," said Rietz, who looked more than a little anxious about me going off on my own. Unfortunately, I was the only one who'd been invited, so bringing him along wasn't an option.

I wasn't too concerned, personally. After all, a party that Couran was scheduled to attend would certainly be heavily guarded. I'd already noticed an unusual number of guards by the gate, in fact, so I seriously doubted I had to worry about being attacked partway through the festivities. Frankly, I was more worried about committing some sort of horrible faux pas myself!

I set off into the castle, leaving Rietz and the others behind. I was stopped by the gatekeeper, but I'd been sent a formal letter of invitation this time around, so I was able to show it to him and get admitted right away.

Castle Perreina appeared just as ancient as Castle Canarre, though maybe just a little bigger. As I passed through the gate and neared the keep proper, I heard the sound of a commotion coming from within.

Oh, no—I'm not late, am I?

I hurried off toward the entrance. When I got inside, I found the main hall packed with nobles, all seated and chattering away with each other. I was, however, relieved to see that nobody was bringing in food yet. In other words, the party had yet to begin in earnest.

A few of the other guests cast skeptical glances my way as I walked past them. I could tell they were thinking something to the tune of, "What's this brat doing in here?" I was fairly certain that most of them were high-ranking nobles, too, so their attention was

I WILL USE MY APPRAISAL SKILL TO RISE IN THE WORLD

making me quite uncomfortable.

"Oh, Ars! You made it!" cried out a familiar voice. I turned to look in the direction it had come from and found Lumeire making his way over to me.

"This place must be full of new faces to you, so let me give you a quick introduction. First, do you see the small-statured man sitting over there? That's Rulrook Dolan, the Count of Perreina," Lumeire said, pointing at a middle-aged man with a small build and white hair.

I gave Rulrook a quick appraisal. For being so small and slight of build, his Valor was remarkably high. His Politics was up there as well, though his Intelligence was nothing to write home about. I could definitely tell that he was an upstart noble, just like my father had been. He struck me as a fairly capable man, all around, and I could tell that having him on our side would prove beneficial, even setting aside the resources he could provide.

Lumeire proceeded down the line, naming all of the influential nobles one after another. Almost all of them had stats that were notably higher than the average person's. I suppose I should have expected as much from a gathering of counts, really. There *were* one or two that certainly didn't impress me, though, and I was also a little concerned to find that nobody's stats stood out to me as truly exceptional.

"Has Lord Couran not arrived yet?" I asked.

"He's around, but he seems to be out of the hall at the moment," said Lumeire. "He'll be here to give a speech when the party officially commences, I'm sure."

Sounds like that speech will be the perfect opportunity to appraise him.

I was excited to learn what sort of person the late duke's son was.

AS A REINCARNATED ARISTOCRAT

After finishing his explanation, Lumeire returned to his seat, and I sat down to his right. His wife, incidentally, was sitting on his left side. It seemed that many of the prominent nobles at the party had brought along their spouses, children, and siblings.

There were still plenty of people I hadn't appraised yet, but just as I was getting started on that, I heard what sounded like the crashing of cymbals. The nobles' chatter quickly ceased, and everyone stood up. I followed their example, and Lumeire leaned down to whisper, "Here he comes!" into my ear.

The silence was so absolute that I heard the tapping of his approaching footsteps long before I saw him. Finally, the door at the very end of the great hall swung open and a blond-haired man stepped through it. The moment he entered the hall, every noble present bowed in unison, with me frantically imitating the gesture a second later. That had to be Couran, surely, but I was too flustered to confirm it in the moment.

"Rise," said the man in a deep, dignified voice that carried an unmistakable air of gravitas. I raised my head and took another look at him. His outfit was truly extravagant, and he stood before the hall of nobles with an imposing presence that made it feel like he owned the place *and* them. I estimated that he was in his early forties; and his face was peppered with scars. Noble-born though he may have been, it was clear at a glance that he'd been through more than his fair share of battles.

He was Couran—he had to be, so I appraised him on the spot.

I WILL USE MY APPRAISAL SKILL TO RISE IN THE WORLD

> Couran Salemakhia
> Age: 45
> Male
> **Status:**
> LEA: 99/99
> VAL: 97/97
> INT: 78/79
> POL: 80/81
> Ambition: 93
> **Aptitudes:**
> Infantry: A
> Cavalry: S
> Archer: B
> Mage: B
> Fortification: A
> Weaponry: C
> Naval: A
> Aerial: B
> Strategy: C

To be honest, his stats were jaw-dropping. They were far beyond what I'd imagined, and I had already been expecting a lot from him. The persistent rumor was that his younger brother, Vasmarque, was favored by the late duke because he was far more talented than his older sibling. If that was true, and these were Couran's stats, I couldn't even guess what Vasmarque's stat block looked like.

Then again, it was always possible that the duke just hadn't had an eye for talent. Plus, parents tended to have skewed perspectives on their children's abilities.

AS A REINCARNATED ARISTOCRAT

"I thank you all for coming here today," said Couran, kicking off his speech. "On this evening, we close the curtain on the two hundred and tenth year since the Summerforth Empire's founding. Tomorrow, we shall witness the dawn of a new year. Unending strife and bloodshed await us. Our empire is not what it once was, and I do not believe it will ever return to its former glory."

Couran paused for a moment, then continued, "Once, the great men of House Salemakhia ruled over this land of Missian as kings, not subservient proxies to some far-flung greater power. I intend to win the battle that looms before us and take back what is mine by right. I shall then unite these lands under my banner, secede from the empire, and re-establish the Kingdom of Missian!"

He wants to bring back the Kingdom of Missian? Is that what he's been after this whole time? I guess it's not too surprising, considering the state of the empire.

"I believe that my brother, Vasmarque, intends to do the exact same thing," Couran went on. "However, Vasmarque is a craven fiend! A man such as he is unworthy of the kingdom he seeks to establish! We *will* triumph, my brothers in arms, and our first battle has already been won! We have seen through Vasmarque's schemes and put an end to them before they could play out!"

Couran went on to explain the details of Vasmarque's plot to deceive Rulrook, the Count of Perreina, into thinking that Maasa had betrayed Couran's cause. He took care not to rebuke Rulrook for siding with the enemy, and even framed the speech as praise, congratulating him for his choice to join the winning side. Rulrook stepped to the front at that point to offer his own speech, apologizing for his support of Vasmarque and swearing to spare no efforts in supporting Couran's cause.

"I, however, was not the one to see through Vasmarque's cow-

I WILL USE MY APPRAISAL SKILL TO RISE IN THE WORLD

ardly scheme," Couran continued once Rulrook was finished. "That honor belongs to the youngest of us—a man with talent far beyond his years. Step forward, Ars Louvent and Lumeire Pyres."

For a moment, I was too stunned to react. I had *not* expected my name to come up like that! Lumeire whispered, "Let's go" into my ear as he stood, helping me shake off my panic and stand up along with him.

Why are we going up to the front? Am I supposed to give a speech?! Nobody said anything about a speech!

My one saving grace was that Lumeire had been called up with me. Hopefully, he'd be able to save my skin. It wasn't that I was afraid of public speaking—I actually had quite a bit of experience with it, in fact—but speaking in front of a crowd of nobles who were *all* my superiors on the social ladder was a completely different question! I was afraid I'd be too tongue-tied to spit a single word out!

Despite the terror I felt, I managed to walk up to the front of the hall and stand next to Couran. Seeing him up close only reinforced the air of majesty that he projected. This was our first meeting, in any case, so I decided to err on the side of formality and bowed.

"It is an honor to meet you in person," I said. "Ars Louvent, at your service."

"Yes, I suppose this *is* the first time we've met. I am Couran Salemakhia," said Couran with a smile. He then turned his gaze back to the crowd. "As you can see, Ars is still but a child. Nevertheless, he has done an exemplary job serving as the lord of a territory in Canarre known as Lamberg. *He* is the one who saw through Vasmarque's treachery."

A round of applause ensued, at Couran's prompting. He then went on to praise me to the high heavens without ever actually offering any specifics as to *how* I discovered the nature of Vasmarque's scheme.

Maybe hiring mercenaries to get a job like that done isn't considered the most honorable approach among the high-ranking nobles?

Soon after, Couran's focus shifted to Lumeire, who he praised just as lavishly for choosing me for the task. He asked Lumeire if he had anything to say, and Lumeire happily obliged with a bland but inoffensive, "I pledge to do everything in my power to support your cause, Lord Couran." He got a round of applause for it, so apparently, it went over well.

It seemed my ordeal was finally over, and I was just about to return to my seat when Couran surreptitiously passed me a letter.

"No need to come if you'd prefer not to," he whispered in my ear. "But personally, I'd be quite pleased if you did."

To come to what, *exactly? Is this letter another invitation?*

I was immediately worried. When a man who was several steps your superior on the social ladder said, "No need to come," your presence was absolutely mandated. The fact that he handed it to me on the sly meant it probably wasn't something he'd want others seeing, so I stowed the letter in my breast pocket for the moment. I'd make a trip to the toilets or go outside for a breath of fresh air to read it privately later.

The party carried on, and it wasn't long before food was brought out for us. It was all delicious—no surprise, considering Couran was in attendance. It was either the best or second-best meal I'd had since my reincarnation, most likely.

A performance was scheduled after dinner. I found a program affixed to one of the walls and discovered that said performance was scheduled to drag on for a very long time. It seemed they planned to keep going until the stroke of midnight. I excused myself before

I WILL USE MY APPRAISAL SKILL TO RISE IN THE WORLD

the entertainment got started, made my way to the restrooms, and found a private corner in which to read the letter.

When the magical dancers scheduled for the third act conclude their performance, I would like you to excuse yourself from the party and come see me. I have something to ask you, as well as something to ask of you, the letter read.

Instantly, my worries compounded. Turning a request from a lord of his standing down would be hard, no matter how unreasonable it might be. I'd have no choice but to do whatever he asked. I brooded over my options as I stowed the letter and returned to the party.

I arrived back in the hall just in time to catch the performance's opening act. I sat through the first two of them, after which the magical dance troupe Couran had mentioned in his letter took to the stage. They cast and combined magic of all types and aspects, and frankly, it made for quite the spectacle.

Couran led the audience in a round of applause after the performance finished, then excused himself to visit the restroom. That was my cue to slip out as well, and the moment I did, I found Couran waiting for me just outside.

"I'm glad to see my offer caught your interest."

"I wouldn't even dream of refusing," I replied.

"Well then, follow me."

Couran led me out of the keep, then all the way outside the castle walls. A tall, slender man was waiting for us there.

"This man's name is Robinson Renjee, and he is my most trusted retainer," said Couran.

"Robinson Renjee, at your service," the man said with a rather flamboyant bow. I quickly returned his greeting, then appraised him. His Leadership and Valor were both unremarkable, but he had an Intelligence of 88 and a Politics score of 91. It seemed Couran's trust in him had been well-earned.

The three of us set off down the city streets.

Where in the world are we going? And why do we have to walk this far in the first place? Didn't he just want to ask me for a favor?

"We're almost there," said Couran. "You'll have to forgive me for being so circuitous. I wish to ask a favor of you that I'd rather not let your fellow lords overhear."

The bad feeling I had about the situation only deepened. What sort of favor would he not want the other lords to hear? Was I about to get taken advantage of by a pedo?! I'd have no hope of fighting back if things went in *that* direction! I'd just have to go limp and take it! The more I thought about the situation, the more anxious I became.

"We've arrived," Couran finally said as he stepped in front of a small, unremarkable-looking store. It struck me as old, unfashionable, and definitely not the sort of place you'd expect the son of a duke to frequent. We walked inside...only to find that there were no other customers at all, and for that matter, not even a storekeeper.

"A gold coin bought us the run of the place for the evening," Couran explained as he plopped down onto a nearby chair. "Please, make yourself comfortable."

I took a seat on a chair that faced him.

"Now then," said Couran. "I am about to subject you to a simple test."

A test? What's he talking about?

"Lumeire told me that you have the power to perceive people's strengths and talents. He told me you saw through to the hidden genius that lurked within a Malkan boy and a slave girl. I have a favor to ask that could only be granted by someone with a power

I WILL USE MY APPRAISAL SKILL TO RISE IN THE WORLD

like yours, but before I say anything more, I would like to verify that your power is real."

I get it now—this is all about my Appraisal skill!

I was relieved to conclude that he wasn't going to do anything untoward after all. I was *also* confused about why he'd bothered calling me all the way out here, in that case, but the relief was still winning out.

"All right," I replied. "But how exactly would you like me to prove it?"

"A sound question. First, I would like to hear about your power in more detail. Once I know more, I can decide how I'd like to go about testing it."

I quickly explained how my Appraisal skill worked to Couran.

"Leadership, Valor, Intelligence, and Politics, along with their aptitudes for a variety of roles," he muttered when I finished. "I see. Frankly, that's even more than I had hoped for, and it makes testing your power quite simple. I would like you to appraise both me and Robinson, and tell me the results. I know Robinson's strengths better than anyone else, and needless to say, I'm quite acquainted with my own as well. If your information proves accurate for both of us, I will choose to believe your story. Be honest with me—if your power tells you that I have a weakness, then do not hold back for politeness's sake."

It really was a simple test. That was no trouble for me at all. I figured that the numerical scores my skill gave me would only serve to confuse him, so I chose to summarize what they meant about their capabilities in more ordinary language instead.

"I see... I am convinced. You do indeed possess the power you claimed," said Couran with a nod when I finished speaking. "Now then, let's move to the real matter at hand."

"A-All right," I replied nervously.

"No need to be so guarded! I suppose seeking out such an excess of privacy made you nervous. I promise you that I won't be asking anything dreadful of you, so you can rest easy," said Couran. Apparently, I'd been doing a poor job of hiding my state of mind.

"You inspected the capabilities of your fellow nobles at the party earlier, didn't you?" he asked.

I'd been expecting a request at that point, not a question, so it took me a second to collect myself and answer him.

"Yes, I did," I eventually replied. I had no idea what he was getting at, so I figured I'd be better off being honest.

"Tell me, what did you make of them?"

"I...well...let's see... I thought they were an impressive group of individuals."

"Did you really? Nothing about them struck you as lacking?"

"Lacking?"

If I were to answer that question honestly, I'd have to admit that, yes, I had been rather underwhelmed. I hadn't been lying about them being impressive, but none of them other than Couran himself had been exceptional. I'd been expecting to see some real talent gathered up there, and to be completely frank, I was a little disappointed.

When I stopped to consider why that might have been, though, it struck me that most nobles had their titles handed down to them. It wasn't all that common for an upstart to claw his way up the ranks and obtain a noble title, so really, it wasn't too surprising at all that most of them were essentially ordinary people. In any case, I decided to reply honestly, and told him that I had indeed had a thought or two along those lines.

"I'd expect no less," said Couran with a nod. "And I do not deny

I WILL USE MY APPRAISAL SKILL TO RISE IN THE WORLD

it. Few of my allies are incompetent, but fewer still truly excel. That applies not only to the counts, but also to the vassals who serve them—very few have made names for themselves. Even amongst my own direct subordinates, only Robinson here has proven himself truly worthy of praise."

Couran clearly had an eye for talent as well, though nothing quite as easy or precise as what my skill provided me with. Finally, his decision to have the conversation away from prying eyes was starting to make sense. I couldn't imagine any noble would be pleased to hear their lord describe them as unremarkable.

"The greatest thorn in my side is rather evident," Couran continued. "I speak of the lack of anyone suited to serve as my tactician, of course. I believe myself to be more clever than the average person, and Robinson's intellect is readily apparent, but neither of us has the experience required to fill the role. Vasmarque, on the other hand, has a man on his side named Remus. Not only was he my father's closest advisor, but he's also the pillar that has kept Missian stable for decades."

Couran paused there, then sighed before admitting, "Vasmarque himself is remarkably intelligent as well. I've never once surpassed him academically. Worse still, his right-hand man, Thomas, is just as much of a prodigy as he is. And that's not even mentioning *her*... Oh, but I suppose she was exiled? In any case, as I'm sure you've surmised, Vasmarque holds the upper hand in terms of his advisors' wisdom by a substantial margin. Our forces are roughly equal in terms of strength, which means that whoever has the more capable subordinates will surely come out on top."

"You mean to say that, as things stand, you're going to lose?" I asked.

Couran nodded gravely and replied, "That brings me to my request. I have heard that your power has enabled you to recruit a host of truly talented retainers into your service. Do you know of anyone you would endorse to become my personal tactician?"

"Anyone I can endorse? I'm not sure," I carefully answered. Anyone I chose to name here would go on to serve under Couran—in other words, I'd be giving them up to him. I wasn't about to just hand over *my* people that easily.

"Of course, I appreciate that you wouldn't want your own prodigies stolen away from you," Couran clarified. "Instead, I have a proposal: I would like you to participate in my next council of war."

"Your council? You want *me* to be there?"

"I do. Ordinarily, only the most influential of nobles would be permitted at such a conference, but I would like you to attend…and to bring someone with tactical expertise along with you."

"Are, umm…? Are you sure someone as inexperienced as me should be present at a council like that?" I asked.

Couran shrugged and replied, "I'm sure some of those present will be unamused, but talking them down will be my responsibility. Moreover, whether or not a proposal is accepted at a council of war hinges upon whether the proposal has merit—*not* upon who made it. If you have a useful perspective to contribute, then my people will accept you. As I said before, while none of them truly excel, none are outright inept, either. They can tell the difference between a good suggestion and a bad one."

"There's just one other thing I'm somewhat concerned about," I said. "If I were to attend, it's possible that I may wind up bringing a Malkan along with me. Do you believe that would pose a problem?"

If I were to accept his proposal, I planned to bring Rietz and Rosell. That said, Rietz was a Malkan, which meant he was likely to be the subject of prejudice even at the council itself. I wasn't convinced the lords there would listen to him at all.

"I see," said Couran. "So that Malkan of yours is one of the ones you believe could make a decent tactician, eh? You're right to be concerned, in a sense. I imagine that some of my subordinates *would* look upon him with scorn. That said, as I stated a moment ago, what he says would carry far more weight than who he is. If he puts forward an unmistakably sound proposal, then I don't imagine any would oppose him, and even if they did, they would be quickly overruled by the majority. In the worst case, I can always silence them myself."

"That's good to hear," I replied. Inwardly, though, I was still shocked.

Me? At a council of war? Is Couran seriously desperate enough to turn to a literal child for this sort of help?

Like Pham had said, I had no interest in boarding a sinking ship, and I was less than convinced that my help would be enough to turn the tide of war in his favor. Rietz and Rosell both had astonishingly high Intelligence scores, yes, and Rietz would surely be suited for the task, but Rosell was a lot less of a certain factor. After all, he was just a kid.

Worse still, his Intelligence score had plateaued recently. It had only gone up by one point over the past year, bringing it to a current score of 90. He studied tirelessly day after day, and he seemed to be getting smarter, but my Appraisal told a different story.

I was beginning to understand that "Intelligence," as far as my skill was concerned, was determined exclusively by one's ability to come up with the sort of plans that would prove helpful in a battle. Rosell, meanwhile, had literally no practical battlefield experience, so it was no wonder his Intelligence wasn't improving. That meant thrusting him into a real-life council of war out of nowhere would probably end very poorly.

That left me with only Rietz to my name. Would he be able to carry Couran to victory on his own? Couran had named three notable tacticians who were supporting his brother, and when it came down to it, Rietz was more of an all-rounder than a specialized tactician. It seemed very likely he'd find himself at a disadvantage compared to them.

The one major counterpoint, of course, was that however much I talked about not boarding sinking ships, I was more or less already aboard this one, so jumping off could prove dangerous in its own right. Did I even have it in me to betray Couran? Would Lumeire be able to do something in his capacity as count if I convinced him we were doomed? Would it even be possible for me to join up with Vasmarque on my own if things got really bad?

I guess I'd have to get in contact with his chief retainers through some sort of back channel. But even just getting him to accept a secret message from a no-name noble on the other side would probably be hard!

"I appreciate that my offer has given you a lot to think about, Ars," said Couran. It was like he'd seen right through me...and like he knew that I was seriously considering the merits of betraying him. "I would not dream of making an offer such as this without a corresponding promise of compensation. Assuming you bring me the tactician I need, and assuming said tactician leads me to victory over Vasmarque, I shall grant you the title of Count of Canarre."

"Huh?"

My jaw dropped.

Me? The count?!

"Is that even a possibility?" I asked. "What about Lord Lumeire?"

"He would be made count of a larger county. I must confess

I WILL USE MY APPRAISAL SKILL TO RISE IN THE WORLD

that Canarre's proximity to the border makes it somewhat less than desirable in the eyes of the nobility. House Pyres has ruled over the county for five generations, and I imagine the current count views the region with no small amount of fondness, but if granted a more desirable title and territory in exchange, I trust he will not be discontent."

I could become a count if the war goes well... I could become the sort of lord who lives in an honest-to-goodness castle...?

Lamberg was a pleasant enough territory, to be sure, but it had its limits, and those limits were absolute. If I remained in my current station, then I would always live with the looming threat of a more powerful lord deciding to snuff me out on impulse. I would never escape my status as small-time nobility.

Becoming the Count of Canarre would mean moving *several* steps up the social ladder, all at once. There was a degree of risk that we would lose the war, certainly, but making contact with Vasmarque and stabbing Couran in the back was also a gamble.

Thus, I made my choice.

"Understood. I accept your offer."

Afterword

Thank you for choosing to purchase and read this book! This is the author, Miraijin A, speaking!

I was inspired to write a story about medieval territory management by a certain historical simulation game set in the Sengoku period of Japanese history. The game casts you as one of the many lords (or "Daimyo") that ruled over Japan at the time, then tasks you with uniting the country under your banner. The first game in the series was released almost forty years ago, and the latest one is the fifteenth such title. It's an incredibly popular franchise!

I consider myself a *huge* fan of the series, and while I haven't played every single game that's been released, I *have* sunk literally hundreds of hours into the ones I've tried. That probably goes to show just how much I like the games. They allow you to play as the likes of Oda Nobunaga and Tokugawa Ieyasu—historical figures so famous that everyone in Japan knows about them.

Playing as the Oda or Tokugawa clan means that you start the game with an abundance of skilled subordinates, so taking over Japan is relatively easy. When I first discovered the series, I enjoyed that level of difficulty, but the longer I played, the more I grew unsatisfied. I wanted a challenge.

My solution: I chose to play as a figure so obscure that only the most hardcore of history nerds would have even heard of him. I won't say precisely who I picked, but his stats were low, and his retainers' stats were all laughably low as well. Making *him* the ruler of Japan was a grueling task.

That difficulty, however, just made victory all the more sweet. I quickly became obsessed, and pulled many accidental all-nighters playing the game nonstop. The sense of achievement I felt when I finally made my no-name noble the ruler of Japan is something I'll never forget. *As a Reincarnated Aristocrat, I'll Use My Appraisal Skill to Rise in the World* is a story that came to me as I thought back on the time I chose to play that game as a petty, insignificant lord.

This work will be my fifth published series in Japan to date. That I've had so many of my works published in the two years or so since I first became an author is something I never would have even dared to dream about. I started writing as a hobby, more or less, so I find the fact that so many people read and enjoy my works deeply moving.

To everyone who purchased this book, everyone who read and supported the web novel version of the story, to my editor, who did their absolute best to support me throughout the writing process, and to jimmy, who drew the most wonderful illustrations I could have ever asked for, I offer my most sincere gratitude. Thank you all so, *so* much.

And with all that said, I hope to see you again in the next volume!

Author
Miraijin A

Full-time author Miraijin A speaking! I'm sure plenty of people will pick up this book without having read my other works, so I'd like to introduce myself. I was born and raised in Kumamoto Prefecture, where I still reside, I'm a man, and I'm in my twenties. I enjoy reading, watching baseball, playing video games, watching anime, etc. I also love light novels, and after reading enough of them, I felt the urge to start writing one of my own! I sincerely hope you enjoy this book!

Illust.
jimmy

I'm jimmy, and I draw day in and day out! I hope you like the book!

The Dawn of the Witch
The Remedial Student and the Witch of the Staff

Five hundred years of conflict between witches and the Church has finally ended in an uneasy peace, but pockets of violent resentment linger throughout the land...

Saybil is a magic student with no memories of his life before he met a mysterious silver-haired woman in an alley. Now he travels with his teacher, Loux, another student named Holt, and the beastfallen Kudo for "special training"... but this field trip may not be as routine as it seems!

Kakeru Kobashiri presents a new high fantasy series set in the same world as the smash hit *Grimoire of Zero*!

Volume 1 Available Now!

© Kakeru Kobashiri / Kodansha, Ltd.